Need You
for Always

Need You for Always

HEROES OF ST. HELENA SERIES

MARINA ADAIR

Montlake
Romance

Published by Montlake Romance, Seattle

www.apub.com

Amazon, the Amazon logo, and Montlake Romance are trademarks of Amazon.com, Inc., or its affiliates.

ISBN-13: 9781503948259
ISBN-10: 1503948250

Cover design by Shasti O'Leary-Soudant / SOS CREATIVE LLC

Printed in the United States of America

*To all of the men and women
who put their lives in harm's way to protect
our freedoms.
You are the real heroes.*

chapter
one

"You need to get laid," Emerson Blake explained to the line of uniformed soldiers funneling off the party bus and into the St. Helena VFW dance hall.

She'd always had a thing for a man in uniform. It was something about the way they perpetually looked ready—for anything—that had her happy spots singing.

But there was no singing to be had, not today anyway, because these men and these uniforms smelled like mothballs. And the lei in question? That had more to do with the bundle of flowered necklaces in her hand than belting out a hearty "Oh My" anthem. Not to mention her body hadn't so much as hummed in months and she had no idea why.

Okay, so she had a pretty good idea why, but that would be fodder for thought for another rainy day. *This* rainy day was to be spent catering to the few hundred seniors who had come out in support of the Veterans of Foreign Wars monthly wartime mixer.

With an open bar, live band, and Copacabana theme, the turnout was bigger than Emerson had anticipated, or prepped for. Heroes from every one of the past five wars were present, which meant that every single silver-haired lady over sixty was there, ready to be seen and heard. Including Mother Nature herself, who sent Emerson a *you can suck it* reminder from the universe in the form of an icy blast of wind that blew into the dance hall—and up Emerson's grass skirt.

"Have you been lei'd?" she asked the first man in line.

"Not since I was stationed at Pearl Harbor," retired gunnery sergeant Carl Dabney said, waggling a bushy brow. "So don't try to give me one of them no-salt-allowed yellow leis. I want a pink one."

"If I give you a pink one, you'll go home in an ambulance," Emerson said, handing him a yellow one. The old man refused to take it.

"If I can't have any salt, what kind of message is that sending to the ladies standing at the salsa bar?"

"That you have high blood pressure?"

"That I'm a pansy, *hashtag real men wear pink*!" Carl was in his early nineties, carried a cane and a gun at all times, and was a regular customer at Emerson's food cart in town. He'd also, according to Emerson's little medical printout, compliments of Valley Vintage Senior Community, survived three wars, two triple bypasses, and a stroke—which made him far from a pansy. It also meant he was stubborn enough to beat death.

Too bad for him, death didn't have anything on Emerson.

"Yellow means low sodium," she explained, and Carl snorted as though he could take on sodium and the entire periodic table without even dropping his cane. "I can always give you a white one."

He looked the white lei over carefully. "What does that one get me?"

"Low sodium, low fat, and if I see you with alcohol anywhere near your person, silver star or not, I get to kick you out. No refund."

He wasn't sold. And wasn't that just great. With three years of the finest culinary training Paris had to offer and five generations of family recipes in her arsenal, Emerson should have been well on her way to cementing herself as a serious contender in the world of Greek cuisine. Yet here she was, still in her small hometown of St. Helena, California, the entire fate of her career—and her reputation—hinging on her ability to corral disgruntled seniors while wearing a pair of coconut shells.

Because when your mother's ALS goes nuclear five months before graduation and you forgo finishing culinary school to take care of her, shells are bound to happen. Not that she regretted one second of it, but after her mother's death nearly two years ago, the rebound had been brutal—on everyone. Unable to ignore what her family needed, Emerson had given up her dream of finishing school to help with the aftermath, to be there for her sister, Violet, who had only been four at the time, and her father, who had lost his best friend.

Emerson had become the family glue, and she was okay with that—most days. But today she needed things to go her way.

Not that catering the VFW's monthly mixer was the most glamorous job Emerson would have asked for. In fact, she hadn't asked for it at all, but they'd been desperate for a caterer who wouldn't mind getting into costume, and Emerson wanted to take her business to the next level.

Eighteen months ago, after realizing the only position open in wine country for a chef lacking the right pedigree was a line cook, Emerson had taken the money her mother had left her and bought a food cart and food license. It gave her the chance to cook the kind of cuisine she was passionate about, authentic Greek street food, and gave her the illusion she was in control of her own life.

Which she so wasn't.

Illusions could be dangerous, and Emerson knew that better than most. But even though she'd accepted that life didn't always play fair and dreams died, every day for everyone, she was determined to keep this one alive. Determined to make her mother proud—make their dream of a Greek streatery fleet a reality and in turn make her mark in the culinary world.

So the Pita Peddler was a cart and not quite the pimped-out food truck they had dreamed of. So what? It was a start. A small one, but a start nonetheless.

Food doesn't have to be pretentious to be delectable, it just has to have heart. That had been her mom's motto. One that Emerson tried to embrace. She had delectable down, but she wasn't sure she had enough faith left in love to nail the last part. But she was trying.

So no one was more surprised than she was when her "little pita cart" had turned out to make serious dough—and fast. Dough that had risen and doubled in size, and now this year Emerson had bigger plans. Plans that needed the extra two grand this VFW event would bring her. If catering the occasional kid's birthday or wearing humiliating costumes meant upgrading her food cart to a twenty-seven-foot custom-designed gourmet food truck with Sub-Zero fridge and freezer, dual fryers, four burners, a Tornado speed-cook oven, and a twelve-thousand-watt diesel generator all wrapped in Pita Peddler Streatery vinyl—then she'd shell up.

Emerson handed out a few more leis, ignoring the goose bumps covering every inch of her bare skin—which was nearly all of her inches. Behind her, the wind picked up, scattering a thin sheet of water over the marble floor of the entry to the dance hall, her leis whipping her in the face. Outside, the late-autumn storm continued to pound the sidewalk, bending the branches of the maples that lined Main Street and rushing down the already full gutters.

No wonder it was so packed inside. With the potted palm trees, pineapple party mugs, and bottomless-mai-tai bar, it was like a tropical paradise in the middle of an arctic typhoon.

Double-checking to make sure all essential body parts were securely tucked in, Emerson took a deep, humbling breath and held up the yellow lei again to Carl. "At least with this you can do some body shots off Ms. Beamon."

Carl peered through the door at Ida Beamon, owner of the local wine bar Cork'd N Dipped, who was already inside and standing by the bar. Dressed in a blue-and-white-striped sailor's dress and red flats, she looked like a one-woman USO. She was also wearing a yellow lei. "You think she's packing tonight?"

"I heard in the ladies' room that she swapped out her holster for a garter belt and she's looking to score." Emerson wiggled the yellow flowers again. "Last chance."

He looked at the lei and frowned. "Real men wear—"

"Pink, yeah, yeah," Emerson cut in, then looked at the large group of seniors still waiting to be checked in and sighed. It was only a matter of time before a riot broke out, and if Carl kept yammering on, it would only get worse. She'd seen it happen too many times with her sister's Lady Bug troop—one bad bug could lead to an angry swarm.

Time to get tough. "You can either take Ms. Beamon on a twirl around the dance floor or have me escort you out. Your choice."

Carl studied the yellow lei thoroughly, then sized Emerson up, most likely to see if he could take her. She flexed her guns and narrowed her eyes. "Remember when your grandson Colt came home with a busted face senior year? That was me. And I was only a seventh grader."

She might be small but she was scrappy.

With a resigned sigh, *smart man*, he gave the lei one last skeptical glare. "If I promise no salt, do I have to wear that?"

"Rules are rules." Emerson leaned in close—real close. Close enough that Carl could see the seriousness in her eyes, and if that didn't work, she hoped he'd be too distracted by her coconut shells to argue. And wasn't that a man for you—one well-calculated breath and his eyes glazed over, his mouth snapped shut, and he stopped yammering. "You got to get lei'd before you can do a body shot, Carl."

"Not much point in body shots if I can't salt her up first," Carl grumbled, but he took the lei anyway, dropping his twenty on the table before hobbling off.

One down, fifty to go, she thought, taking in the still-growing crowd.

"With rules like that, I'm glad I came." A cocky but oh-so-sexy chuckle came from beside her.

Emerson closed her eyes. It didn't help. She could still feel the weight of an intense, masculine, and very amused gaze as her whole body instantly heated and—

Oh boy, hummed.

Because it wasn't just any low, husky chuckle. It was the same panty-melting chuckle from her past that had spurred her every teen fantasy. In her more recent past, say, oh, five months ago, it had whispered wicked promises in her ear.

Promises that took an entire night to fulfill and five months to forget. Not that she'd forgotten. Far from it. But she'd tried.

Never one to run from her past, or anything, for that matter, Emerson opened her eyes and—*sweet baby Jesus*—the wry amusement and combustible heat in those dark blue pools made her knees go weak. And *that* pissed Emerson off. More than the wet grass skirt that was bleeding green dye down her legs.

Emerson didn't do weak, not even for a guy who looked like Captain America, G.I. Joe, and an underwear model all wrapped up in a big, badassed army-of-one package.

Oh, Dax Baudouin wasn't just insanely handsome. Handsome she could handle. He was also dark, inside and out, and dangerous in that mysterious way that tempted her even when she knew better. His body was massive—everywhere—and today it was soaked. All the way through.

Like he hadn't bothered to get naked before showering.

His white button-up was wet around the collar and down his chest, the material translucent, clinging to his hard-cut upper body and hinting at the impressive collection of tattoos that were hidden beneath.

Great, now she was thinking about him naked. In her shower. His smirk said he knew it. Just what she needed, a little game of I've Seen You Naked to make her already humiliating day that much more so.

Clearly, karma was bitch-slapping her for her one transgression.

Then again, Dax Baudouin was one hell of a transgression to have, but she had known that the second she'd agreed to go back to his hotel room. He had been her first and only one-night stand, a no-panties-allowed kind of affair that had blown her mind. It had blown some other parts too, but she didn't want to think about that here. Not with her goal of a gourmet food truck just in arm's reach.

"Dax," she said, forcing what she hoped was a professional and unaffected smile. He smiled back. It started as an amused twinkle in his eyes, then spread to his face and—

She was toast.

That was all it took: a single flash of those perfect teeth and her body started humming. There was no other word for what happened to her whenever he so much as shot a dimple her way. It was as if he jump-started her entire body—brought it to life.

His gaze took a long trip down her body and back up, the corners of that smile turning up farther, and Emerson could practically hear the gears turning in his head, trying to come up with the perfect smart-ass remark about her attire.

"Now back to those rules," he said, inspecting the different-colored leis.

"Yeah, no."

He laughed softly. "No? To getting laid or the drink?"

MARINA ADAIR

"No to both the lei and the drink." To be as clear as possible, she added, "And no, you can't mow my grass, put a lime in my coconut, or any other unoriginal comment you were going to say."

"I'm very original." He leaned forward, resting his hands on the table, which did amazing things to his biceps. "Creative, even."

Didn't she know it. "Why are you even here? Shouldn't you be off in some war-torn country defending mankind from the super-villains of the world?"

"I've had four tours of the most recent foreign war, which automatically puts me on the list." He leaned in. "I get a plus one, if you're interested."

"I'm good." She crossed her arms and that made his grin grow.

"As for defending mankind from supervillains? Someone else is handling that today," he said as though it would be just another day at the office. Emerson snorted.

As an army Ranger, Dax was a weapon of mass destruction in a sea of already lethal weapons, handpicked and trained by Uncle Sam to fight the battles that very few soldiers were equipped to fight. He'd been to some terrible places, seen the worst parts of human nature, yet he kept going back, his need to serve stronger than his fear of death. On the rare occasion when he wasn't on supersecret missions or hiding out in caves, he lived in San Diego, a good nine hours south of St. Helena, which was why she'd agreed to the one-night stand to begin with.

And okay, she'd just watched one of her best friends, Shay, marry Dax's older brother Jonah in an incredibly romantic ceremony overlooking the Golden Gate Bridge, and all the talk of forever and partnership and a kissy-boo future had gotten to her. Not that she wanted a kissy-boo future, but sometimes she thought about what it would be like to not have to fight every battle alone.

Then she'd seen Dax at the bar looking bigger than life in his dress blues—as out of place in all of that happiness as she was—and before she knew what was happening they were . . . bonding. Over Jack and Johnnie Walker.

In a momentary lapse in judgment, she'd found herself in his room, her bridesmaid dress around her waist like a Hula Hoop, staring down her one secret fantasy, who had offered her something she'd desperately needed.

Escape.

One night to forget about everything, be selfish, and lose herself without the fear of *losing* herself, because she wasn't looking for forever. Good thing, since Dax was not a forever kind of guy.

"If I give you a lei, will you go away?" she asked.

"Is that your way of saying you don't want to talk about the wedding?"

"First rule about one-night stands," she said as though she were a foremost expert on the subject. "What happens between the wedding party, stays between the wedding party. No postexpectations, no postconversations, and no ties."

"Actually, first rule of one-night stands, Emi, is that they last all night. You cut out before dawn." He lowered his voice. "And to be clear, you liked my tie."

She had. A whole lot. Almost as much as she'd liked him. Which was why she'd cut out. Somehow, if she was the one to walk, it felt like she was still in control of her emotions—in control of her life.

"I had things to do."

"At three in the morning?"

"What did you expect?" She laughed. "To cuddle and hold hands while swapping embarrassing childhood secrets and life goals? And it isn't like you called me the next day anyway."

He grinned. Big and wide, and he slipped something out of his pocket. A phone.

He gave a few confident swipes of his finger, and a second later, hers rang. She leveled him with her most lethal glare. When it kept ringing, she crossed her arms, *so* not going to play this game.

Dax stood there, patient and unfazed, as though he was confident she'd answer as it rang and rang until it went to voice mail. Emerson could hear the muffled message she'd recorded and threw her hands in the air. "Oh for God's sake, hang up the—"

He held up a silencing finger. *Beep.*

Emerson had a finger of her own to hold up, but since she was working, she refrained.

"Hey, Emi," he said into the phone, charm and swagger dialed to full. "Wanted to let you know that I had an amazing time the other night—"

"Five months and nine days ago."

He flashed her a *do you mind, I'm busy here* look. "I'm in town for a bit and I'd love to see you. Say grab a drink, maybe after you get off work? I know the perfect place, coconut shells welcomed."

Then he ended the call, slid the phone into his back pocket, and smiled. "You were saying?"

"You're infuriating."

He shrugged as though he'd been called worse, then slipped a twenty into the cash box and took a lei, a pink one, and held it out for her. She rolled her eyes.

"Now slip this flower necklace around my neck so I can go get us a drink."

"There is no *us.*"

"If you say so."

"I say so." But she didn't sound all that convinced. Maybe it was because as she said it she swayed closer. "And I'm not going on a date with you."

Dax held out the lei and wiggled it at Emerson. When she crossed her arms and shook her head, he slid the lei over his head and winked. "Who said anything about a date?"

Normally, Dax wasn't all that big on actively engaging the unexpected. They were called unidentified threats for a reason in his line of work—*former* line of work, he had to keep reminding himself, now that his career as an army Ranger was unexpectedly over. But after a month of bed rest and three weeks of dragging his sorry ass out of bed, working out until he passed out, working out some more, then crashing only to start all over again the next day, the unexpected was looking pretty tempting.

Especially since Emerson's coconut shells and wisps of dyed straw did little to camouflage the lethal bod beneath. And that mouth. *Man*, that mouth was sharp and smart and, if memory served correctly, so talented it should be registered as the eighth wonder of the world.

And his memory about her mouth and that night was photographic. Sparring with Emerson was like walking into hostile territory. It put him on edge, pumped him full of adrenaline, and had him jonesing to gear up for some hand-to-hand combat.

Full-body combat with Emerson, yeah, he remembered that too. Every second. The way her skin tasted, how she gave that breathy little sigh when he got it right, which made him want to get it right over and over. And over again. He especially remembered how, for such a small thing, she liked to talk a big game during sex—often and dirty. His personal favorite was when she ordered him around.

Fifteen years in the army had taught Dax how to take an order and, in more recent years as squad leader of a highly trained and elite team of soldiers, how to issue them. But never in his life had he been turned on by a direct command.

Move those hands any slower, Ranger, and I'll make you drop to your knees and give me twenty. And I'm not talking about pushups.

Dax found his gaze dropping to Emerson's hands and felt his lips curl up again into what he was pretty sure was a smile. It felt odd because he hadn't used those muscles much since being back stateside—awkward and a little rusty, but damn good.

"Oh no," she said, pointing to his mouth, her voice taking on that feisty edge he loved. He hadn't known her all that well growing up—she was a few years behind him in school—but he'd heard enough to know she had bite. "Aim that somewhere else. As I said, there will be no date, no repeat of that night, and absolutely no talking about it."

"But I love it when you talk."

She opened her mouth to argue, and when he gave those feisty lips all of his undivided attention, she closed it. Then pulled out her cell, her fingers swiping furiously across the screen. With a satisfied huff she stuck it back between her coconuts, and a second later his phone buzzed.

Not Interested in what you're selling.

He did a little swiping of his own. Hit Send, making her dig between those pretty shells.

Your coconuts say differently.

She looked down at her shells, perfectly in place, and scowled. He slid her another wink designed to rile her, and mission accomplished. Her eyes narrowed, her nostrils flared a little, and she got an intense expression that looked really similar to the expression she wore just before she exploded.

She leaned in, providing him an inspiring view of her coconuts, and with a quiet steel to her voice, said, "You, me, Johnnie, and Jack in San Francisco. It was a fun escape." He'd call it a hell of a lot more than fun but decided now was not the time to argue. "You and me here in St. Helena? Surrounded by the gossip mill, our crazy

NEED YOU FOR ALWAYS

families, and, well, life? That sounds . . ." She shivered—and not in a good way. "Suffocating."

"More complicated maybe, but I wouldn't say suffocating." Although thinking about sex with Emerson had his chest acting strangely.

"Complicated defeats the purpose," she said. "So let's agree that it was epic—"

"Epic, huh?"

"—and go back to being two people who happened to grow up in the same town."

"Two people who grew up in the same town." He tried that out, then looked at her mouth and shook his head. "Won't work. I've seen that cute tattoo on your a—"

She pressed her hand to his mouth and looked around. "Well, make it work, because no one in town knows what my tattoo looks like, and I like it that way. So as long as you are here, and gossip is still the town's leading commodity, this"—she dropped her hand to flap it between them—"is never going to happen."

When put that way, Dax saw her point. No strings only worked when there was nothing tying them to more than a casual, fun, and fuck-yeah kind of party—a hard thing to accomplish when surrounded by a shared past.

And Dax treated ties the same way he treated unidentified threats: avoid if at all possible, but if forced to engage, proceed with caution, use the appropriate level of force, get crafty when things get sketchy, and if all else fails, pop smoke.

Hands down, this was a pop-smoke kind of situation. But he'd always had a hard time walking away from a challenge—especially one with a smart mouth. So he closed the rest of the distance, pressed his lips to her ear, and whispered, "Never is a long time, Emi."

Satisfied when he heard her breath catch, he gave her a parting wink and headed toward the bar on the other side of the room, a thousand and one WTF questions going through his head. He'd only agreed to recuperate at home because, one, St. Helena Hospital had one of the top orthopedic specialists in the state, and, two, if he hadn't come home, his family would have come to him. Sharing the occasional meal on his terms seemed a hell of a lot easier than sharing bunk space with his two brothers.

He'd also agreed because he had a plan. A good one. Get in, get better, and get out—avoiding as many firefights as possible. The plan was working. His blown-out knee was still tender but healing, and he had a potential job lined up that would take him far enough away so that he could process the last few years without one of his eight hundred relatives asking what was wrong. Or one more little old lady dropping off another casserole. He wouldn't be working special ops in the military anymore, but he'd be engaging bad guys nonetheless. As long as his doctor signed off, which he'd make sure *would* happen, he was pretty sure the position was his. So a distraction right then probably wasn't smart, seeing as last time he'd been stupid enough to get distracted he'd ended up with a hunk of shrapnel in his leg.

Sure, the shattered kneecap still hurt like a bitch and the images were tattooed on the insides of his eyelids, but at least he'd come home. Others weren't as lucky. So in honor of buddies who'd never get that chance, guys who deserved it more than he did, he'd set up post in St. Helena. Not forever. *Jesus*, he couldn't take forever in a town that spewed sunshine and rainbows, but long enough to get back on his feet, so to speak, stuck for the next month in a house he'd sublet—spitting distance from one brother and hollering distance from the other. Not to mention the myriad of other relatives who also called St. Helena home.

Dax spotted his brother Adam over by the bar. Being an elite smoke jumper for the Napa County Fire Department, Adam was a hero in his own right, but not a soldier—past or present. Didn't stop him from holding up the bar like he owned the place, though.

"I didn't know you were coming," Dax said.

"Wasn't. Then I heard you were coming." Adam was usually the most laid-back of the brothers, but tonight he looked like a force of nature in his SHFD T-shirt and his ball cap pulled low. "On your bike."

On an expired license went unsaid, because they both knew Dax hadn't been stateside long enough to renew it. "It was just a few blocks."

"Explain that to Jonah. Because last he knew I was your ride today, then he gets a call that you were spotted driving your motorcycle with a jacked-up knee down Main Street."

Two minutes and he already had a headache. "How did he know?"

"Nora Kincaid posted it on the town's Facebook page. It's under her Damn Fine Vintage album if you want to check it out."

Dax blew out a breath. He shouldn't have asked. Nosy Nora had been perched outside his stoop since he got home, trying to catch a picture of the missing Baudouin brother. Keeping a secret from leaking in St. Helena was like trying to stop Niagara Falls with a tampon.

"Is he pissed?" Dax asked.

Jonah was the biggest tight-ass of the group. Loved every letter of the law. All that black-and-white text really revved his engine. Not a surprise since he was also the oldest and acted like he carried the entire universe on his shoulders. Yup, the local sheriff was big, badass, and when packing that brother-knows-best attitude, could be intimidating. And irritating as hell.

He was also one of the best men Dax knew. Honest, tough, loyal, and a man who got things done. Jonah could find gold in a shitstorm, herd feral cats, and swim through land. He was that good.

"Called me nine times. When I didn't answer he came over waving his phone, acting like I'm your keeper. Interrupted the best nap I've had in weeks." The way his brother's hair was tucked messily under his cap and the relaxed, just-been-laid stance he had going on told Dax that his nap was done in tandem. "Said he'd arrest you next time."

"What did he expect me to do? Take the senior shuttle?"

"Be smart enough to know that nothing good will come of you driving that bike with your knee. Or, I don't know, you could always call someone who owns a car and ask for a ride," Adam suggested.

"Jonah's on duty, it's your day off, and based on your T-shirt being inside out, you were otherwise occupied." Dax shouldered his way past Adam to order a beer. He might be the baby of the brothers, but he had three inches and thirty pounds on the both of them.

"And yet I'm still here," Adam said, giving the bartender a nod. "Next time call Shay. She's all smiles when she gets to help someone in need."

"Yeah," Dax said, running a hand down his neck. How did one go about explaining that his brother's wife was kind of crazy? Pretty as hell, sweet, funny, perfect for Jonah, but crazy as hell when it came to her animals. "Did that. I ended up going to PT with a Shetland pony on my lap. On the return I got stuck with a flock of geese who were left behind in the migration. I got suckered into goose-sitting for two days. Two days of honking and feathers, bro."

Now it was Adam's turn to run a hand down his face, only he was hiding a stupid grin. "It's called a gaggle, and I heard the mama has a thing for pecking at the boys."

She also had a thing for sneaking up on him when he was in the shower—and his boys weren't covered. "Which is why I came alone. Mr. Fallon is in town, he wanted to meet me in person, but I didn't want to show up covered in feathers or holding a bag of frozen peas."

Mickey Fallon was the former chief of the San Francisco Police Department and an old army buddy of Dax's commanding officer, who was also at the party. Three years ago, Fallon had been asked to head up a security company in Silicon Valley that provided elite detail teams for private sector businesses, so when he'd e-mailed Dax and asked if he wanted to meet up for a beer, Dax had jumped at the chance. He was more than qualified for the position, but he was the only outsider in the running, and if he wanted his transition into civilian life to go as smoothly as possible, then having Fallon's blessing would go a long way toward securing this job.

"Well, you can meet him holding this," Adam said, trading the bartender a bill for a drink. It was tall, fruity looking, prissy as hell, and had one of those umbrellas sticking out of the top. And it was pink—the umbrella and the drink.

"What the hell is this?"

"You in a glass." Adam took the cold draft off the tray, clinked rims, then took a long swallow. "Now, if you want one of these," he said, holding up the beer, "you need to man up." When Dax didn't make a move for the glass, Adam went serious. "You applied for a job with Jonah's former boss. And you didn't say a word. To me or Jonah. We want to hear these things from *you*, not the grapevine. It sucks having to pretend we know what the hell's going on in our own family."

This was not the conversation Dax wanted to have tonight. "Because I'm still in the application process." And because he didn't want to spend the next five weeks defending his decision to live a good two hours from home and his family.

"We knew that convincing you to stay for the long term was a pipe dream, but to apply with Jonah's friend for a job that would take you to San Jose and not say a word?" Adam shook his head, which made Dax feel like he was ten all over again.

"This isn't a for-sure thing," Dax explained. "And I knew if I told you guys I was applying, Jonah would want to hook me up. Help out. And I didn't want his name to sway the decision."

Jonah hadn't always been a small-town sheriff. Prior to working in the sheriff's department, Dax's older brother had been one of the top detectives at SFPD. He was respected, admired by everyone he talked to, and a real honest-to-God hero. If Dax wanted those kinds of expectations hanging over his head, he would have stayed here in St. Helena. "I wanted to get it on my own merit."

So that there wouldn't be any misconceptions about exactly who they were hiring. Dax was good at his job—better than good. He had been one of the best snipers in the army and had no doubt he could out-shoot, out-train, and out-strategize any of the competition. It was when he wasn't combat ready that he fell short.

Both of his brothers had a charisma about them. *Baudouin charm*, as his stepmom called it. A way of making people feel safe, involved. Making people want to be better, do more just from being in their presence, which made them powerful leaders. Dax didn't have that.

Didn't want it.

By nature, snipers clung to the shadows, a position that fit Dax's personality well and had earned him the name Wolf. He liked being a part of a team, liked the rush of a mission, but didn't want the responsibility again that came with being a squad leader or looking through the scope of the gun and being the one to decide if he pulled the trigger. Nope, this time around, he wanted to do his job, do it well, then be able to clock out and go home without fear of closing his eyes.

Simple, straightforward, clean-cut.

"Too bad for you, Fallon had dinner with Jonah," Adam said, and Dax's stomach knotted. "And it looks like they're headed this way."

Dax turned to look at the entrance, disappointed he couldn't catch a glimpse of Emerson through the door. Just his luck, he *could* see his big brother leading the former chief right toward him. Chest puffed out, superhero complex in full effect, Jonah walked right over and gave Dax a hug. It was a handshake/bro-hug combo that was a little heavy on the back smack part.

"You made it," Jonah said as though this were his meeting. "Dax, this is Mickey Fallon. Mickey, this is my brother Dax. And like I was saying, you couldn't ask for a better addition to your team."

Fallon reached out a hand. "After spending the day with Jonah here, I'm starting to realize that a Baudouin is just what our team needs."

chapter
two

Emerson wasn't much for sweating the little things. She'd long ago learned that stressing over variables she couldn't change was a big energy suck. It also clashed with her tough-girl persona. But with fifty pounds of shaved lamb shank and an entire day's profit hinging on a faulty heating system, she felt the first bead of perspiration slide between her breasts.

Today she'd set up her cart in front of town hall to attract the tourists who were in town for Crush, wine country's harvest season. The big clock above the pillars of town hall told her she had fifteen minutes until Twofer Tuesday began, and with her own twist on her mom's famous lamb gyros, she wasn't surprised by the line of hungry customers roughing the harsh wind, waiting for her to open.

With one last attempt at relighting the pilot light, which failed the second the wind passed through the duct, Emerson slammed the access panel. Telling herself it would take more than a temperamental starter to take her down, she raced down Main Street toward Cork'd N Dipped.

"Sterno," Emerson announced as she pushed through the wooden door. "Where did you store the big ones I ordered last month?"

"Used them to keep the hot buttered wine steaming last weekend," Ida Beamon said from beneath a display of chocolate plantains. "But I think I have some of the fondue size left."

Ida had frosted hair, violet bifocals, and was wearing enough pink feathers on her shirt to be confused for a flock of flamingoes. She was also the owner of St. Helena's only wine and chocolate bar—and most likely the artist behind the dipped plantains.

"Those will do." They'd have to. She was desperate, not a new feeling for her, and with the clock ticking, it was time to get creative.

"They're in the kitchen pantry, next to the his-and-hers fondue skewers," Ida said.

"Thanks." Emerson raced past the glass walls of wine bottles and into the commercial kitchen she subleased from Ida for her business. In order to make her mom's dream a reality, she'd needed a commercial kitchen to secure her food licenses—and Ida had the only one on Main Street that wasn't being used regularly. So in exchange for a few hundred bucks a month and catering a couple of events at the wine bar each year, Emerson wound up with the female Willy Wonka as her kitchenmate.

And a resident duck as her neighbor. As Emerson flicked on the light, she found Norton on the center island, beak covered in pistachios, tail lowered to the metal tabletop, looking ready to defend the baklava he'd discovered. The baklava she'd spent two hours making.

"Norton! Down!" Emerson commanded, even snapped her fingers and pointed from the bird to the floor.

Norton puffed out his wings and, tail straight back, parted his beak—duck for *What? What?*—then went back to pecking the baklava. In fact, the plate was practically pecked clean and he was already eyeing the other full tray.

"One more peck at my profits and you will end up a pillow. Got it?" To her frustration, all she got was a good look at the duck's backside when Norton gave tail before going for the tray. "You want to play dirty?"

Emerson pulled a squirt bottle out from the pantry and fired. Once, twice, all the while making a *psht psht* sound, just like the Dog Whisperer did on the show Ida watched while prepping for happy hour. And because Norton was more concerned with proving himself a dog instead of a water fowl, he hopped off the table and scuttled his tail feathers right out of the kitchen and through the doggie door.

Quark! Quark! Quark!

Emerson slid the remaining tray of baklava onto the top shelf of the pantry for safekeeping, then located the his-and-hers skewers, which had interesting places to secure the fruit and meat. Next to them were the fondue cans. They were small, too small for what she needed, but they would have to do. She grabbed every last one, located a candle lighter, just in case, then made her way back to the front—snatching a stick of chocolate-covered bacon because, yeah, it was going to be one of those days.

"You got any duct tape?" she asked.

"Yup." Ida set down the fresh fig she was dipping in a vat of bitter-smelling dark chocolate and walked to the register to pull out some tape. "Add some of those nautical ropes I bought for last week's coastal wine tasting and I'd say you were looking to get lucky."

Emerson laughed while bagging her stuff. She wouldn't mind getting lucky right about then. With her cart, that was. "The Pita Peddler's pilot won't light. I think there's something wrong with the starter."

"Uh-huh." Ida studied Emerson's outfit and frowned. "Seems to me like you're looking to be noticed. Even before you picked up that dating starter kit."

Emerson was wearing her uniform—KISS MY BAKLAVA tee and leggings—but she'd swapped out her usual black skirt for a short denim one with a million zippers and pockets, and, because attitude leads to altitude, her American flag Converse high-tops. And okay, so she'd seen Dax jogging around the community park yesterday, all hot, sweaty, and breathtakingly shirtless. That didn't mean she'd applied mascara for his sake.

Emerson dropped the lighter inside when Ida grabbed the bag and held it hostage behind the counter. "Lunch starts in ten minutes, Ida."

"Promise me you'll wear the cork costume on Saturday night, and I'll give you the bag."

A subtle throbbing started behind Emerson's forehead. "What's Saturday night? And why am I wearing a cork costume?"

"Saturday night the girls and I are throwing a party. It will be our first weekly Blow Your Cork Singles Night," Ida said as though the words *party* and *the girls* didn't inspire terror in townspeople everywhere.

The girls referred to Ida, Peggy, and Clovis—a blue-haired trifecta of trouble. All three were kissing seventy, stubborn as hell, and loved to stir up serious trouble. And when men and alcohol were involved, it usually wound up in someone pulling out the cuffs—sometimes even the cops.

"The dance at the VFW was a bust," Ida said with force. "Can't make friendly with the Johns with all of those younger Janes from the active living community sniffing around, looking for a sugar daddy."

"You mean the active living community that requires you to be fifty-five or older?" Emerson asked, because she could either give Ida two of her rapidly disappearing minutes to hear her out or the older woman would hold her Sterno cans hostage. Worse, Ida would follow Emerson out to the cart and talk her ear off while every patron in line listened.

"At fifty-five I could dance without wheezing, laugh without wetting my unmentionables, and my nipples still pointed up instead of looking like they were beacons for finding water." Ida cupped her ample water beacons and lifted them heavenward a good twelve inches. "Anyway, liquoring the men up only to have you pop right out of that top. Pastor Sam nearly had an aneurysm seeing you in those shells." Ida shook her head. "We want you on the ticket to bring the guys in, but unless you're in a cardboard box, you'd steal the ones with real teeth."

"As tempting as *that* sounds," Emerson said, dying a little inside at the glimpse into her future, "I can't cater your event Saturday. I have the farmers' market all day, and with so many tourists in town for the harvest, I've been doing a second serving out by DeLuca Vineyards."

Crush only lasted a few months, and with the weather turning colder and it getting darker earlier, Emerson was working every angle she could get before winter made her job a whole lot harder.

"Now can I have the bag?" Emerson held out her hand.

"I'll pay you a hundred dollars more than you'd make at the winery, plus twenty percent of tips if you look like a cork every Saturday and serve tapas," Ida said as though she were back in the old country, negotiating fava beans for ten cents a pound.

Emerson couldn't believe she was even considering spending the evening with the geriatric mafia, especially after what was going to be one exhausting week, but an extra hundred bucks was a hundred bucks closer to her goal. Not to mention the tips from the night would be huge.

She estimated how much she'd make at the vineyard, added a hundred, then said, "Six hundred bucks, you hire someone to do cleanup, I get *half* of the tips, and no costume. Now give me the bag."

Ida held out the bag, but when Emerson went to take it, the older woman's bony hands gripped tighter. "Six hundred, I handle cleanup, *forty* percent of tips, and the costume is nonnegotiable."

Sadly, a cork didn't even come close to her most embarrassing costume request, and passing on a regular six-hundred-plus-tips gig for one that would end in a few weeks' time wasn't smart business.

Emerson took a deep, calming breath, resigning herself to suiting up, and said, "Deal." Grabbing the bag, she hurried back to her cart, mentally adding the mechanic's time and estimated parts it would cost to fix the cart's heating system, and sighed. It seemed as though every time she got a step closer to her target, there was always some kind of setback.

After taping the Sterno cans together to make two superburners, she placed them under the chafing trays. One flick of the lighter and she was back in business. Feeling very MacGyvery and a bit smug that she had five minutes to spare, she opened the blue-and-white umbrella, which was the national flag of Greece, and turned to the first customer, who was offering up a toothy grin and a twenty.

Seeing the customer, Emerson immediately went into crisis-management mode. A mode she had become familiar with over the past two years.

So much for her five-minute lead.

"What are you doing here, Violet?"

Her six-year-old sister, Violet Blake, stood on the other side of the cart in a pink fuzzy jacket, two curly pigtails, and glittery fairy wings strapped to her back, swishing happily back and forth. Their twenty-three-year age difference raised eyebrows, but surprises happened. And Violet had turned out to be the best surprise. "It's Pixie Girl. And Dad said I could have some baklava."

"Sorry, baklava is for humans only." She ignored Violet's pout and zeroed her gaze in on her dad, who forced an innocent grin from behind his youngest. "It's the middle of the school day," she pointed out.

Roger Blake shrugged as though not seeing the problem with this. His peppered hair was windblown, his Hawaiian shirt slept in, and his feet were in flip-flops. The frayed cargo shorts and sleepy eyes only added to the beach bum image he had going on. "We're taking a field trip."

"The principal gave me two days off on account of fairy dust landing in Brooklyn's eye," Violet informed the line as though she hadn't just confessed to being suspended. "Only it's Taco Tuesday at school, and I like tacos, so I didn't want to leave."

Roger rested his hand on Violet's slim shoulder. "Who wants a taco when we can have dessert for lunch?"

"So Dad brought you here, after getting suspended, to celebrate with dessert?" Emerson asked and both dad and daughter nodded. Emerson dropped her head and took a calming breath. It didn't help.

This wasn't the first fairy-inspired incident, and because she was afraid it wouldn't be the last, she resisted the urge to high-five her sister for giving Brooklyn a dose of her own medicine—an act that would be as irresponsible as buying her a dessert to celebrate her first elementary assault charge. Emerson knelt down and looked her sister in the eye. Long and hard.

"Want to explain how glitter wound up in Brooklyn's eyes when you were banned from bringing glitter to school?"

"Fairy dust," Violet corrected while toeing at the ground with her pink Converse. "And Lillianna Starlight gave me some this morning."

"Imagine that." Emerson looked Lillianna Starlight right in the eyes—and he had the decency to look ashamed. "I didn't know you still talked to Lillianna."

Chocolate-colored pigtails bobbed. "I sent her a message through fairy mail yesterday and told her how Brooklyn told the whole class that fairies weren't real. Then this morning a letter was under my pillow that said all nonbelievers needed was a little love and a lot of fairy dust."

Eyes never leaving Lillianna's, Emerson piled some lamb into a pita and rolled it up. "Take this and go wait over there while I talk to Dad."

Violet looked from the gyro to Dad and back to Emerson. "What about my baklava?"

"You're lucky it isn't tabbouleh. Now go, before I change my mind."

Horrified at the thought of being forced to eat something green, she hustled her little fairy butt over to the bench and sat down, wings flapping in the breeze.

"Not you." Emerson caught Lillianna by the cuff of his shirt. "I thought you had an interview today at Bella Vineyards."

Roger shifted back on his feet. "It was for a delivery manager, which means I'd miss breakfast and seeing her off to school."

"The last job offer was a nine-to-five, and you passed because you'd miss picking her up from school. If you're not careful, you'll end up passing on your whole future, Dad." The once sought-after vineyard manager had found a logical, rational, mature-sounding reason to pass on every opportunity that came his way. When in truth Emerson knew that going back to work meant finally letting go, admitting they'd lost the battle, the fight, and the most important person in all of their lives.

"Plus I'd miss twilight walks with Pixie," he said quietly, and Emerson sighed. The soul-deep kind of sigh that started in her toes and moved its way out through her heart. Her dad was so busy making sure he took the right steps in moving forward, he was stuck in the same place he'd been the day his soul mate died. And he'd kept Violet right there with him.

"Violet," she gently corrected. "And I thought we were done with this."

"We were," Roger said, running a hand though his hair. "Then that Brooklyn girl started giving Violet a hard time."

"Because she wears wings to school, only answers to Pixie, and talks to daisies and grass blades at recess," Emerson said with a quiet intensity to ensure Roger finally got it. "The only thing worse for a first grader would be a 'Kick me, I'm socially inept' sign on her back."

Roger winced. "I thought about throwing those damn wings out when she was sleeping, but then I remembered your mom made them for her that last Halloween." He shrugged helplessly, looking as lost as he had the day the real Lillianna had died. "I figured, what could it hurt?"

Emerson felt her throat tighten. "A lot, Dad. She can't mourn someone she is convinced lives under a toadstool. And it isn't healthy for her to only socialize with imaginary friends."

"She socializes with me."

Which was the equivalent of hanging with Peter Pan. And they both knew it.

Violet had been an unexpected miracle baby, and her parents had embraced that every day of Violet's little life. When her mom's ALS had taken a fatal turn, Lillianna had been determined to make every day she had left with her girls magical. And she had, sharing every family recipe with Emerson, taking Violet on backyard fairy hunts at twilight, making sure that when she was gone her daughters would have a lifetime full of happy memories to combat the heart-wrenching ones.

After her death, Roger had taken on the responsibility of Violet's happiness. Leaving every other responsibility to Emerson. Not that she would change it for the world. Emerson loved taking care of her family, knew that she was the only thing keeping them from falling completely off the grid. And she wanted Violet to experience some of what she'd had as a child, but sometimes being the only realistic one in a family of dreamers made things difficult.

Take Lillianna Starlight, for example, the fairy who slept under daisy petals and traveled by shooting stars. Emerson wanted Violet to remember their mom, remember their walks and the love she had for make-believe and magic. Unlike her father, though, Emerson worried that the make-believe was holding Violet back. Keeping her from moving on.

Her heart a little heavier than it had been moments ago, Emerson made up one of her mom's famous lamb gyros with extra tzatziki, just the way Roger liked it, then packed up two pieces of baklava to go. "At least stop giving her things she can assault her classmates with."

He took the bag and smiled. "Will do."

The Sterno didn't last as long as Emerson had anticipated. Neither did her lamb, since she was only two hours into the lunch shift and nearly sold out. At this rate she'd have her food truck by the end of next month, a thought that had her smiling as she greeted the next customer in line.

"What can I get you?"

Mrs. Larson, the refurbish part of St. Helena Hardware and Refurbish Rescue, looked at the nearly empty dessert tin and frowned. "Two wraps, and please don't tell me you're out of baklava. I'm having an old pipe organ from a condemned church in Colusa delivered today and I was hoping to put Walt in a sugar coma for a few hours while I had it moved to the back warehouse. One look at the size of those pipes and he'll start sputtering up a storm."

Emerson reached under the cart counter into her secret-stash cabinet and pulled out a bag with "Larson" written on it. "I know how much Walt loves his baklava, so I set aside a few pieces for you."

"Aren't you a sweetheart?" Mrs. Larson took the bag and clutched it to her chest, her silvered bob bouncing as she wiggled with excitement. "I know the second Walt sees how lovely the pipes will look in the ceiling-to-floor headboard, he'll fall in love with it. He just doesn't have the same vision I was blessed with."

Emerson wasn't as confident in Walt's ability to call what sounded like a bizarre twist of taking it to church "lovely," but she was certain his love for his wife would overcome his need to toss the organ out.

Walt had made it clear to the entire town that even though his wife had turned half of his hardware shop into a scene from a Dr. Seuss story with her eclectic rehabbed furniture, he was still her biggest fan.

To Emerson, that kind of unwavering support ranked a solid fifteen on her swoon-worthy scale.

"Anything else?" Emerson asked.

"Well, yes." Mrs. Larson looked around first before lowering her voice. "Walt's sixty-fifth birthday is next month and I'm throwing him a small family party. I was hoping to surprise him with that cake your mom used to sell at the farmers' market. The orange one with the liqueur frosting?"

"Orange sponge cake with Metaxa frosting?" she asked, her throat suddenly going tight.

Mrs. Larson snapped her fingers. "Yes, that one. It's Walt's favorite."

It was Emerson's favorite too. Her mom had made it for her on every birthday.

Emerson held her smile firm, but her insides sank at the idea of replicating her mom's special-occasion cake. "I can try, but I can't promise it will taste exactly like my mom's," she admitted. It was one of the few recipes Emerson didn't know by heart, and it had sadly gone missing, along with the journal her mother had made for her.

Its disappearance was one of life's mysteries Emerson couldn't seem to get past. She'd racked her brain, torn up the house, interrogated Violet. Then sadly realized that just like her mom, the journal—*her* journal—had been reduced to a collection of memories.

Last year, when it seemed that the memories were starting to fade, Emerson had tried to re-create it—without luck. The result was a delicious cake. Just not Lillianna's-orange-Metaxa-cake delicious.

"I'm sure you'll make it magic, just like your mom." Mrs. Larson reached over the cart to pat Emerson's hand. She had complete faith in Emerson's ability, but Emerson wasn't so sure. She continued smiling anyway.

Mrs. Larson smiled back, turned, then did a double take as she realized something. "My, don't you look pretty today, wearing lipstick *and* serving your mom's man-bait lamb wraps." Hand to her chest, her eyes twinkled with intrigue. "Why, Emerson Blake, who are you trying to trap?"

"It's called Chapstick. People wear it in the cold months to avoid chapped lips," she deadpanned, wondering just how bad she normally looked, while ignoring the fact that she had made her mom's notorious man-bait lamb wraps. The same recipe that had snagged Roger's heart.

"Uh-huh," Mrs. Larson said, clearly not buying a word of it. And wasn't that the epitome of food cart culture? A good cart with voicey food brought the customers back day in and day out, making it feel like serving family. And family, as Emerson knew, never missed a thing—especially if it led to gossip. "What do you think?" Mrs. Larson asked, looking over Emerson's shoulder.

"Tempting enough to bring me over," a sexy voice said from behind.

Emerson didn't have to turn to see who it was, because her chest fluttered—and when she did turn, those flutters became annoying pings whose reach was a little too south for her liking. Dax towered behind her, his wide shoulders blocking out the sun and his super-powered testosterone blocking her ability to think clearly.

He wore a pair of longer running shorts and one of those tight, clingy shirts that runners wore during marathons. And it was cling-ing to him, all right. He was sweaty and sun kissed and looked ready for anything.

"Well, look who it is," Mrs. Larson said, tilting her frosted head way back to look up into Dax's face. "You *are* home. Figured the rumor mill had it wrong since you haven't returned a single one of my calls."

"Something must be wrong with my phone, since I haven't received other calls as well," he said, his eyes firmly on Emerson, who busied herself with making up and bagging Mrs. Larson's order. "But it's good to see you, Aunt Connie." Dax pulled his aunt in for a hug. "I have been busy, but I'll try to stop by next week."

"I'll have to bring over one of my spaghetti casseroles in the meantime." Mrs. Larson released Dax, but not before patting his rock-hard stomach. Emerson could have sworn she heard Dax groan. "Look at you, wasting away. I bet you haven't had a real meal since you've been home."

Emerson smothered a laugh. Wasting away her butt. The man was built like a fine-tuned machine—with enough muscles and charm to have a woman drooling.

"Hey, Emi." His eyes dropped to her tank top and he smiled. "No coconut shells? Too bad. Although today's special looks . . . appetizing. I'll take two, since I'd hate to waste away."

And because his eyes were glued to her KISS MY BAKLAVA offer, she said, "Sorry. I'm all out."

"You have to compliment her, dear," Mrs. Larson whispered, patting his arm. "Then she pulls out the good stuff." With a kiss to her nephew's cheek, she waddled away with her order in hand.

Dax turned back to Emerson and offered up an amused grin. "The good stuff, huh?" His eyes roamed over her, from her high-tops to her Chapstick and everything in between. "What kind of compliment lets me taste your baklava?"

"My baklava is in pretty high demand, as you can see. Nearly sold out. And the line starts back there."

Dax took in the long line of customers, which wound and disappeared around the corner. "But you'll be *all* out before I get here," he said.

Emerson smiled. "I know."

ch⬤pter
three

"How much do I owe you?" Dax called out, setting his napkin down on the worn steel counter made from the tailgate of a '48 Ford pickup.

Stan O'Malley, owner of Stan's Soup and Service Station, came in from the garage floor wearing a blue mechanic's jumper, holding a carburetor in one hand and a rag in the other. Both mechanic and jumper were covered with a day's worth of grease. "It's on the house."

Dax looked down at the two empty bowls of blue-ribbon chili, three sides of corn bread, and empty bottle of soda and reached for his wallet.

Stan waved his rag at the offering. "How I see it, I still owe you and Kyle for all those years you'd come help me work on my bikes. Probably clocked over a few hundred hours here."

Dax laughed. "That was senior year alone."

Kyle was Dax's best friend, and Kyle's grandpa's shop had been Dax's escape in high school, the only thing that kept Dax out of finding real trouble after his dad's heart attack. In fact, witnessing the kind of man Stan was, hearing his war stories and the talk of his brotherhood, had piqued Dax's interest in joining the army.

"Just think of lunch as a welcome-home gift," the older man said, rubbing the rag over his bald head, spreading more grease than he eliminated.

Arguing with a man who was stubborn enough to make it through the jungles of Vietnam with a shattered vertebra was a waste of energy, so he slipped his wallet back in his pocket. "Thanks, Stan."

"Just glad you made it home safe and in one piece."

Dax tapped his knee. "That could be argued." There were a lot of other places he could tap too, but since they weren't external scars, he kept that to himself.

"Broke but still ticking and my grandson says it should heal up just right. I'd say you did good, son."

That was up for debate, which was one of the reasons Dax had come to Stan's for lunch. "You got any bikes back there that need a second opinion?"

"I got a pumpkin-basil soup that needs some help, and that's it. I stopped doing bikes a few years back. All those dot-commers moved up with their fancy weekend warrior hogs, hovering over my shoulder while I changed their oil like I was birthing Jesus." He flapped a hand. "Not worth the trouble."

Stan lifted the lid on a large pot, and a warm blast of nutmeg and basil scented the air. He wasn't just one of the best mechanics Dax knew, the old-timer was a master with the spoon. His soups had been written up in just about every foodie magazine on the planet. "You still good with a knife?"

Dax lifted a challenging brow, and the old man handed him a butcher knife and pointed to a stack of pumpkin needing dicing.

"I can't cook worth shit," Dax admitted, rolling up his sleeves and washing his hands.

"I remember. Assumed that's why you're here. Hungry for some hearty food."

He couldn't dice worth shit either, but slicing vegetables was better than the alternative—sitting at home and crawling up the walls.

Hanging with Stan was also smarter than his new favorite hobby, an afternoon game of Where's Emi?, which consisted of tracking down Emi's food cart at one of her fifteen locations around town and checking out how short her skirt of the day was.

Yesterday she had been parked across from the community park wearing a tight black number that, when paired with her knee-high boots, blew his mind. But today the sun had been out, the autumn air surprisingly warm, and she had opted for a spot by the fire station and a summery little orange number that flirted with the breeze—sans those usual leggings.

He'd considered dropping by for lunch, which smelled amazing, but the line for food was worse than the other day. Today it went down Main Street, wrapping around Pope Street and into the senior center parking lot. Not to mention that every time he ran by, she pretended to ignore him, and he pretended not to stare at her ass. Or check out her baklava.

"Just chop them in big chunks." Stan handed him an apron and Dax went to work cutting. "The seeds go in that bowl. And when you're done, I'll send you home with some for later."

"That's okay," Dax said, thinking of the dozen or so casseroles shoved in his freezer. "Between the friendly pop-ins and endless casseroles, I've had enough small-town hospitality to last me through the winter."

Stan laughed, going into a gravelly cough at the end, and Dax realized how old his friend appeared. The man had always looked older than time, but to a lost teen kid, Stan had seemed like an immortal warrior—battle scarred and range tough.

Today, though, he seemed shorter, a little fragile even. And Dax didn't know what to do with that information. So he filed it in his to-process pile, which was already backlogged until 2057.

"When I was overseas, all I could think about was comfort food," Stan said. "Then I got back stateside and the smell of those tuna salad casseroles the church ladies would bring by made my insides itch." Stan patted Dax on the shoulder and held his hand there for a moment. The air went thick with understanding and a genuine empathy that, for once, Dax didn't mind accepting. "People just showing they care, not understanding that sometimes the care is suffocating. It's why I started making soup. Stopped the covered-dish parade." Stan paused. "And a whole lot more."

With a final pat to the back, Stan said, "Now get chopping. I've got a food critic coming by for dinner and I got to get that squash marinated and roasted."

"Yes, sir."

"Oh," Stan called over his shoulder before disappearing into the garage. "Make sure you return those casserole dishes."

"Return them?" That would mean having to go to each and every house, being invited in for more neighborly visits and gut-churning chats. "I don't even know who brought me what."

Stan chuckled. "Might want to figure that out soon, son, or else you'll have a whole other kind of parade marching on your door-step. And they'll be carrying condemnation and sharpened knitting needles."

Later, as Dax was finishing up with the last of the pumpkins, a tall figure appeared in the doorway wearing a big hat, a sidearm, and a smug look that was all big brother and respected sheriff rolled into one.

"You should have Mickey add kitchen helper to your résumé," Jonah said, taking off his sheriff's hat and setting it on the counter. "I bet it would be great for undercover work."

"Stan needed help, so I'm pitching in," Dax defended, tightening the bow on his apron, grimacing when he tried to move his stiff knee. Everything below his knee ached and everything above it was sore. He needed a solid night's sleep but knew going home to his empty rental would only make him antsier.

"You sure he's the one who needed the help?"

Dax set down the knife to argue, then picked it back up, because according to the gas-pump clock over the door, he'd been in that coffin-sized work space for over two hours, chopping pumpkins, onions, celery—not a single slice was the same size, and Stan would probably have to toss it all out—but Dax hadn't itched once.

"Can I get a bowl of the chili?" Jonah asked. "Heavy on the cheese but light on the onions. Shay and I are driving out to Sonoma to get a schnoodle when I get home."

Dax wasn't sure if schnoodle was married code for sex or another furry friend Shay was taking in. But since either option gave him a rash, he silently filled the order and slid the bowl across the counter.

Jonah took a spoonful. "The other night seemed to go well with Mickey. You hear anything back yet?"

"There are a few other guys in the running, applying from other teams, but he said as long as my doctor gives me the all clear, I shouldn't have anything to worry about." Dax opened up two sodas and slid one to Jonah. "Thanks for the other night. The intro really helped."

Jonah lifted his bottle before taking a swig, and instead of lecturing Dax about not coming to him in the first place, he just said, "Glad it worked out."

"Fallon said they'll make their final decision by the time I finish PT."

"What are you going to do between now and then?" Jonah took another bite of chili. "Since you've been home a little over two weeks and already you're going nuts."

"Who says I'm going nuts?" Jonah merely eyed the apron and piles of vegetables. "Okay, maybe I have a little cabin fever."

Bullshit and they both knew it. Dax needed that job. Needed it to start sooner than later. More than anything Dax needed to feel useful again, and sitting on his ass watching the rain fall was slowly killing him—no matter how many pumpkins he chopped.

"That's why I brought over this." Jonah handed him an unaddressed envelope from the Napa County Sheriff's Department. Wiping his hands on the apron, Dax opened it to find a flier for a department-hosted event. "What's this?"

"Close-quarters battle training for the department. The deputy in charge relocated to Reno and we have a few new guys who are applying for the two open positions in my department, and I want to see how they work under pressure. As the new sheriff, it falls to me to secure some guest instructors until we can fill the position. I think with your background in weapons and CQB, you'd be great."

Dax studied the flier, thought about what it would be like to teach a bunch of deputies about the latest and greatest in guns, then remembered that the job would mean working directly with his brother in the middle of Mayberry.

"Not interested."

Jonah leveled him with a look that was all business. "If you want to work with civilians, then you need to get involved in the community. Prove to Fallon that you can acclimate to civilian life, make connections, and that you're willing to be an active participant in the neighborhood."

Dax wasn't looking to make connections—he was looking to do a job that had the least chance of connecting. Which was why he was applying for corporate security. The only people he'd have to connect with would be his team and high-value suits. "Did Fallon say something?"

"Other than you being the exact kind of badass the team was looking for?" Jonah shook his head, and Dax could see the pride behind his brother's eyes. "Nope. I just know that the difference between the guys who make it and the ones who blow out is their ability to adapt. I also know that teaching these classes would be a good way to blow off some steam while you're waiting to get back in the game." Jonah stood and put his hat back on. "And maybe some options in case the game you're looking for has changed. Oh, and here."

Jonah handed Dax one more piece of paper. This one was pink and way too official looking to be anything other than his big brother's way of sticking it to him.

"A ticket, man? What the hell?"

"Driving the bike out front on an expired license and registration is against the law." Jonah tipped his head. "Now you have a good day."

Exhausted from another day as the local food-cart girl, Emerson walked the narrow flight of steps leading into her apartment, engaging in her nightly ritual of wondering if today was the day the mail was finally going to deliver good news or bad news. She'd definitely prefer no news to bad news.

Her apartment wasn't much, but it was cozy and quiet—and hers. Located above the Boulder Holder, a lingerie shop for the curvier set, Emerson had one bedroom, one bathroom, and a one-car garage big enough for her food cart. She also had exactly one neighbor—her best friend, Harper Owens.

Who was curled up on Emerson's couch, watching the latest made-for-television killer-sharks film.

"Remind me to file a complaint with management. The security around here sucks," Emerson said, dropping her keys into the bowl by the front door and hanging her backpack on the hook.

"You bet," management said, holding a container of what Emerson was fairly certain were lamb empanadas to her chest.

Harper's grandmother owned the century-old Victorian. A few months after Emerson's mom had passed, the older woman had spontaneously decided to rent out the second studio, which she'd been using as an overflow storage space, for, wouldn't you know it, the exact amount Emerson could afford.

It was a handout and everyone involved knew it—but numb and desperate for a quiet space to grieve, a place where she didn't have to be the strong one, where she could process and make a life plan, she'd signed the lease and wound up with Harper as her property manager.

Harper pulled out a flaky pocket of heaven and took a huge bite, then closed her eyes. "God, this is so good. What is it?"

"My dinner," Emerson accused in her scariest tone. Unconcerned, Harper took a bigger bite, moaned a little louder, then offered up the container as if *she* was willing to share.

Unsure of how karma would react to harming a person who wore a knitted kitty sweater, pink leggings, and smelled like unicorns and Play-Doh, Emerson snatched one of the empanadas and plopped on the couch. The first bite was heaven. Flaky crust, hearty filling, and a taste that reminded her of crisp fall days with her mom.

Eyes on the screen, Harper said, "I heard Mr. Dark and Mysterious is in town."

Emerson choked on her bite. She wasn't a big talker, didn't need girl time or ice cream binges to chat it out. In fact, she was content to take everything she felt, did, or witnessed to the grave. Too bad Harper was a ninja master of ferreting out secrets. Those big blue eyes, swishing ponytail, and sunny smile were too powerful a force for even a cynic like Emerson to resist. If Harper got wind of a secret, she was on it like white on rice.

Which was why Emerson schooled her features and shrugged as though Mr. Dark and Mysterious hadn't asked her for a replay of their night together. "Huh."

"Don't 'huh' me. The guy you had wall-banging sex with, followed by wild shower sex with, and then—"

"I get it." And reliving it all over again wasn't going to help her keep her distance, which was imperative.

"Yeah, you got it all right." Harper snorted. "Which is why I find it odd that he's back, a few minutes away, *and* he was at the VFW dance that *you* were working, and you said not a word about it."

"Because there wasn't anything worth mentioning." Emerson snatched the last empanada and shoved it into her mouth. "I need to focus on my truck, not get distracted in the final mile by some guy—"

"Last time you called him a sex ninja."

She'd called him worse in her mind. "I was drunk."

"Which is how I know you were telling the truth," Harper said with a knowing smile. "When you get tipsy you get all mushy, and girly, and chatty. You even let me do your nails and makeup."

Which was why she didn't drink often. First, she was, surprisingly, a lightweight. Second, she went from a fighter to lover in two shots of whiskey—just ask Dax. And most importantly, growing up with a sick mother meant weekly trips to the ER, where she'd go from sound asleep to ready to go in seconds, which had taught Emerson the risk wasn't worth it. Being in control and ready for anything had been the key to surviving her childhood.

"Winter is right around the corner," Emerson said. "If the rain gets here before my truck, then I am back to dressing like a clown and catering kids' parties full-time until spring." And that would feel like taking a huge step back. Something Emerson wasn't willing to do.

The Pita Peddler, although a money maker, was a seasonal business. Her single umbrella didn't offer much protection from the elements, and water-soaked falafel didn't rate high in customer satisfaction.

"So you're almost there?"

Emerson smiled. "Almost." According to her plan, she was just six thousand dollars, or three private VFW parties, shy of her goal. Which meant that come January she would be trading up and accomplishing what she and her mom had dreamed of.

"Good, because look what came in." Harper pulled a certified letter from the back pocket of her jeans and waved it in Emerson's face.

"Oh my God!" Emerson grabbed the letter, a punch of excitement slamming against her chest. "Is that from—"

"Street Eats?" Harper's grin was so big it shone. "Yup. The mail guy needed a signature, so I pretended to be your roommate."

Emerson looked at the empty pastry box in the kitchen, the mango-colored backpack sprawled across the table, and the stack of Harper's laundry on the chair waiting to be folded, and figured it wasn't that far from the truth.

Emerson ran a finger across the side of the envelope, hesitating at the back flap. Inside could be a rejection, or an opportunity of a lifetime, and Emerson wasn't sure which she wanted more.

Street Eats was the nation's most competitive and prestigious food truck competition. Hundreds applied, only a few were lucky enough to be accepted, and this year it was coming to wine country. The cook-off would attract thousands of foodies and some of the best gourmet food trucks from around the country. The top chefs in her field would go head-to-head in her own backyard, showcasing their cutting-edge eats, and Emerson dreamed of being one of them.

A lot of things had changed since she'd applied last year. Violet had started school, her dad had found every reason in the world not to get a job—in fact, her family seemed more dependent on her now than ever. Plus, she was still shy a gourmet food truck. And short on cash to get one.

Harper scooted to the edge of the couch. "Open it before I combust from nerves!"

With a deep breath, Emerson pulled out the letter and—

"No freaking way." She held up the gold script invitation certifying that Emerson Blake, culinary school dropout, had an exclusive golden ticket to live out one of her life's greatest dreams. "I got in."

"You got in!" Harper, being 100 percent chick, let out a huge squeal, then pulled Emerson in for one of her infamous hugs. It was warm, long, and full of all those female bonding sounds other women seemed to make when they hung in large groups. Emerson had never been big on large groups, or female bonding, but knowing it would go faster if she didn't resist, she allowed the embrace—but didn't return it. Counted to three. Gave a closing pat to her friend's shoulder, then tried pulling back.

"Um, Harper?"

Harper finally released her and clasped her hands in front of her face. "This is huge, Em!"

"I know." With a sigh, she dropped her head on the back of the couch, because it was also a year too early. Emerson had dreamed of competing in Street Eats since watching the first show with her mom and coming up with a plan for their Greek streatery fleet. Serving her food in that arena would be all the endorsement she'd need to get her truck into big events throughout San Francisco and Silicon Valley. One of last year's competitors had gone from one truck on Main Street, USA, to six trucks in the six biggest cities in the country. He even had his own show on television.

"Then why didn't you tell me you applied?" Harper asked, and Emerson slid her a sideways look. "No way! You didn't tell me because you weren't sure if you were going to do it, and that constipated look you have, yup, that one right there"—she pointed in accusation at Emerson's face—"that says you have somehow convinced yourself the responsible choice is pass up the biggest opportunity of your life, which is insane since you have been talking about this for years, about how you would dominate and kick some serious culinary butt. *Butt* that cannot be kicked if you don't show up." She grabbed Emerson by the shoulders. "Why aren't you going to show up?"

"Because it is a food truck competition, not a food cart competition." The *duh* went unsaid but it was thick in her tone.

"You said you were almost there."

"Yeah, almost there as in three months out." Emerson took one last look at the letter, then folded it up. "Street Eats is one month away."

"Whew," Harper said, sitting back and making a big spectacle out of putting her hand to her heart. "And here I thought you were going to say it was because your dad is still unemployed and Pixie Girl got suspended for lobbing a lethal glitter bomb in class."

"You know?"

"The entire mommy community knows. Brooklyn's mom had it all over her mommy blog by lunch," Harper explained as though it wasn't a big deal. Although Harper wasn't a mommy herself, she managed the Fashion Flower, the only kids' craft and clothing boutique in town, which made her the great Mommy Oz of wine country. It also explained the Easter egg outfit and preschool teacher vibe she had going on. "But if a truck is all that's stopping you from checking the yes box, then let's get a truck."

"Sounds great," Emerson said, clapping her hands and mimicking her friend's sunny tone. "You happen to find an extra six grand in the mail when you were snooping?"

"No. But . . ." Harper reached under the couch and pulled out Emerson's laptop. "I happen to know of someone who can help."

"Oh, please God, no," Emerson moaned, but it was too late. The screen flickered to life and a spreadsheet complete with a running balance, remaining deficit, and an animated trench coat dancing next to the target amount filled the screen. It was the same fund-raising mascot and propaganda presentation Harper used to persuade her preschoolers to sell cookies for art classes or collect coats for charity. She had convinced her students, some of their parents included, that if they all reached into their pockets to help, the Coat Crusader could turn pocket change into social change.

Anytime someone needed cash for a cause, Harper and her *you can do it* coat friend came to the rescue. "He prefers Coat Crusader," Harper clarified. "But he is a miracle worker, so I can see how you'd make that mistake." Back to the spreadsheet. "I had you at ten grand shy, but you only need six." Her fingers clicked away, then she looked up and smiled. "Two seconds at work and already the Coat Crusader found you four grand."

"When did you do all of this?"

"The second I saw the letter this morning, I knew you'd get in," Harper said so sincerely Emerson felt herself shift on the couch cushion. "Which is why when I spoke with Grandma Clovis, we decided you need to go see this potential client." Harper pulled out a candy bar wrapper with an address scribbled on the inside.

"What's this?"

"Your missing money," Harper said. "Last week Giles' grand-nephew came home from the hospital."

Giles was four thousand years old and a Rousseau, which meant he was related to half of the town. He'd dated the other half until he'd snagged himself Clovis Owens and gave up his ladies'-man lifestyle for the only lady he'd ever loved. "She said that his grand-nephew is supermoody and a total handful, running his family ragged. So they were talking about hiring someone to cook a few meals each day."

Emerson felt for the boy's parents. Although Violet had been a miracle child, she'd been a turd until she turned two. Fussy, colicky, refusing to sleep or eat on any normal schedule. She also had a wail that could be heard from Mars. "Did Clovis say if they are looking for food delivery or more of a personal chef?"

Because, *holy hell*, this could work. Sure, the first option would be easier to manage, cooking up their meals for the day and delivering them each morning. She'd worked her way through culinary school doing just that. Made good money too. But the latter option had her heart thumping, because even though it would be more time-consuming, if their schedules matched, being a private chef could bring in some serious cash.

"I think they need someone to make fresh meals on-site. Nothing says home like a fresh-made meal."

Emerson couldn't agree more. And not just because she wanted the business. She'd seen the power that a home-cooked meal made with love could have on a family. Some of her happiest memories had been around her family table. Her mom had made mealtime the most important event of the day, a time of exchanging stories and love, and Emerson tried to pass that along to her customers. "Do you know how long they'd want a chef?"

"At least a few weeks. Maybe four."

"Four weeks?" Emerson tried to play it cool. No sense in getting excited until the job was secure. "Do you know their budget? Because three meals a day, seven days a week, would cost about three thousand dollars." Which would be huge for Emerson but a bargain in a town where the average personal chef charged upwards of three grand—*per week*.

"I don't think that would be a problem," Harper said, and Emerson wondered if maybe she'd gotten lucky after all.

Dax had spent the last fifteen years wading, waist deep, through the bowels of humanity in some of the most dangerous hellholes on the planet. He knew when to fight, when to regroup, and when to get out of Dodge.

Most importantly, he knew when shit was about to get real.

This was one of those times. Yet instead of lying low, getting in and out unscathed, he'd abandoned every hard-won instinct and fired the first shot. Maybe it was suburbia fever, or maybe they'd missed a chunk of shrapnel in his head, but damn if he wasn't excited to see the ticking bomb on the other side of the door.

Granted, this bomb was more of a bombshell, equally as lethal but certainly more fun to look at. Her dark auburn hair was loose and curly, her dress surprisingly feminine, and she had on a pair of black leather boots that were sleek, above the knee, and ended a scant inch before her dress began. Little Miss Bite Me was dressed to impress. She looked sophisticated, sexy as hell, and as if she were about to kick him in the nuts.

Nothing new, he thought, keeping a close watch on those pointed boots since he was within kicking distance. Emerson had been four years behind him in school, a scrappy little thing with a lethal glare who never failed to give him a hard time when he deserved it. Which was saying something since Dax had been voted Best Wingman in a Bathroom Brawl.

"Morning," he said, resting a shoulder against the door frame, sure to plaster on a big smile.

"You," Emerson accused, taking in his bare feet, workout shorts, and, if he wasn't mistaken, his tattoos. "What are you doing here?"

"I live here." He pointed to the bullet-shell doormat his step-sister, Frankie, had given him for a housewarming present.

"Alone?" she asked, and he could practically feel her willing him to say that, yes, he was just visiting, and behind him was a happy and homey family in desperate need of her services.

She was going to be disappointed.

"Yup. And you"—he tapped his watch—"are very punctual. I like that. Shows me you don't always have to be the one in control."

He stepped back in invitation. "Now, would you like to do the interview in the kitchen, or maybe in the hot tub?"

"Unless you're a fussy child, then this interview is over." She paused to glare, and it was a good glare. One that would have had most men squirming. Dax was just amused, and it must have shown because she threw her hands up and said, "Scratch that, you are a child. An overgrown child in need of a time-out. Interview definitely over."

And then, because she looked like she wanted to inflict bodily harm, he said, "I'm not opposed to spanking or a time-out, hot-tub style, as long as you play lifeguard. But we'd have to add the right verbiage in the contract."

"Didn't you hear a word I said?"

"Sorry. Still thinking about that verbiage."

"Is this fun for you? Finding amusement at my expense?" she asked, and he could tell this was nowhere near amusing for her. There was something about the way her voice shook that told him he'd screwed up. That she wasn't angry, but genuinely upset. "What part of my life being crazy did you miss?"

"I didn't." In fact, part of the reason this plan was so good was that it would help them both out. "I knew you wouldn't come if you knew it was me, so I asked your friend to keep it quiet."

Wrong thing to say, he realized, because her eyes went so frosty he felt his nuts shiver. "Do you have any idea what I had to do in order to make this appointment? How much money I am going to miss out on because I had to cut my prep work in half to get here on time?" She lifted her arms to the side and looked down at herself. "I'm in a freaking dress."

"It's a pretty dress," he said, feeling like a grade-A jerk.

"That I *bought*. For an interview. With a potential new client." There went that anger again, which was a hell of a lot better than the disappointment he'd seen. "Who doesn't exist. God, you're a jerk."

This was not going as planned. Dax had expected her to see him, get a little pissy, then a whole lot bossy. Then they'd work out some kind of arrangement to stop the never-ending covered-dish parade through his house so he could finally get some peace and quiet, and Emerson would make some cash out of the deal. It was win-win all around. And if they happened to get a little hot in the kitchen, so what? They were grown adults with enough chemistry to launch a land-to-air rocket.

But there wasn't going to be any cooking—in the kitchen or otherwise—if he didn't fix this.

"I *am* a jerk and I'm sorry. There is a job offer and you didn't waste your time."

He pushed off the wall and stepped onto the porch. She didn't budge. Nope, Emerson jabbed her hands onto her hips and strained her neck to look up at him. "Go on," she said, and the fact that her bossy tone was back told him he hadn't blown this completely. So he decided to go for honest.

"I suck in the kitchen. A decade and a half of eating in a mess hall means I suck in the kitchen."

This made her happy. "You can't cook anything?"

"I can grill," he said a little defensively. "And I cook a mean almond-crusted salmon with fingerling potatoes." He grinned. "I should make it for you sometime."

"Your make-it-happen meal? I'll pass, thanks," she said and then laughed at his expression. "Whenever a guy wants to seal the deal with a lady, they invite her over, lower the lights, and cook that one dish that was on the cover of *Maxim*. Voilà, her panties hit the floor before the salad course is served."

She was good. "Fine, no salmon. Bottom line is, I'm in town for another four weeks, and if I have to eat one more tuna casserole I'm going to weigh three hundred pounds." He placed a hand on his stomach and she rolled her eyes. "Seriously, we don't need one more fat security guy on the street."

"Security?" she asked, confusion creasing her brow. "What about the army?"

He lifted the leg of his shorts to expose a raw scar going from his thigh to below the kneecap. "The doctor said this would make it a little hard to jump out of choppers." Although he hadn't needed some fancy stethoscope wearer with letters after his name to confirm what he'd known the second he heard the first mortar explode behind him. The shrapnel had torn through his knee and shattered what had been one hell of a career in the making.

Spending the rest of what had been a high-octane career sitting behind a desk was not an option. And training more kids to put their trust in some guy like him? Nah, he had enough nightmares as it was.

"Must have hurt like a bitch," she said and he had to laugh. Emerson didn't faint or fuss or ask him stupid questions like if it hurt or if he was pissed his career was over. Didn't even ask him how it happened. Instead, she raised a brow, admired the scar for what it was, and said, "So a mall cop, huh? Do you get to ride one of those Segways?"

"Private security," he clarified, because that sounded way more manly. Then he crossed his arms, sure to flex his biceps and send that Special Forces tattoo dancing. She seemed fond of that one. "I'll be protecting politicians and Silicon Valley hotshots."

Usually this got women going. Not Emerson—she just yawned. "So you'll play with civilian-approved toys instead of federal toys. Isn't that trading down?"

When put like that . . .

"Security was always my plan B." One that he'd never imagined he'd have to implement. Dax had gone into the service expecting

MARINA ADAIR

to be a lifer, but his one bad decision had changed everything. For a whole lot of people. "Better than plan C."

"Which is?"

"Hiring myself out as a male model."

She laughed, and what a great laugh she had. Bold and uninhibited and showing all of those white teeth. She cleared her throat, then her face softened. "I'm sorry. I know how much it sucks when plan A doesn't work out. And I want to save you from your crazy family." Something about the way she said it made him believe her. Made him wonder if her food cart was her plan A or if, like him, she was living her backup life.

"Look, I have four weeks to get myself ready if I'm going to secure the job." After his meet and greet with Fallon, Dax was certain he was a front-runner. "Not easy when every person on my family tree has dropped by to check in on me, bring me cake and covered dishes, or invite me to dinner. My great- aunt Luce showed up yesterday morning with her cat and enough toaster waffles and bacon to feed my entire squad. The woman sat with me until I finished the entire plate." It was as if his pores were seeping bacon grease and syrup. "I swear, one more cheese-covered casserole and I will bust out of my pants."

She released a big sigh, her gaze going back to his knee, so he hobbled a bit for added effect. "So you're looking for a personal chef?" And bingo, she was interested.

"More of a personal assistant. Someone to stock the fridge with good food, make healthy meals, pick up prescriptions."

Her face went flat, her eyes were back to frostbite again. "Sorry, I don't have time to run your errands, Ranger. Call someone else."

She turned to leave, so he reached out and grabbed her arm, and the sparks that shot off had every inch of him standing at attention. She turned to look at him and, *yeah, honey,* that kind of heat was nuclear grade. "I don't want anyone else."

He didn't want people in his space, asking him to retell the story, looking at him like he was a broken soldier every time someone found out the real reason behind his return. He wanted the sexy, sharp-mouthed chef in front of him. "I'm offering you four grand for four weeks of meals and a few errands." Her gaze didn't look as chilled as it had moments ago. Her eyes even dilated at the price, something he took as a good sign. "You want the job. I want you to take the job. So just say yes."

He recalled liking the way she said yes. Loved when she screamed it.

Emerson waffled for a long moment, glanced at her POS car, then back to her dress, and finally looked him dead in the eye. No BS present, she said, "I can't work for someone who knows what my tattoo looks like." He dropped his gaze to her boots and the cute little daisy he remembered that sat above her right ankle. "Not that one and, hey!" She snapped her fingers in front of his face. "Don't look."

He didn't need to. Every branch and slope of that tattoo was also firmly cemented in his mind. All he had to do was close his eyes and he could picture the elegant vine of purple flowers that he had traced from her right shoulder, curving down her back and over the gentle slope of her ass to her other hip.

With his tongue.

"And stop picturing it," she demanded, poking a finger in his chest. "This is why I can't take you on as a client. Sex makes things weird."

"Then we did it wrong. Which means, for the sake of my ego and pride, we need to give it another try."

"Sorry, you're not my type."

Too bad she was looking at his chest when she said it.

"Emi," he whispered and she slowly met his gaze. "I was your type when you were screaming out my name."

She ignored this. "I'm done with that type. All mysterious and intense."

"What you see is what you get."

Now it was her turn to laugh. "Dax, you are a human puzzle. One of those superhard round puzzles. Of Darth Vader's cloak. All dark, and complicated, and brooding. I have enough complication in my life. I want someone who is nice—"

"Check."

"Sensitive—"

"You'd eat sensitive for breakfast."

"Rock solid." He flexed a little, even though he knew she meant stable. "And makes me laugh."

"Knock knock," he said.

"Good-bye," she said, turning toward her car, those hips of hers swishing right down the walkway and toward the street.

"So is that a no on the job or the sex? Or both?"

His only answer was the slamming of a car door.

ch🍳pter
four

"A sshole," Emerson said as she pushed through the front door of the Fashion Flower. A warm blast of cinnamon-and-crayon-scented air greeted her, along with the sunny jingling of a bell and a collective gasp so loud it was as if all the oxygen were sucked out of the room.

It was Watercolor Wednesday at the kids' boutique, so the room was filled to capacity with kid-sized easels and three-foot-tall Picassos vibrating with titillation over the masterful use of the naughty word. The moms looked neither impressed nor titillated.

"Apples," Harper said in her singsong voice, shooting Emerson a look. She stood at the head of the room in a sweet-potato-colored dress, green tights, Mary Janes, and an apron that read FLOWER POWER. Both teacher and apron were covered with a light smattering of what Emerson assumed was dirty paint water some kid had flicked at her. She looked like Rainbow Brite with a boob job. "What Emerson was trying to say was 'apples,' which is what we are painting. Can we say it together?"

"Apples!"

Harper clasped her hands in the universal sign of Teacher Approved. "Great, now let's get creative."

Seventeen hands shot up simultaneously. Harper pointed to a little girl in the front who was wearing paint-stained overalls. "But you said we was painting pumpkins for fall."

Smile never faltering, Harper said, "You're right. I did. And now you have the choice to paint a pumpkin *or* an apple."

Seventeen hands shot up again. Harper pointed to a bean of a kid with buckteeth and a ball cap. "Can I paint a pumpkin with an apple on it?"

"Sure," Harper said and there went the hands again. "Pumpkin or apple, those are your two choices."

Several sighs and a loud raspberry sound later, the hands dropped and paintbrushes were moving across the paper.

Emerson felt a tug on her arm and looked down to find a little blonde looking up at her. Goldilocks ringlets piled on her head, she had a pert nose, the perfect amount of freckles, and a familiar know-it-all expression.

Brooklyn Miner was the spitting image of her mother, Liza. And look at that, not a single indication of glitter-induced irritation in those wide eyes.

"My sister can't talk either so my mom says if she opens her mouth like this"—Brooklyn made a big O with her lips—"then she can say it right. Apple. See, perfect. You should go home and practice."

"Really?" Emerson said, leaning down and lowering her voice. "Because my mom said if you open your mouth really wide, then—"

"Okay," Harper interrupted, grabbing Emerson by the arm and dragging her away. "Brooklyn, it is paint time, not talk time." They didn't speak again until Harper pulled her to a quiet corner, insulated between the fleece Woombie swaddles and a display of Molar Munchers with bling.

"How did it go?" Harper asked in her inside voice.

"It didn't!" Emerson hissed. "There is no way I'd take on a client who I've had sex with. You know that."

Emerson must have used her outside voice, because Harper's eyes darted around, then she pulled her farther back behind the plushy dolls. "Which is why I didn't tell you. I knew you wouldn't go for it with him, and Em, you so need to go for it. Have you seen that body?" Harper laughed. "Of course you have."

"Killer abs aren't a qualification for taking a job."

"Doesn't hurt, though." Harper lowered her voice further. "Did you know he was in some kind of explosion or attack and his family begged him to come home until he was healed?"

Based on the scar, Emerson figured it would have had to be pretty bad to take a guy like Dax out of commission. Then there was his shell-shocked look, which Emerson knew all too well, the one that signaled a deep pain that had never really healed because there were no visible scars.

That reached out to her on an elemental level.

"Did you know he was looking for a personal assistant?"

Harper knew everything Emerson had been through the past few years, which was why she was so upset. She was the one person who made life easier, who understood just how many different ways Emerson was being pulled, and just how complicated her life had become. Harper would never do anything to make Emerson's world harder, yet today she had. And Emerson wasn't sure what to make of that.

Harper rested a hand on Emerson's shoulder. "This will be different than it was with Liam."

"Yeah, because I'm not doing it," Emerson clarified. "And what happened to never speaking his name in my presence?"

Liam was a celebrity chef in San Francisco who Emerson had met shortly after coming home from Paris. He was also her biggest regret.

Sensing that her daughter needed a break from the stress at home, her mom had signed Emerson up for a week-long seminar with the world-renowned restaurateur. Liam had taken immediate interest in Emerson's drive and talent, even convinced her to come on as his personal assistant while he opened his new eatery in Napa. One too many late nights in the kitchen led to blueberry crepes in bed, and before Emerson knew what had happened she and Liam were making plans for forever.

Then her mom passed and her father's world fell apart, and Emerson knew that her family needed her at home. Too bad Liam's idea of forever didn't extend to her loved ones. He took one look at what forever with Emerson would include and offered it, and her job, to a fancy-and-free twenty-two-year-old pastry chef named Lena.

Emerson had learned the hard way that love didn't always conquer all, and that she would never again work for someone she was personally invested in. She also learned she was too talented to be picking up dry cleaning.

"Wow." Harper let loose a low whistle. "Never thought I'd see the day where the girl who beat down Jimmy Wagner with a water wiennie for pulling her pigtail would let some guy walk all over her dreams."

"That is not what I'm doing." Although it totally was and they both knew it. "Between Violet getting suspended and my dad interviewing, I won't have time to be a gofer."

"You won't be a gofer. We're talking stocking the refrigerator and picking up prescriptions," Harper said, making it clear she knew exactly what kind of interview she'd sent her on. "And what if it gets you your truck faster?"

"There's always next year." Wow, saying that hurt.

Harper lowered her voice to that disappointed level that made Emerson squirm. "Two years ago you didn't apply because your mom was sick. Last year it was because your family needed you."

"They did," Emerson defended. She couldn't even imagine what would have happened to her family if she hadn't stepped in and picked up the pieces. She thought Harper would have understood that. "Violet wasn't even talking to humans, my dad slept all day and stared at the garden all night, and—"

Harper placed a silencing hand on Emerson's arm. "I know. I know what it was like, what you went through, and how incredibly selfless you have been. Just like I know that if you don't make some space for yourself, you'll be in this same place in five years. Maybe even ten."

Wasn't that exactly what she'd told her dad the other day?

"As your best friend, I can't let you do that."

Not one to be told what she could or couldn't do, Emerson was about to explain where Harper could shove that BFF entitlement when Harper reached behind the counter and pulled a weathered notebook out of her backpack.

Emerson felt her stomach bottom out.

It wasn't just any notebook. It was small, leather bound, and the spine was worn from use. Across the front in blue script was *The Greek Streatery Fleet.*

"Where did you get this?" She took the journal and ran a finger down its side. She didn't need to open it to know what lay beneath the cover. Every family recipe, every idea, and every dream she and her mother had made for their streatery was in her palms. "I thought I had lost it when I cleaned Mom's things out of the attic."

"Your mom gave it to me before she passed," Harper said quietly. "Made me promise that if you had the chance to do something amazing, I wouldn't let you talk yourself out of it. So I'm playing the mom card, Em. What would Lillianna want you to do?"

Emerson swallowed hard as she opened the cover, and her eyes burned. There on the first page, framed by chef's-hat scrapbooking trim, was the hundred-year-old handwritten recipe that had started it all: her great-grandmother's baklava. Beneath the recipe was a photo of a young Emerson, standing on a kitchen chair, helping her mother glaze the phyllo layers with honey. And beneath that, in beautiful script, was her mother's favorite saying:

If ever in doubt, eat the whole tray.

It was still dark when Dax awoke, hot and sweaty and tangled in the sheets, gasping for breath as if he'd just had a weekend-long sex marathon with a bossy little chef. And he wished to hell it had been a smoking-hot sexathon that had his heart pounding out of his chest.

He threw the covers off and grabbed for his knee, hoping to catch the cramp before it settled into his entire leg. Too late. His muscles tightened and a thin sheen of sweat covered his entire body.

Dax looked at the bottle of pills on his nightstand. Completely full, not a single one missing. He could take one now. This was the exact kind of situation the doctor had prescribed them for, to take the edge off the pain. Problem was, it would take the edge off everything—and pain was the only thing keeping him grounded.

It was also an acceptable alternative to the memories.

He swung his legs over the bed and sat up, letting the cold air from the open window roll over his body, every sharp gust bringing his heart rate closer to normal. He straightened his left leg, nearly passing out as a shot of bone-gritting heat exploded from behind his kneecap. He rotated it to the right, then *holy hell* to the left, just like his doctor showed him, and gave the stretch exactly two minutes to overpower the cramp.

When *that* didn't work, he cursed his weakness, kissed the extra two hours of sleep good-bye, and grabbed his running shoes.

The only thing that was going to help was a fast ride on his bike. Not turning his leg like some ballerina.

Giving his knee a few minutes to adjust to holding his weight, Dax pulled on a pair of jeans, grabbed a T-shirt from the hamper, and—smelling the pits first—tugged it on while heading toward the front door. One step outside and he knew he'd made the right decision. Sitting idle, being surrounded by walls and memories, was slowly driving him crazy.

He stepped off the front porch of his rental, a 1920s Craftsman bungalow that sat right off Main Street, and grimaced through the stiffness as he headed down the driveway.

The early morning dew still covered the ground and glistened off the oak trees lining the road, leaving the air cool and fresh, almost cleansing to his lungs. When Dax had been in the Middle East, roasting in an army-issued bunk, he'd dreamed about mornings like this. When the only people awake were the vineyard workers, and the hot air balloons were slowly rising off the valley floor, and the world seemed at peace.

Only now that Dax was home, surrounded by what seemed to be a snapshot of one of his favorite memories, he wasn't sure how to tap into that peace.

So he'd outrun it.

His fingers twitching to crank the throttle, Dax got to the curb—and stopped short when he spotted Lola.

Lola had been Dax's treat to himself a few years back. His Indian bike was a handcrafted work of innovation. With her sculpted chrome exhaust, polished midnight body, and incredible 119 feet per pound of throttle, she was trouble on wheels. And the exact kind of rush he needed when stateside.

Only today she was wearing a boot.

A big-ass, bright orange boot that had ST. HELENA SHERIFF'S DEPARTMENT engraved on the side.

Unconcerned about the time of day and saving the barrage of oncoming f-bombs for his brother, he fished out his phone.

"Want to tell me why you're calling me at five in the morning?" Jonah breathed into the phone. His voice was groggy and thick with sleep—which made Dax happy.

"Because you're the only loser who would answer his phone at five in the morning," Dax said. "Come on, man, Lola?" He looked at his pristine bike with that god-awful lock on it and wanted to cry. "It's abuse of power. Plain and simple."

"I'll let the sheriff know," the sheriff said with a chuckle, and Dax heard a lightness to his brother's voice that he hadn't heard much since their dad died. He would have been happy for him, but messing with another man's bike was on the same level as messing with another man's woman.

"Make sure you tell him that it's a total dick move," Dax said.

"He'd tell you so is driving around town before the doctor gives you the go-ahead," Jonah said, and Dax could hear the prick smiling.

"I have PT today," Dax reminded him. "What do you expect me to do? Walk?"

"Nope." And because his big brother had a solution for everything, he added, "Frankie should be there twenty minutes before your appointment."

"So I can ride on *her* bike, but not my own?" Because like him, Frankie believed that vehicles with more than two wheels were made for pussies.

"She's borrowing Nate's truck." Despite the fact that Nate was a DeLuca, he was a stand-up guy and made Dax's sister smile, so Dax chose to overlook the fact that he was born into the wrong family. "And Shay's got you covered next week."

"Actually, Sheriff, I've got you covered right now," a muffled but definitely feminine voice came through the phone. "Put your hands where I can't see them."

Dax threw up a little in his mouth. "Jesus, man, I don't need to hear this, and I sure as hell don't need help setting up a damn carpool. Come unboot my girl."

Jonah didn't give him an affirmative that he was headed over, but when Dax heard the phone hit the ground and some questionable noises follow, he decided to hang up and start running, because it was going to take more than a few miles to erase those sounds from his head.

ch**🍳**pter
five

Just because it felt like Dax was taking a round to the knee didn't mean he had to show it.

"This is what you get for running on it," Kyle said, laying into Dax's leg, then applying a tooth-grinding pressure to the back of his knee.

Kyle O'Malley was one of Dax's oldest friends. He was built like an MMA fighter, had the hands of a butcher, and could teach the Taliban a thing or two about the art of torture. He was also the best orthopedic specialist in the county, but before that he'd been in the air force as a pararescue, which was the only reason Dax was putting up with his BS.

Sure, he wasn't G.I. Joe, but any guy who had the balls to parachute into a hot landing zone to rescue a soldier he'd never met had earned the right to be heard.

"I told you not to overdo it and what do you do?"

"I took a brisk walk," Dax lied. "Just around the block." *And across town. Twice. Outrunning some of the slower-moving cars.* "It felt good to work it out."

Kyle leaned his entire being into the stretch, and Dax was certain the man was six feet one of solid lead. "Does it still feel good?"

About as good as waterboarding. "Nothing I can't handle."

"Then I'll take it a little deeper," Kyle said and when Dax didn't call his bluff, he took it from waterboarding to *wake me when it's over.*

On a good day, PT hurt like a bitch. Today wasn't a good day. Dax was tired, aching, and in desperate need of a beer. Or a six-pack. And not that he'd admit it out loud, but pushing that hard this morning on virtually zero sleep had been a crap call. Especially with an hour of PT on the schedule.

Dax had overcome pain before. Had been slapped around by some of the biggest hellholes in the world with no hope of getting to a hospital in time and never once thought he'd break. Not even for a second. He'd been shot at regularly, fractured every rib in his body, twice, and stared down death more times than he cared to admit. But right then, lying stateside on some cushioned mat, he admitted he wasn't sure he could survive Kyle—and those fingers of torture.

But there he was, flipping pain the proverbial bird, because this was the one stipulation to getting the job in San Jose. He had to complete his recovery before the doc would sign off.

No clearance meant no elite team. And Dax didn't have another backup plan.

So for the next hour he gritted through the torment, listened to Kyle go on and on about how stubborn he was, and didn't even break a sweat when he felt that first shot of pain move up his leg.

And after Kyle handed him his ass, he handed him a good-patient lollipop, which Dax was pretty sure wasn't a compliment, then he held his water bottle hostage until Dax dragged himself off the mat. Which was just humiliating.

"Stop being stupid," Kyle said. "You're on civilian land now."

"Tell my trigger finger that," Dax said and Kyle knew enough to let it go.

Sending up a silent prayer that he wouldn't puke until he made it home, he headed toward the patient drop-off area, where Frankie would be waiting.

Dax held his breath as he went through the ER because, *Jesus*, nothing said "hug the toilet" quite like a double dose of ammonia and stale carpet. One foot in front of the other, each step feeling like a mile, he finally pushed through the door and nearly wept when he made it outside. Less than positive about making it to the curb without embarrassing himself, he plopped down on the nearest bench and, palming his ball cap in his hand, hung his head.

A brisk breeze caught the sweat on his skin and he finally, *finally*, felt himself exhale.

In and out, he let the cool air fill his lungs, then empty until the ground stopped shifting and his hands stopped shaking. Major improvement over two seconds ago.

"Hey, Mister," a small but high-pitched voice said from beside him. "You going to throw up? Cuz if you are, I'll hold your lollipop."

Dax opened his eyes, surprised to find a little person sitting next to him dressed in some kind of uniform. She was reaching for the lollipop he was white-knuckling in his hand. He wasn't sure what pissed him off more, that a kid in pink glittery wings was able to sneak up on him, or that he looked pathetic enough that she was going to attempt to steal his candy.

"You selling cookies?" he asked, taking in the sash of badges and patches across her chest. He could go for a box of cookies. And some peace and quiet.

"That's Girl Scouts. I'm a Lady Bug." She pointed to the red-and-black bug embroidered on her top.

"So is that a no on the cookies?"

"No cookies, but"—she dug into her pockets—"I got a gumball that I won at the store last week." She also dug up a penny, pencil shavings, and some pocket lint.

Dax looked at his watch. Frankie was late, and being this close to a little person was making his palms sweat. It wasn't that Dax didn't like kids, he just never knew what to do with them. They were small, smelled weird, and were too trusting for their own good. Take Lady Bug, for example—here she was chatting up a tattooed guy who was asking if she had cookies.

He turned his attention back to her and wondered what it must look like with her sitting next to him, bright eyed and bobbing curls, while he was dangling lollipop bait.

He shoved the lollipop into his pocket. "Aren't you too young to be here alone?" Because *that* sounded so much better than the cookie question. "I mean, shouldn't you go find your mom?"

"Can't," she said, swinging her legs, and Dax noticed her red-and-black polka-dotted high-tops. "I'm waiting."

"Me too," he said, *not* swinging his legs, but searching the lot for Nate's truck, just in case he'd missed it among the five cars in the lot, because, yeah, St. Helena was a hive of activity today.

"Want to wait together?" she asked.

"I'm good. My sister's almost here," he said as if that wasn't the pussiest answer a guy could give.

"I can wait with you. It's more fun that way." Her eyes were straining to see through his pocket, as if she could stare hard enough that the material would melt and she'd catch the lollipop. "We can share the gumball and the lollipop."

"Don't like gumballs," he said. "And the lollipop is mine." He'd worked damn hard for it and wasn't about to hand it over to some kid who had been flitting around in wings all day.

"I'm here on a field trip to learn first aid with my Lovelies." And there went the feet again. "Did you know that a cluster of lady bugs are called lovelies? So we are the St. Helena Lady Bug Lovelies Six-Six-Two."

Dax wasn't sure if she expected him to give his rank and file, so he asked, "You're a bug?"

"Nooo." She dragged out the word long enough that the ache in his leg was now piercing his head. That, combined with the look she gave him, as though he were the slow one, was enough to bring back the nausea. "I'm a fairy."

"Right. Then can you fly away, fly away, fly away home?"

She ignored this. "You can only see me because I used fairy dust this morning."

"Then how come I can see your wings?"

This stumped her. Kept her quiet for all of two point one seconds, then she opened her mouth again. "Watch."

Dax didn't want to watch. He wanted to go home. He needed a shower, a beer, and to get laid. Right now he'd settle for ten seconds of silence, but she was already sliding off the bench. Feet together, hands fisted at her side, she wiggled her body and, *Jesus Christ*, the wings started vibrating and those little freckles on her nose twitched, and she actually looked like a fairy. "Are you watching? Look, I'm getting ready to fly."

"Yeah, I see," he said, giving up. He pulled the cap low on his head and pulled his phone out of his pocket. "I need to call my sister."

Obliviously not accustomed to social cues, the fairy climbed up on the bench again. "Brooklyn says there are zombies in the hospital and that they eat fairies," she said as though that had anything to do with the price of tea in China.

He scrolled though his phone and stopped at Frankie's number. "Brooklyn sounds like a shit."

"That's a bad word." She said it all scandalized as if he'd just stolen ten years of fairy magic from her, but she was smiling with glee.

He shrugged. "Sometimes you got to call it like it is, and she is a shit, through and through." And then, because she took a lungful of air as if she was getting ready to tell him another story that had zippo to do with the last, he said, "Did you know that zombies can't walk in water?"

She went quiet. Really quiet. Quiet enough that he was certain the conversation was over, so he hit Dial. It rang exactly once when the fairy said, "Water, huh?"

"Yeah, it's like their Kryptonite."

"What's Kryptonite?"

"Just take this to scare them away." He handed her his water bottle. "Somewhere else."

"I'm running late," Frankie said by way of greeting.

"How late?" Because if she said more than five minutes, he'd consider walking the five miles home.

"My baby alarm went off."

"Your what?"

"You know, it tells me the best time to get knocked up." Dax waited for his sister to laugh, to tell him she was kidding, but when she didn't, he knew she was dead serious.

"Hold up!" Dax looked at the girl, who was looking back at him. He gave her his hardest *do you mind* glare. She obviously didn't, since she swung her legs and leaned in to listen. He cupped the phone with his hand and turned his back on her. "Are you ditching me to get laid right now?"

Frankie snorted. "Like you haven't done it. Besides, this is serious."

"So is the present situation." Between Jonah in bed and now his sister, he was going to need to run to the moon and back to get this crap out of his head. "Pick me up."

"Give me an hour."

"Tell her I can wait with you so you won't be all alone," the little girl said, not even bothering to sound ashamed that she was eavesdropping.

Dax huddled closer to the phone. "That's a negative."

"Sorry, it's the stress of the performance," Frankie explained. "Actually, it might be a few hours. Not that I'm complaining. Sometimes he likes to do it two to three times, just to be sure we are being the most effective with our time."

"Trauma to the ears," he hissed. "Make it stop."

"That's the opposite of what I say."

Dax closed his eyes. "They're bleeding now."

"Do you need a Band-Aid?" Lady Bug 662 said. "I'm learning how to do that today in first-aid class."

"Nate's here," Frankie said. "Want me to ask him how long it will be?"

Dax hung up on another sibling—his second of the day—who reminded him that while they were all happy and in love and getting laid, he was sitting on a bench with a bum knee, an annoying fairy, and no ride in sight—in any sense of the word.

"Violet!"

Dax and the girl looked up to find a pissed-off woman standing by the doors to the hospital. She wore a tiny black tank, an even tinier black skirt, and a matching pair of red-and-black polka-dotted Converse high-tops. Nice legs, nicer rack, and a mouth that made men think certain kinds of thoughts. Full and plump and free of lipstick. And he was a man all right, would have been thinking those thoughts if those lips hadn't been set into an all-too-familiar *screw off* pose.

"Pixie," the girl clarified, not intimidated in the slightest. Dax, on the other hand, noticed that the floor started shifting again, because when Emerson had told him her life was complicated, he didn't know that meant she came with an eighteen-year commitment who wore fairy wings.

"What happened to waiting inside?" Emerson asked, shrugging that backpack she always seemed to lug around higher on her shoulder. The thing was bright blue and bigger than the ruck he took with him on his first deployment.

"There's a roof," the girl said, glancing up. "And I was just waiting with Mister. He's my new friend."

"I can see that." Emerson's eyes went to Dax for the first time, and he could tell she was as shocked to see him as he was to see her—with her freaking kid. "What are you doing here?"

"Physical therapy." He pointed to his knee.

"No, I mean here. With my sister?"

"Sister?" he repeated, and what an amazing word that was. *Sister.* Not *kid* or *mine* or *daughter*. Sister.

He grinned. She glared. Yeah, so he'd taken an extra-long exhale at the news. So what? "Mister needs a ride," Violet said, interrupting. "You can take him home while I go back to the field trip."

Dax grinned, big and charming. Maybe this girl was magical after all. "Yeah, Emi, Mister really needs a ride."

"Nice bike," Emerson said as she pulled onto Dax's street. "I especially love the orange boot, really adds that badass alpha flare you seem to be going for."

"Oh, are we talking now? I figured blasting the radio was female for 'let's ignore each other.'"

"I wasn't ignoring you." Her plan was to slow down to an easy ejection speed and kick him to the curb. The man had parachuted into hostile territory from a few thousand feet up—surely he could handle a two-foot drop at five miles per hour. "Just not a chatty person."

There was no point in talking, period. Talking would lead to a proposition, a proposition to arguing, and arguing to sex. And sex with a guy who was leaving was a bad move.

"Really, because I recall the only thing I could do to get you to stop talking was to put my—"

"And . . . we're here." Emerson pulled alongside the curb, careful to keep her eyes straight ahead out the windshield and not on his hand, which had been gently rubbing his knee since he got in the car. She knew he was hurting. He'd made too big of a deal about walking normal, even opening her door in the parking lot. But she knew better. Knew all of the ways people deflected from their pain—covered it up.

"Want to come inside so I can thank you properly?" He went to move his leg and winced. Emerson glanced over and wanted to kick herself. He wasn't in pain, he was in agony—the sweat beading on his forehead was a dead giveaway.

"How bad is it?"

He looked down at his crotch and grinned. "Pretty bad. Want to see?"

She leveled him with a look that did nothing to deter that teasing grin. "Your knee? One to ten, how bad is it?"

"One," he scoffed, reaching for the door handle. But when he didn't make a move to climb out, playing the stupid stoic soldier, she felt her resolve crumble.

She leaned over, and as he was about to make some smart-ass crack about how close her mouth was to his stupid stick, she gripped his knee with her fingers. And squeezed hard.

"Jesus, woman!" He tried to jerk away, his whole body jumping off the seat, but she held tight and knew just how bad off he was when he didn't fight harder.

"One, my ass," she mumbled. Then she slowly moved her fingers around the knee and down his calf, following the muscles and manipulating the knots she felt. She also felt just how muscular he was, which said a lot since she was pretty sure, based on the scar, that he'd spent a good amount of time in a hospital bed.

Her heart pinched as her fingers followed the long, jagged scar that started midthigh and dipped well below his kneecap. It was angry and raw and slowly but courageously healing—a lot like its owner.

Emerson made the same pass, and this time his body relaxed, sinking back into the seat.

"God," he breathed, his head falling against the headrest. "That feels good. Don't stop."

Even though she knew that she should, that seeing him like this melted parts of her that had no business melting, Emerson couldn't stop. The caretaker in her wouldn't let her, wanted to help him feel better, take his pain away.

The at-ease look on his face said she was making progress. Then he turned his head and she saw gratitude in the intense blue pools, and a strange fluttering happened in her chest.

Not wanting to go there with him, Emerson loosened her grip, but Dax's hand came down on hers, gently holding it to his thigh, the hairs rough against her palm.

"Just a little more." His graveled voice was thick, his eyes begging her to go on forever, so she ran her hand down his scar, because if the slightest touch meant he was out of pain for a second, she'd do it.

Also because Emerson Blake was a sucker when it came to being needed. Especially by someone she cared about. And no matter how many times she tried to ignore it, she was beginning to care about Dax.

"Where did you learn to do that?" he asked a few minutes later.

The honest answer would have been that she'd spent most of her life learning how to help manage her mother's pain, and the last two years since her passing, managing her family's. But talking about her mom wasn't something she did lightly, and somehow the thought of talking about her mom with Dax scared her. So she gave a nonchalant shrug and said, "Something I just picked up."

Dax didn't pry, just gave a small nod and said, "All the BS aside, I need you to reconsider my offer."

"For the job or the sex?" she joked, hoping he'd laugh and stop looking at her as though she was special. He didn't laugh, and the flutters got worse.

"I'm being serious. You're in the business of making food for a price, and I am a legit customer who's in need of some good food. And a ride now and then, and maybe some more of that." He took her hand and placed it over his scar again. "Don't overthink this, Emi, I need you."

And wasn't that just the thing to say to a serial caregiver? Because even though the last time she didn't overthink things she wound up doing the walk of shame, she found herself asking, "For how long?"

"Just until I finish PT." And when said like that, so honest and genuine with no underlying innuendo, how could she say no?

Emerson thought of her hectic schedule, then of the golden ticket, which was still in her purse as opposed to being in the mail, and finally of the journal her mom had left for her. There were a million reasons to take Dax up on his offer and only one resounding reason to say no.

She had too many skillets on the burner to add a dish as complex as Dax to the menu. Too many people to take care of and too many dreams on the line to mess with a man who had *trouble* tattooed across his chest. And his biceps, lower back, and the sexy tribal emblem that started right above the indent of his lower rib.

Emerson looked at their hands, which had somehow become tangled in his lap, noticed how she was leaning over the center console into him and he was leaning back, and became acutely aware of how close their mouths were—how much closer she wanted them to be.

She snatched her hand back and cleared her throat. "I'll do it, but there will be rules."

He grinned, and it was a high-octane grin that had her hormones vibrating and her body humming. "I love it when you get all bossy."

"I'm not bossy, just helpful," she corrected, and his dimples got in on the action. "Here are my terms. They are nonnegotiable."

"Why am I not surprised?" he deadpanned.

"I'll cook your meals daily, drop them off in the morning, you heat them up as needed. No flirting or 'heating up the kitchen' comments, and no, I will absolutely not perform any other errands or chores or . . ." She held up a hand when his face twitched and he looked ready to speak. "Don't do it. I know you want to, but one wrong word and I quit."

With an amused nod he sat back, but the big jerk was still grinning.

"Although I am your chef, *not* your assistant, I will make an exception and take you to appointments on days when your family isn't available, but it has to work around *my* schedule, and sometimes I will have Violet with me. I get each week's pay in advance, and if you blow it by saying something stupid, then I quit and I get to keep that week's money."

Satisfied that she had addressed all of her concerns, she rested her elbow on the center console and waited for the rebuttal, which she knew was coming. Dax was as alpha as they came. He liked to be in control of his world and set the rules of engagement. But if he wanted her help, then he'd have to learn how to take orders, because the only way Emerson's world kept spinning was when she was the commander in chief. "Deal or what?"

"I don't want to say something stupid, so can you clarify? Was that you being bossy or just being helpful and letting me know that I can speak now?"

Emerson felt her eye twitch.

"I'll take that as a yes," he rushed before she could say anything, "and to your first point"—he ticked it off with a coordinating finger, in case she didn't know how to count to one—"if I wanted to reheat my food, I'd hire a delivery service, not a thousand-bucks-a-week chef.

Second"—there went another finger—"I would never use a 'heating up the kitchen' line. That's too amateur. As for performances?"

Emerson noticed that this particular finger could be taken as an offer. Or more of a visual cue. She chose to take it as a cue and kept quiet.

"Chores and errands wouldn't even make my top one thousand list. And finally, Violet along for the ride is fine as long as she doesn't get glitter on me, because when it comes to my family's chauffeur services, they're fired. Indefinitely. Their kind of help will kill me."

Emerson carefully considered his terms, which was ridiculous since she knew she was going to say yes. Not only was Dax giving her everything she needed, he was being reasonable about his demands. Well, most of them, anyway. And when he spoke, everything seemed so simple. He needed a chef and she needed money.

"I can agree to fresh breakfasts and dinners, but lunch will be tricky because of my cart hours. If a PT session conflicts with my prior commitments, then you reschedule it or find your own way there." She thought about the farmers' market and her most recent catering commitment with Ida and decided she was crazy to take him on. Then again, he wasn't asking her to dress up like a cork. "I need weekends off and I can't start until Tuesday."

Dax studied her for a long moment, as though trying to see if she was hosing him. She'd purposefully chosen the vague "prior commitments" route in case things got complicated and she needed an out. Not that she was going to let them get complicated—she was smarter than that now. But with Dax anything was possible.

"Do we have a deal?" she asked, and then to make sure it came off as an actual question and not a command, she stuck out her hand.

"I can work with that." Dax slipped his fingers around hers and pulled her close so swiftly that her free hand shot out to steady her—landing on his right pec. Which flexed under her palm.

She looked up at him in shock, wanting to ask him what the hell he thought he was doing, but she was afraid she wanted him to do everything she saw written in his eyes.

Before she got to voice her opinion in any way whatsoever, his mouth was on hers and he was kissing her.

To be fair, it didn't take long for her to kiss him back. An embarrassing zero point three seconds was all she needed to go from thinking it wasn't a good idea to not thinking at all. In fact, they reached critical mass with almost zero acceleration. Her hands were in his hair, his on the curve of her ass, and she was considering leaping over the console to straddle him.

In the front seat of her car.

There was nothing more in that moment that she wanted than to lose herself right there, with him, and forget about everything. Dax wanted her, had made it clear that he was open to fun with no future ties. And didn't that sound amazing.

Emerson had been tied down her whole life, first by her mother's disease, then by her death. She'd learned early on that she was powerless when it came to changing the inevitable, yet the hard parts she could have changed—the hospital visits, holding her mom's hand when things became bad, then when things became unbearable— she wouldn't. Not for anything.

Those last few months with her mom had meant everything to Emerson.

But she had a choice now, and didn't that give her the power? Something she hadn't had with her mother or her family or even with Liam.

It was apparent now that if she pulled back and ended it, he'd let her. If she threw her leg over the console, he'd meet her more than halfway. And the thought was thrilling—fun without the stress of forever was a complete turn-on.

That was something she could handle. If—and this was a ginormous *if*—she hadn't just accepted the job. But she had. And this situation was a disaster in the making. Dax could be her client or her escape—sadly, in her world he couldn't be both. And needing all four weeks of income to make a go at Street Eats, she pulled back.

They were both breathing heavy when she asked, "What was that?"

His gaze zeroed in on her lips. "If you have to ask, then maybe I need to show you again."

"No." Her voice wasn't nearly as strong as she'd hoped. "No more visuals. I get it. But there is also a no-flirting clause."

"I'm not big on flirting. I'm more of a take-action kind of person."

"Well, the only action that will happen between us will be professional," she clarified. "So that means that this—"

"Chemistry? Heat? Lust?"

"*Compatibility* needs to be ignored. My life is too crazy."

"I like crazy." He leaned in and teased the seam of her lips. "I also like fun. Let me be your fun."

God, she wanted everything he was offering, but the fun would fade the second they stepped back into reality. The texts, the calls, the babysitting, the sixteen-hour days. It was a lot for *her* to manage. "You wouldn't last two seconds in my world."

"I turned snot-nosed brats into killing machines for the armed forces. I can handle anything."

He sounded so confident and lethal she had to laugh. "You pissed yourself when you thought Violet was mine."

"Did not." She raised a brow. "Okay, maybe I freaked for a second. But she isn't yours, so we're good."

Emerson felt her chest pinch slightly at his comment. Old wounds, she told herself. It had nothing to do with the man saying it. "But she is mine, which means no blurring the lines."

chapter
six

The parking lot of St. Helena Hospital looked like a scene from one of those natural disaster films Harper loved so much. People cluttered the street and the sidewalk, talking in high, frantic voices—and all Emerson could think was, *please, God, no*. Because behind the three flashing fire engines, five squad cars, and endless queue of white-robed patients, each barefoot, and each dripping with water, sat Violet.

All by her six-year-old self. No one looking out for her, making sure she was okay. Nope, she sat on the bench with droopy curls and what had to be the sorriest face on the planet.

"Violet," Emerson called out as she exited her car, but the ear-splitting alarm drowned out her voice.

Heart in her throat, she ran across the lot, scanning the area for the rest of her sister's Lovelies. Fear mixed with intense fury when she found them and their soggy sashes a good fifteen feet away, standing on the opposite side of the exit, huddled around their leader. Who was paying zero attention to the lonely Lady Bug.

"Violet," she called again.

Her sister looked up, and Emerson felt her stomach bottom out because Violet's face went wide with relief that the cavalry was there, then crumpled as she leaped to her feet. "Sissy!"

Emerson had barely made it up onto the curb when Violet locked her little arms around her big sister's waist. Emerson pulled her in tight, breathed in the scent of glitter glue, bubblegum, and wet polyester—and that's when she noticed her hands were shaking.

"Are you okay?" she asked. *God, let her be okay.*

Violet's head moved up and down, but she didn't release her grip. Which was fine with Emerson, because she could use a moment to gather herself. To process the fact that the little soul her mother entrusted her with wasn't hurt. Wasn't crying.

Wasn't dead.

She needed to get a grip. A-SAP. Because it didn't matter if she felt like throwing up or that her heart was beating so hard she was certain it was going to blast right through her chest, Violet needed Emerson's strength right then, not her worry. The poor kid had dealt with more worry than any person should ever have to.

"What happened?" she finally asked, kneeling in front of Violet.

"Someone pulled the fire alarm," Violet said quietly. "And all the sprinklers went off. Then everyone started screaming, and I tried to tell them it was only water and to stay calm like you always say, but nobody would listen. Then Lovely Leader Liza told us to exit the building in a single file."

Emerson felt her pulse beat a little slower because Violet was safe, the alarm had been silenced, and the firemen were now milling around. It was just a false alarm. But it seemed no matter how many false alarms Emerson had lived through, they never got any easier.

"Then why did you separate from the group?" Emerson schooled her features because they'd had this talk before, and she was certain if she lost it right now they'd have it again the second she turned her back. Violet was a wanderer—just like their father. The biggest

NEED YOU FOR ALWAYS

ice cream sundae in the world would be wasted on her since she wouldn't be able to sit still long enough to get through the first scoop. "Rule number seven is—"

"Always stay with the group," Violet said diligently, giving a pretty good impression of Emerson, making her wonder if she really sounded that uptight. But when it came to her family, rules were the only thing keeping Emerson sane.

"You." Emerson pointed to the other bugs. "The group. See the problem here?"

"Rule number two is to respect my elders," Violet said. "And Lovely Leader Liza told me to sit on the bench."

"Why would she tell you to sit by yourself if she thought there was a fire?"

Violet toed at the ground for a good long minute, her fairy wings trailing water on the concrete as she swished. In the tinniest and tiniest of voices, she said, "Cuz someone pulled the alarm," then closed her eyes tight and threw a handful of glitter in the air and whispered, "Wings, take me to Lilly Lane Willows."

Well, hell. Emerson had to close her eyes too, because she was pretty sure that *someone* was silently wishing her way home.

"You're still here, kiddo," Emerson said and she wasn't sure if she wanted to laugh or cry. Violet opened one cautious eye, then the other, only to realize she hadn't magically transported herself to her backyard, and let out a despairing sigh. "Now, you want to tell me why you pulled the fire alarm?"

Violet shook her head. Emerson, not having any of it, flashed the *Don't mess with me, I control your bedtime* face. Just like Emerson had when her mom issued that warning, Violet caved like a cheap suitcase.

"I got thirsty and drank all the water in Mister's bottle. Then I had to go potty, real bad, and my bug buddy was Brooklyn and she said that we'd have to go by the morgue to go to the potty and

I didn't have no water for the zombies so I pulled the fire alarm to be safe," Violet said in one giant rush of words with no pauses, her voice elevating with each syllable.

"Zombies?" Emerson asked, and it was a sad state of affairs that she was neither surprised nor confused by her sister's statement. Living with Violet was like living in a choose-your-own-adventure story. Only Violet did all the choosing.

"Brooklyn said zombies eat fairies." Violet's voice was heart-breakingly low. "And if they ate me, then I wouldn't ever get my wings to grow big. So I made it wet so the zombies couldn't follow. I'm sorry, Sissy, I didn't mean to make everyone mad, but I want big wings."

Emerson felt her heart soften a little, because rule number six was to go to a teacher or trusted adult when being teased. But how could Violet be expected to rat out the bully to the bully's mom?

"I get why you did what you did, and how it would have been hard to go to Mrs. Miner when Brooklyn was teasing you." Emerson took a big, painful breath, and then leveled her sister with a look. "But zombies aren't real, Violet."

She shrugged a slim shoulder, her droopy wing sagging farther under the movement. "I know."

"Then why did you pull the alarm?"

"Just in case," Violet said and now she was looking Emerson in the eye. She was the one getting serious. "You said Bigfoot wasn't real, but then I saw a show on Discovery that has these guys who've seen him. They have video and everything. So what if you're wrong about zombies too?"

Being wrong about fairies went unsaid, but Emerson saw the challenge in her sister's eyes. She might be six, but she was a Blake through and through. Most days Emerson admired that kind of tenacity, but today she was too tired. And too sad.

Making a mental note to address her sister's television habits with their father, then deciding it would be easier to just cancel cable altogether, Emerson stood and took Violet by the hand. "Let's go talk to Lovely Leader Liza and explain the situation."

Emerson tried really hard to keep her cool, even repeated several times on her way over that punching Lovely Leader Liza, who wasn't so lovely and was a shitty leader, in the face wouldn't be a good example for Violet. Not to mention the cops were out in force, so she took a calming breath and said, "Liza, we've got a problem."

Liza turned toward Emerson and flashed that Hollywood smile. Even in her Lovely leader uniform and drowned-kitty hair, she still managed to look the epitome of a Napa Valley momtrepreneur. Her heels were designer and her boobs fake and she had her camera out, probably snapping pics for her mommy blog. "I agree."

Emerson looked down at Violet, who was looking back as though her entire world hinged on what was about to go down, then to Brooklyn, who was grinning. And Emerson knew that grin—she'd used it a time or two when outsmarting kids in her class. Brooklyn had dealt Violet a losing hand, and poor Violet didn't even know she had cards to play. Good thing for the Blake girls, Emerson did.

"I think we might need to clarify exactly which problem you're agreeing to," Emerson said.

"Sometimes it's hard to see past our loved ones' failings." The moral voice of perfect mommies everywhere leaned in, patting Emerson on the shoulder. "Perhaps we should talk about this in private."

Emerson looked at the five sets of eyes on her, then shrugged. "I'm good. Because I know my sister. She wears wings to school, hides her vegetables in the bottom of her milk"—Violet gasped as if Emerson was all knowing—"and pulled a fire alarm because someone told her that there were zombies in the morgue, but she isn't a troublemaker."

"Some would disagree." Liza gave Emerson a long, thorough examination, her brows furrowing, which looked bizarre since her forehead didn't move. "Regardless, your sister has a history of creating problems and with the Loveliest Survivalist Campout coming up in just a few weeks, I'm sure the other parents are concerned."

"Are you implying that my sister's not welcome at the campout?"

"Heavens no," Liza said, waving a manicured hand. "I'm implying that perhaps it would be easier if you removed her from the group altogether."

Violet sucked in a terrified breath and her hand tightened around Emerson's. "Are they kicking me out? Like for always? Cuz I need to get my survivor badge."

"Don't worry, Vi, that isn't happening," Emerson said, ruffling her sister's hair while getting eye to eye with Liza. "She made a mistake, but she wasn't the only one at fault."

Brooklyn glared viciously at Emerson. The kid obviously had no protective instincts, because if she had, then she'd put those beady eyes back in her head before someone knocked them out completely.

"I won the Mommy Choice Award for a wonderful post on my *Whining, Dining, and Diapers* blog titled 'The Scoop on Acknowledging Shortcomings.' It addresses the shortcomings of children as well as the parents." Liza lowered her voice. "I could e-mail you the link."

"Why don't you do that," Emerson said. "And while you're at it, can you send me the link to that article you did on bullying? Because I'd love to post it on the bulletin board at the Fashion Flower next to the surveillance footage of Violet's bug buddy bullying her into pulling the alarm."

Liza made a horrified gasp while clutching at her surgically enhanced chest. "What are you implying?"

Violet tugged on Liza's pant leg, and when the woman looked down, Violet whispered, "I think she means that Brooklyn's a little shit."

Every pint-sized face went round in awe, and Emerson worked really hard not to high-five her. Violet frowned. "What? I was just telling it like it is."

"The Lady Bugs are about manners and building young role models," Liza informed the entire surrounding area. "I refuse to allow my daughter to be exposed to this kind of behavior! And I will not be responsible for a Lovely who doesn't abide by my rules."

"Your rules suck," Emerson pointed out, to the glee of the other four girls. "Lady Bugs should be about making friends and ice cream socials and fun."

Not that Emerson had all that much experience with any of those—she'd been too busy helping out at home. But she wanted different memories for Violet. It was she who'd signed her up for Lady Bugs to begin with. She wanted her sister to experience being a kid, have some fun, and find a space that she fit.

"Not taking field trips to a hospital. I mean, is 'Whoopee, I'm going to see sick and dying people today!' something any of you ever say?"

Not a single kid raised her hand. Not even Brooklyn. Then a little girl with a surgical mask scooted closer to Violet and said, "They didn't even give us suckers."

"Or let us play with the dolls," another one with glasses said. "And the dolls were naked."

"They were first-aid dolls," Liza defended, but the girls weren't listening. In fact, it appeared that every one of them was excited to be heard, which told Emerson that Violet wasn't the only one who was unhappy.

"Last year's Lovely Leader Carol took us to a doll factory, then got us ice cream," Glasses was explaining, and for the first time since Emerson had arrived, the girls were actually smiling.

"Ice cream rocks," Emerson agreed.

"Ice cream and doll factories won't help win the Loveliest Survivalist," Liza said, taking Brooklyn by the hand. "Calistoga Lovelies Nine-Eight-Three knows that. It's why they are seven-time Loveliest Survivalist champions. And they have been begging Brooklyn to join their group since pre-K."

"Well, then what are you standing here for?" Emerson asked.

Liza looked at the group of misfits who had moved closer to Violet and took Brooklyn by the hand. "I have no idea."

Emerson watched Liza blast through the parking lot, completely oblivious to the chaos around her, and she wondered how a woman like that had been put in charge of a bunch of impressionable kids, then wondered why all of the remaining bugs were looking expectantly at her. As if she were the queen bug. And suddenly a bad feeling started in her gut.

Glasses stepped from the group and asked, "Are you going to take us to ice cream, Lovely Leader Emerson?"

chapter
seven

The next week, Dax went out for a run. The cold wind slapped him around and stole his breath, but it did nothing to settle the unease that had been gnawing at his brain all week.

Staring at the walls of his rental was driving him nuts, and Dax was itching to get back in the action, back to the adrenaline rush of a life that left him too busy and too spent to ponder stuff he shouldn't be pondering. Which was the only reason he could come up with for why he was running toward town hall, looking for a certain food cart.

Sure, he still had no idea how he was going to get to PT tomorrow. And he'd scrolled through his phone, a lesson in why it was important to keep up with old friends, because the only people in there who weren't family lived in San Diego or were stationed in another country.

He would have asked Emerson, except he didn't have her number either. The one she'd given him always went to voice mail—as though he was sent there. So he'd woken before the sun, set up camp on his porch, and waited so he could ask her. Hoping to catch her dropping off his food and sneaking away, a direct violation of their agreement—which she'd been directly violating since Monday.

Mission failed. The five-foot-nothing piece of work had outsmarted him. Again.

Oh, she'd been to his house, day three of her little color-coded containers in the freezer bag on his porch were proof, but she must have waited for him to hop in the shower before ringing the bell. Rookie mistake. And one he wasn't going to make again.

So he was headed off to hunt her down.

He ran up Main Street in a hard sprint on his second pass, and when he still didn't spot the Pita Peddler, he continued on past the sheriff's station, not slowing down until he reached the wine and chocolate bar on the far side of downtown. According to his investigation, a sneaky little Greek goddess subleased the kitchen space behind the bar.

He pushed through the front door and entered what could either be a bar or a high-priced brothel. The past-midnight lighting and deep red velvet accents had him thinking it was the latter, until a warm wave of nutty chocolate and fruity goodness wafted past, and if he closed his eyes, he could even detect a hint of fresh-baked pita. He was in the right place.

"Good afternoon?" He phrased it as a question, because the place looked empty.

A frosted bun poked up from under the counter, followed by a set of assessing eyes. They ran the length of him, taking in his mirrored wraparound sunglasses, lack of shirt, and excess of tattoos. "It sure is now. You here about my melons?"

Dax wasn't sure if the woman was senile, hitting on him, or just plain crazy, but he stared her in the eye, avoiding the melons at all costs, which were sagging on display. "I thought this was a wine bar."

"We dip too, anything that goes with chocolate. Only the last batch of melons were overripe and the supplier said he'd send his guy out." She looked at him, hopeful.

"Sorry, wrong guy."

"Huh." She smoothed down her LET'S GET CORKED AND SCREW tee, tugging it to make sure the letters were readable. "Well, it ain't my birthday," she said, sounding genuinely perplexed when she looked at the calendar to find that, no, it was not. Then she caught sight of his running pants, stared at the seams for a good, long time, and grinned the kind of grin that had Dax squirming in his shoes. "You're the new entertainment for the panty raid next week. Clovis said she'd let me test out the top picks." She reached under the counter and came up with a smartphone. "Can I film it for my website? Business purposes, you understand."

Dax took in his attire and understood that he resembled a cast member from *Magic Mike*. "Not that guy either," he said, pulling his tee from the waistband and sliding it over his head, but he heard a few clicks of the camera. "I was just out for a run and forgot to put my shirt on."

"Well, if you aren't here to squeeze my melons or strip, then what can I do for you?" she asked, but he noticed she still had her phone out, still aimed and still ready to roll, as though this was part of the skit and he was about to rip off his pants.

"I'm here to see the resident cook." He took out the business card Emerson had given him the other day.

The woman's eyes narrowed, her smile fell, and she mumbled something about "even in a cork costume" and shoved her phone back under the counter. "Of course you are."

"Is she around?"

"Nope," she said, her face carefully neutral, but her tone told him that even if she were, her answer would be the same.

"Do you have a number I can reach her?"

She crossed her arms and her eyes went on stranger-danger alert. "Cute as you are, Sexpot, I'm not in the habit of playing match-maker or giving out private info to tourists."

"I wouldn't expect you to," Dax said sweetly, pouring on the charm. "And I'm not a tourist." Not really. "The name's Dax."

He reached out his hand. When she just looked at his outstretched offering as though it were a grenade with the pin pulled, he leaned forward and to the side slightly, to engage her while coming off as a nonthreat. "I hired Miss Blake to do some cooking for me while I'm in town."

Nothing changed in her stance, then suddenly her face went bright, like the light had been flipped on, and she snapped her fingers. "Oh my word, I didn't recognize you with all those clothes on."

That was the last thing Dax expected to hear.

"Why, you're Marie Baudouin's youngest," she said, and Dax felt that familiar unease that always accompanied talking about his mother. He never knew what to say or how to feel. His mother had been beloved by everyone in St. Helena.

Except Dax. He'd only been two when she died. Outside of pictures and stories, he didn't really know anything about her, which made reminiscing difficult. And awkward since people expected him to carry that same torch of fondness for the woman they knew and loved.

"She'd be happy knowing the last one of her boys has come home, God rest her soul."

And there it was, the look that always followed the mention of his mom. It was one of respect and warmth, as if all he had to say was that he was Marie's and people accepted him immediately as family. Which was why he avoided bringing attention to that fact when he was home. But today he needed to talk to Emerson, convince her to take him to PT so he wouldn't be stuck listening to Frankie talk about the most effective pregnancy positions. And if knowing he was Marie's helped convince the gatekeeper he was harmless, a legit customer and not some pervy stalker, then he'd go with it.

"The last time I saw you, you had on diapers and were dragging around a doll."

"Action figure," he clarified. "A G.I. Joe *action figure*."

"Your mom was at chemo and I was babysitting. You cried the whole time because your brothers wouldn't let you in their blanket fort." She reached out her hand and Dax, making a mental note to punch his brothers later, shook it.

"Ida Beamon," she said. "I'm too old to babysit, but I still play bunko with your great-aunt Lucinda and Frankie. Although Frankie's too busy with her husband to make it to the game much anymore." She leaned in and whispered, "You know he's Italian."

Yes, and he'd heard enough for one lifetime about his brother-in-law's prowess, but thankfully Ida was already moving on. "I heard you were back in town. The ladies down at the pool canceled senior water aerobics when they read on the Facebook that you were jogging up and down Main Street topless. I had a lady doctor visit that day, so I had to miss the excitement." She gave him a thorough examination. "Wait until they hear I got a private showing."

Unsure of how to respond, he asked, "So you want to help me out and tell me where I can find Emerson?"

"You should come to Blow Your Cork on Saturday. It's a single's heaven. *And* ladies' night." She gave him an appreciative shimmy of the cantaloupes. "You'd start a riot. The other night it was so hopping the fire marshal came by." She pulled out a VIP card and slid it across the bar top. "Just drop my name and this will get you in free of charge. Or you could just come with your aunt."

"People pay a cover charge in St. Helena?" Dax had a hard time picturing any establishment in a town of six thousand asking for a head fee. Almost as hard as it was to picture his seventy-year-old aunt coming to a club.

"Only the tourists," she said as though he were mentally challenged. "But if you're looking for Emerson, she caters all of our events."

"Thanks," Dax said, pocketing the card. "But I was hoping to talk to her before she delivered my next batch of food."

"Seems pretty important to you." Ida leaned forward. "You sure this is just about her flipping your flapjacks?"

At this point, Dax wasn't sure what it was—only that he wanted to find her. Normally he'd have cut out of there the second Ida brought up his mom. But something about Emerson playing stealthy ticked him off—and turned him on.

Hell, at this point he was so bored and antsy, he'd rather spend his day searching down his chef than sitting on the couch watching television. So here he was, chasing her down with no clue as to what he'd do once he caught her. "I'm sure."

"Her number's in the phone book," Ida said.

"Already tried that one, it goes to an answering machine." Which she either wasn't checking or had selective caller block installed. "Tried her cell too."

"Only two reasons a woman like that doesn't return your calls," Ida said. "Either she's playing coy." Not likely—Emerson didn't know the meaning of *coy.* "Or she isn't interested in what you're selling."

Or she knew it would mess with his head. Regardless of the reason, Dax was intrigued.

"But," Ida went on, "because you showed me a little skin earlier, I'll tell you that she has a home number that she always answers." Ida pulled out a piece of paper and scribbled it down.

"Thanks." A grin as wide as the valley split his face as Dax reached for the paper. Ida tapped her cheek, so he leaned across the counter and gave her a peck, then moved toward the door.

"But it's Thursday so she won't be home," Ida called after him, and Dax stopped.

"You going to tell me where she is?"

That got a toothy grin. "That information will cost more than a kiss."

"I'm not taking off my clothes," Dax clarified, knowing that this little favor was going to cost him. That was how it worked in small towns. Ida did him a solid, and before he left, Dax would have to return the neighborly favor. He just hoped it had nothing to do with her melons.

"She closed up the cart early and headed to the community park."

It took Dax less than three minutes to jog to the park and two seconds to locate his target.

His person of interest was huddled around one of the public barbecue pits at the far end of the park. Alone. Bent at the waist, her hands moving a mile a second, she was like a homing beacon, drawing him in.

Her hair was pulled through the back of a camouflaged ball cap, and she wore a sweater, also camo, that fell off one shoulder, revealing the thin strap of what his gut was telling him was a bra. Solid black. Like her skirt, which in her current ass-to-the-sky pose was pulled high enough to show him the curve of her cheeks and if the lace was a matching set—were it not for the camo leggings she had on underneath.

She should have looked ridiculous with that knockout body covered from head to her patriotic-themed Converse in multicamo. Instead she looked sporty and tough, while managing to crank the sexy to full throttle.

"Should you be running with your knee?" she asked, her eyes firmly affixed to what was happening in the barbecue.

Dax walked around to look at her from the front and found himself smiling. Her hat was pulled low. Not low enough to hide the way her face was pursed in concentration—or the ash smudges on her forehead and right cheek—but low enough to know she meant business. And since she was trying to light the pit with a hunting knife and a flint rock, he took a big step back.

"Thank you for your concern," he said, leaning against a nearby picnic table. "We could have talked about this, say, a few hours ago when I was sitting alone at my table, reading the instructions for how to microwave my made-fresh meal."

She hit the rock again and a spark the size of a flea ignited, then fizzled in the wind. She swore, then commanded the wet twigs she was calling kindling to combust. When that didn't work, she narrowed her gaze—at him. "What did you expect me to do? Feed you?"

"Depends." He smiled, and man, she was cute when she was flustered. And she was flustered all right—he could almost see her feathers ruffling when he gifted her with a wink. "Would you be wearing that skirt?"

"Yup." She waved her blade in the general direction of his boys. "And my knife."

She was crazy. Crazy and bossy and so damn adorable he found himself shrugging. "I'm pretty good with knives, better with lace, and a ninja at stoking up fire." He pushed off the table and walked closer to the pit, studying her piss-poor excuse for a tinder ball. "Need help?"

The look on her face said she'd rather singe off her dominant hand than admit she needed help from him. With anything. Which was really a shame because Dax was having fun. And that restless feeling that had been suffocating him all week was gone, replaced with a lightness that he could only attribute to excitement.

"You just admitted you can't work a microwave," she pointed out.

"And you just waved your knife in my face, which in my world is a call to arms."

She didn't move a muscle, didn't even meet his gaze, but still managed to project that *screw off* vibe that had him grinning.

He leaned in, getting close enough that he could smell her shampoo, close enough that he could feel her heat seep through his clothes, and whispered, "Don't worry, Emi, you're safe. I don't want to shock you with the size and heft of my combat-ready blade."

She swatted him away like a pesky bug and went back to striking her flint—and ignoring him. Three more failed attempts and she glanced to her right, so Dax leaned over her shoulder too, grinning when he saw a wilderness survival book. It was opened to a picture of a mother and child making a fire. Below the diagram was a list of what one should have on hand in their pack. Dax wanted to point out that matches and a lighter should be at the top of the list, but refrained.

"We had a deal," he said, taking the top sticks off of her pile and restacking them to make a proper pyramid. "I didn't order takeout. And what's up with not returning my calls?"

Emerson looked up at him and worried her lower lip—she had amazing lips. "I'm not avoiding you," she said and he lifted a single brow on that lie. "Okay. I am avoiding you. But not for the reasons you probably think."

"Then you're not avoiding me because of that kiss?"

"Okay, so it is just what you think. But it's also because my week went from crazy to insane," she admitted begrudgingly, smacking his hand away when he tried to discard some of the wetter wood shavings. "I was going to return your *calls* today."

He could have called her on that lie too, except the way she emphasized the plural made him feel like he needed to get a life. One that didn't include playing cloak-and-dagger with the crazy cute girl. "What if I was calling you to say I was lactose intolerant?"

Now it was her turn to laugh. "You're a man, you'd never admit that."

"I would if it were a deathly allergy."

She paused, giving him all of her attention, and even though he knew she was messing with him, he still felt himself falling into those emerald-green pools. "Is that why you were calling? To tell me milk hurts your belly?"

He scoffed. "No, I was calling to ask you for a ride to PT today."

Her expression went soft, then flooded with guilt, and suddenly Dax felt like a jerk. "I know I said I'd give you a ride, but I can't today. I have to learn how to make fire, then help my sister with a diorama on the three-toed sloth, and I still have to prep for tomorrow, all before I turn into a pumpkin."

The strain in her shoulders and the exhaustion beneath her eyes said she was telling the truth. His little army of one needed a break. Yet instead of offering her some creative recreational ideas for how to blow off steam, the go-to for him in these situations, Dax found himself reaching for the bright blue rucksack at her feet.

He looked at the zipper, knew that opening it would be willingly following her down her rabbit hole of crazy, and hesitated. Dax could make fire with a candy wrapper and a ray of sun while cuffed and held at gunpoint—in a blizzard.

That wasn't the problem.

Making fire would be stepping into the role of hero, and he'd long ago given up that title. But something about the determined set of her jaw, the way her tired hands continued to strike the knife even though he knew she'd never get that wet tinder lit, had him unzipping the bag.

It wasn't like he was saving an orphanage of children from armed rebels. He was lighting a barbecue, for Christ's sake. Nothing that would require gratitude past a hot little kiss.

"I can reschedule for tomorrow," he said, digging past the flashy camping gear to locate the useful tools in about two seconds flat. He grabbed the flashlight, its battery, and a piece of steel wool, and tossed the rest of the useless weight to the ground. "Maybe after dinner."

"I'm not having dinner with you."

"Is that a yes to PT then?" Because he could deal with the dinner part later.

"I'll have to check my calendar," she said noncommittally.

Played that game. "Go ahead and check," he said, pulling off a thin strip of the steel wool and tugging it until there was ample flow for oxygen to pass through. "I've got time."

And that was the heart of the problem, he thought. Dax had spent the past decade going full force, running headfirst into hostile territory. There wasn't time in his line of work to stand idle, at least not without increasing his visibility, not to mention the chance of getting himself, or his men, killed.

Small-town living was all about the slow pace, being neighborly, and smelling the roses. Dax was pretty sure that smelling any more roses would send him into anaphylactic shock. So he picked up a few pieces of drier wood lying under an oak tree, placed them on the other side of the pit, and went to work.

"So about PT?" He scraped a stick on the side of the barbecue until he got to the dry center, collected the fibers into a little ball, stacked some of the smaller twigs, then finally the branches. Satisfied with his pyramid, he unscrewed the top of the flashlight and took out the batteries.

"Fine," she said. "I can take you tomorrow after I close down the cart. Now stop messing with my things. I have work to do and you're taking up all my working space."

She reached for the flashlight and he gave it to her, keeping the batteries and turning his back on her and the wind. He stacked the batteries on top of each other, then laid the steel wool on the contacts of the batteries, and poof.

Dax was in business.

"Oh my God," Emerson said, trying to look over his shoulder. "It's glowing."

He quickly moved the flame to his tinder ball, and with a few strategic, controlled blows it started smoking.

"Fire," she said, shoving him aside. "You made fire. In like two seconds. Is that even possible?" Since she seemed to be asking herself, he remained silent, then she lifted those big eyes his way, and Dax felt his throat cave in, because Emerson was looking at him as if this was more than a hot-little-kiss kind of moment. More than using a Basic Survival Training 101 skill.

She was looking at him as if he'd just stepped in and saved her day. And worse, he felt that addictive rush that came with playing hero. The one that gave even the most grounded soldier enough of a complex to make life-altering mistakes. And it was working. Dax felt himself surrender to the moment. "Want me to show you?"

She nodded, her smile so animated he felt himself being pulled into her sexy vortex. "I want you to show me *and* my friends how to survive in the wild."

Not the cozy little rendezvous he was imagining, but still, something he could work with. "It will cost you."

Emerson looked at his expression as if trying to read his thoughts, and since they centered around him and her, in the wild, under the stars, naked and making heat, he was glad for all of the interrogation training he'd received. And when he was certain she was going to tell him to screw off, she glanced at her watch and let out a long sigh. "Fine, I'll drive you to PT and cook you dinner."

"Breakfast and dinner," he countered, then added, "at my house as agreed upon," when she seemed like she was sifting her way through the loopholes. Her clenched jaw said she was doing just that. "And no more stealthy aid drops on my porch step."

She didn't counter as he'd expected, just zeroed in on something over his shoulder and said, "Deal. I take you to PT and cook you two meals a day. In your house. As agreed upon. And you promise to help me and my girls survive in the wilderness."

"Babe, I survived four tours in the middle of the desert with only my sense of humor and sand fleas to keep me company." He'd also had his squad with him, but he didn't like to talk about them with people who couldn't understand. "I think I can handle teaching a few ladies how to make fire and set up a designer tent."

Something about the way she smiled, then eagerly stuck out her hand, as if she didn't want to give him the chance to change his mind, should have had his internal warning system nearing DEFCON 1. But he was playing hero. And heroes didn't hesitate, because they naively thought themselves invincible. So he took her hand, pulled it to his lips, and kissed it. "I take that as we have a deal?"

"Oh yeah," she said a little too smoothly for his liking. Then she reached into her bag, pulled out another ball cap, and placed it on his head. This one was red and said LOVELY. "Sealed with a kiss even. On the hand, but binding enough."

She went on her toes and looked over his shoulder. "Hey, girls, let's get this meeting started by meeting your new Lovely leader."

"Oh, goodie! Do we call him Lovely Leader Mister?" a familiar and whimsical voice asked.

Dax slowly turned around, and DEFCON 1 didn't even begin to describe the situation. He'd faced down a mob of terrorists with only one clip, broken into a terrorist camp to rescue a captured squadmate, even watched a piece of shrapnel blow through his knee with enough force to take him out. Yet he'd never been as terrified as right then—staring down a small mob of pint-sized troops in red bows, pleated skirts, and glittery sneakers.

"I don't see why not," Emerson said, sending him a cocky grin. "He is a part of the Lovely now."

"Excuse us." He took Emerson by the elbow and led her behind the barbecue pit. "No way. I said I'd help your girlfriends, not a bunch of little girls who all happen to be friends."

She shrugged, not giving a shit that he was about to hyperventilate. "Semantics. Plus, if someone hadn't told my sister to pull the fire alarm when she saw a zombie, neither of us would be here."

"I told her to squirt potential threats with water, not pull the . . ." He paused, looked at the girl with corkscrew curls and fairy wings, and found himself smiling. And damn if she didn't smile back. "Pixie pulled the fire alarm?"

"Violet, and don't encourage her," Emerson said, turning them so the girls couldn't overhear. "They evacuated the entire hospital, and their Lovely leader quit, so unless I want to be another person who disappoints my sister, then I am their new Lovely leader. Which in all my spare time should be a snap, so unless you want to find a new chef, then you are my co-Lovely."

Dax knew jack shit about kids, even less about little girls. No sane person would put him in charge of any squad in his condition, let alone one made up of a bunch of freckle-faced Lady Bugs. Then again, he'd already decided Emerson was crazy, and it must have been rubbing off on him, because he said, "The conditions have changed. Time to reassess. I want two fresh-cooked meals a day, free cuts on your food cart line for lunch, you take me to PT, *and* . . ." He dragged out the word dramatically, making sure she understood that this *and* was as nonnegotiable as his stance on John Wayne being the best Green Beret on film. "I want to share one meal a day with you. At my kitchen table. No microwaves, casseroles, or weapons allowed."

Emerson opened her mouth to say no, hell no if her constipated expression was accurate, but then a little girl with Kool-Aid-stained lips and blonde curls tapped Emerson's thigh.

"Lovely Leader Emerson," she said, her voice so high it would send military dogs running. "Do we have to be near the smoke to make fire? Cuz I have asthma and my mom said the smoke will make me sick and I don't want to get sick cuz then you'd have to take me to the hospital and I don't like hospitals."

Dax smiled. "What's it going to be, Lovely Leader Emerson?"

Knowing she needed his help, she skewered him with a glare and said, "Fine, one meal a *week* with you and before you go smiling, all smug and irritating, note that even though I won't have my knife, it's still not a date."

chapter
eight

"No way. It's green."

Normally Emerson wouldn't even address the childish comment, just explain how greens were good for a growing body. But today she wasn't shopping with her picky kid sister. Today she was shopping with a 250-pound superfancy soldier who went squeamish at the sight of anything that grew in nature.

"It's kale," Emerson said, taking a head off the shelf and stuffing it into a produce bag. "It's supposed to be green."

"Yeah, well, the only thing that's green in the army is MREs, and I bet they taste better than that." Dax picked up some kale, then set it back on the display.

Emerson stared him down. This "quick" trip to the market to restock his fridge with healthy choices had already gone over her allotted time. He was due at PT in less than thirty minutes *and* they only had five things in the cart: a case of Bud, a couple of T-bones, coffee, and two containers of Muscle Milk. "You can't shoot down kale. You already nixed squash—"

"Too mushy."

"Broccoli—"

NEED YOU FOR ALWAYS

"Green," he pointed out as if she were the slow one.

"Asparagus—"

He lifted a finger. "Green." Up went another. "It comes from outer space. And it makes my pee smell funky."

She lifted her own finger to indicate the GROWN IN THE NAPA VALLEY sign. "They're locally grown and good for you."

"Negative," he said, not believing a word. "Anything that smells that funky can't be good for you."

"I gave you asparagus in last night's dinner," she said, thinking back to the meals she'd dropped off over the past few days. Meals that she'd woken up at four a.m. to prepare. "And the spinach in the chicken breast."

"I picked that out," he informed her sternly as though he didn't sound like a finicky eight-year-old. "Had you been there, cooking for me as promised, you would have known that."

He had her there. She always went to her clients' houses, did a full preference and allergy chart to ensure what she cooked was high quality, high flavor, and highly enjoyable—based on the client's palate. She'd skipped that step with Dax, which was completely unprofessional, and now she needed to make it right. Hence the shopping trip.

"Well, I am eating with you tonight—"

"Part of the deal," he reminded her. "And after sticking me with a bunch of squealing girls for an hour, I think I deserve some dessert too."

The way he said it, all smooth and full of innuendo, had her stomach fluttering—and her warning bells blaring. "Just think of how good the community service will look on your résumé. Lovely Leader Mister."

He glanced around at the other customers, then lowered his voice. "Co-leader. And if word gets out about me and my Lovelies, the guys will replace my bullets with tampons."

She leaned in too, even grinned. "I'll be sure to e-mail them a photo then."

Yesterday, Dax had looked like a real hero working with her troop. Ten minutes in and she knew that even though working side by side with him and watching him patiently mentor her sister was going to pull a few heartstrings—and create some pretty steamy fantasies of being stranded in the woods with a highly trained, highly attractive Special Forces guy with the most talented hands she'd ever seen—Dax was going to be the difference between her girls coming home from the campout proud and coming home disappointed. Which was why, no matter how talented he was, this was now, more than ever, a hands-off operation.

"And no dessert."

Undeterred, he followed her around the produce section. "How about a movie then? *The Green Berets* with John Wayne. A classic."

"Movie equates to a date, so no."

"You sure? Those Green Berets are a bunch of badasses." He grinned. "Want to know the difference between a Ranger and a Beret?"

"The Berets eat their vegetables?" That stopped him short. "Which we need to balance out the ten pounds of meat you picked out." She picked up a bunch of carrots. She could make some wonderful glazed carrots with cardamom and ginger. "How about these?"

Even Violet ate carrots without complaint. Sure, they were either cooked in butter and brown sugar or dipped in a sauce, but she cleared her plate.

Dax, however, was not of the same school of thought, because he crossed his arms over that massive chest. "A guy with perfect vision eating carrots would only come off as bragging."

"Are you shitting me? Is this another one of your lactose tummy ache BS statements?" His expression said that this was, in fact, not BS at all.

How was she supposed to make him complete meals if he only consumed red meat, beer, and caffeine? It wasn't as if she could hide things in his food like she did with Violet, or tell him that the onions were little bits of cheese that didn't melt. He'd see right through that.

Or would he?

Emerson picked up a bunch of fresh-picked broccoli and paused to study her latest food critic, who was leaning over the berry display, poking through the strawberry containers. He was built like a Humvee, had the arms of a piano mover, a killer backside, and the confidence of a guy who could handle anything that came his way.

As long as it wasn't green.

Dax rested his hands on the display case to find the perfect box of berries, and would you look at that. The fabric of his shirt pulled taut across his arms, and up his back. The sheer amount of exposed muscle and ink was enough to make her thighs quiver. Then his right biceps danced, flexing up and down in a seductive rhythm that could charm women from the far corners of the earth.

Women like me, she thought, unable to look away.

"Impressed?" he asked, glancing over his shoulder to watch her watch him and proving that exactly nothing got past Mr. I Can Track a Single Target in Four Thousand Square Miles of Desert with Perfect Accuracy.

"I can paralyze you with a stalk of celery," she pointed out.

"How about I just ram him with my cart?" Nora Kincaid, St. Helena's own Perez Hilton and the self-appointed director of the town's social media presence, asked. "Maybe my pie dish will fall out."

The older woman placed herself directly in Dax's path. She was five feet on a good day, wore a church dress and flowered hat, and she bared her teeth before poking Dax in the stomach with a cucumber. No pie dish fell out and not a single thing jiggled. He was solid under there. So Nora upped her game and poked him in the front pocket of his pants.

This time he did move, fast and with purpose, dropping his hands to cover his goods. "What the hell?"

"My thoughts exactly," Nora said, her beady eyes going beadier. "You might have perfect vision, but your manners could use a smack to the forehead." She looked at Emerson. "They got a vegetable for that?"

Emerson wanted to tell Dax that it was called humble pie, because he looked so thoroughly confused. Then again, seeing him sweat it out would be entertaining, but they were on a tight timeline.

"Hey, Ms. Kincaid," Emerson said, stepping forward. "We were just talking about your carrot parsnip pie." Dax looked at her with the most adorable *huh* expression ever, so she smiled encouragingly. "He liked it so much he ate it all in one sitting."

This made Nora's lips retract back down into something some might consider a smile. "Did you now?"

"Yes, ma'am," he said, so absolute Emerson thought he was about to salute. "It's why I didn't want any of Emi's carrots." He slid her a sideways glance. "Wouldn't want to mess with perfection."

"Well, bring me my dish back and I'll bake you another one," Nora said loud enough for the three silvered ladies picking through the brussels sprouts to overhear—not that she had to say it loud since the trio was practically leaning over the wooden case to listen in.

Something Nora noticed, because before Dax could utter another "Yes, ma'am," she had her phone out and Dax posed under the carrot display holding a bundle by, yes, the green stems. A click of the camera and a few frantic swipes to her screen later, she said, "Perfection, huh?"

Dax hesitated, and Nora's lips went up again and the cucumber came out.

"Uh, yes, ma'am," Dax said and Nora lifted a painted-on brow, then cupped a hand to her ear. "Perfection?" When Nora gestured for him to say it louder, he did, and thankfully dropped the question mark at the end.

With a satisfied nod, Nora placed the cucumber in her cart and toddled off, but not before grabbing a few pounds of carrots.

"It's the orange one," Emerson said quietly.

"I know what color carrots are."

She grinned. "I meant the pie dish. Nora always serves her pie on an orange plate. She says it matches the carrots."

"You sure?" Dax asked, his forehead furrowed as though doing a mental search of his fridge to see if he remembered an orange platter.

"Yeah, when my mom passed she brought one to my dad every week for a month straight. My suggestion is scrape it down the sink and give her the plate back, then don't answer the door when she knocks again."

"Noted," he said, then shook his head. "I still don't get it. That's like bringing a six-pack to game night and then expecting the guys to give me back the empty bottles."

"It shows how little you know about women," Emerson said and shifted her gaze slightly to the eggplants, which were conveniently located just left of his biceps, and reached around him to pick one. "Do you like these?"

"I know all the important stuff about women, and yes, I like. Very much," he said, his eyes squarely on her hindquarters. She cleared her throat and he lifted his gaze to her hand, but not before perusing her other produce. "Oh, that. What the hell is that?"

"Eggplant. It doesn't smell, isn't green." And it was the first thing outside of dessert she'd ever mastered in the kitchen.

"Is it mushy?" he asked, looking hesitant, then took it and weighed it, as though he was the resident expert on mush factor. "Because it looks like it would be mushy."

"Not the way my mom taught me to make it." And when he didn't look as though he was about to object, she added, "I slice it really thin, cover it with feta cheese and a bunch of yummy Greek seasonings, roll it up, and bake it. We used to eat it at least a few times a week." Just thinking about those meals, that time with her mom when she wasn't even big enough to reach the counter without a kitchen chair, made her smile. "Even Violet likes it."

She waited for him to answer, but he just stood there, balancing the eggplant in his palm while silently assessing her. And he had the weirdest look on his face that no matter how hard she tried to translate, she couldn't. Then he gently nodded and said, "How can I say no to your mom's recipe?"

"Nearly everything I cook is one variation or another of my mom's recipes," she admitted.

He placed the eggplant in the cart and led them to the other side of the produce section. "Did your mom own a restaurant?"

"It was always her dream, but her health wouldn't allow for her to be on her feet that long. She did a lot of catering for family and friends, though. Had more offers to cater than time," she said, determined not to make her mother come off as a victim. Because that would have been the furthest thing from the truth. Her mom was one of the strongest, most dignified and determined people Emerson had ever met. Around town she was known as the sweet, soft-spoken Greek lady with the mouthwatering dolmas and contagious smile.

What most people missed was that under her mom's velvet exterior was a power and courage that were awe-inspiring. Traits that Emerson worked tirelessly to embody—without much luck. "It was her idea to open the food cart. The next step in the master plan is to upgrade to a food truck."

"Food truck?" he asked and she could hear the confusion in his voice. The same outdated underlying question everyone had when they first heard her plan. "Like the burrito wagon that used to come through base?"

"No." Definitely not. "A state-of-the-art, gourmet food experience on wheels. A mobile way to bring top-quality eats to everyday people."

"I knew what you meant, I was just giving you a hard time," he said with a smile. "And your idea is smart. How far you've come is impressive," said the most impressive person in her life right then. "What do you think your mom would say?"

Over the years, Emerson had been bombarded with that same question. However, few took the time to listen to her answer. They were too busy telling Emerson *their* opinions of exactly what her mom would be feeling.

Proud, impressed, tickled pink. She'd heard it all from the time she was seven and her mom was diagnosed with ALS.

After her mom's death it only got worse. Family, friends, sometimes even strangers would approach her to give their condolences, which usually led to a story about losing their own loved ones or how missed Lillianna would be. In those situations, Emerson found herself swallowing her own emotions to take on the role of nurturer.

With Dax it felt different. For a guy who seemed to have the emotional capacity of a rutting stallion, his compassion and understanding went much deeper than she'd expected. Maybe it was firsthand knowledge of the complexity of losing a parent, since he'd lost both, or maybe he was showing her his hidden layers.

Either way, Dax seemed to get her in a way that was refreshing, and she found it incredibly appealing.

"She'd probably tell me it's about time," she said and found herself laughing, because she could almost hear her mom saying those exact words. "Then she would tell me that if I was a real chef, I would find a way to get a grown-ass man to eat his vegetables."

And there went the double-barreled dimples that excited and confused her all at the same time. Because when Dax smiled like that, real and from the heart, she wasn't sure how to react. Dismissing him when he was being a flirt was easy. Ignoring the way her heart fluttered when he engaged fully was impossible.

"So tell me, Ranger. Are there any vegetables that don't scare you?"

He thought about it for a long minute and, smile dialed to dangerous, said, "I like corn."

She didn't have the heart to tell him that corn was a grain, so she grabbed a couple of ears and tossed in an avocado just to throw him. "We'll start with the eggplant and work up to kale."

"You don't look so good. How bad is it?"

Dax wasn't sure how to answer that. His chest burned, most of his organs felt like they were shutting down, and he was pretty sure he was two seconds from losing his lunch.

"I can handle it," he said, gritting through the pain.

"Sure you can," Kyle said, taking the weights from his legs and setting them on the floor. "That's what all the G.I. Joes say right before they pass out. So why don't you lie down on the mat and we'll cool down."

"I can do one more rep," he said but realized that he was already on the floor, his back pressed hard into the mat. "Why is it I feel fine until I come here?"

"That pain you're feeling is a good sign," Kyle said, putting a death grip on his kneecap and leaning into him like he was a man sled and this was the NFL.

"And here I thought dying was a bad thing," Dax joked, but no matter how hard he tried to laugh, he couldn't.

"That pain right there"—Kyle pressed farther just in case Dax didn't know exactly what pain he was talking about—"that's the nerve endings coming back to life. It means you took well to the surgery and now your body's healing."

Kyle released a fraction, then pressed in an inch farther. Dax sucked in a breath. "You want me to stop there?"

"No way." Dax pressed through the next thirty seconds, ignoring the dots of light piercing his vision, and when he felt his leg finally hit the mat, he allowed himself to breathe. And that's when a new wave of pain rolled through him like a tsunami.

"Your flexibility is improving too. All signs that—"

"You're an asshole?"

"I was going to say that things are on track." Kyle squeezed out the knot that had formed in Dax's thigh from the strain. "But you need to do more stretching at home and less pounding the pavement."

"Okay," Dax said like he did every session, knowing he wouldn't stop. Running was the only outlet he had left, and unless the doctor wanted him to officially lose it, he couldn't give it up. But he'd try more stretching.

Maybe get his crazy cutie of a chef to assist him.

"Take some of those pills the doctor prescribed tonight or in about two hours you might embarrass yourself."

Dax opened his eyes, and it took a moment for Kyle's two bodies to merge back into one. "Not happening."

"It will make the recovery more manageable." Dax remained silent and Kyle shrugged a shoulder. "Yeah, I didn't take them either."

A silent understanding passed between them, and every reason Dax had for coming home, for entrusting his recovery to Kyle instead of some physical therapist in San Diego, was confirmed. Only someone who had marched in his shoes before could understand his need for the pain, because with pain came clarity, and right now Dax needed something in his life to make sense.

"Just know that in order to heal, your body actually needs rest." Kyle held up a hand. "Which I know for guys like us feels like crawling our way out of our own skin. Slowly. But your injury is like a woman, it makes its own set of rules that change hourly and gets pissy when you don't listen."

Dax knew a woman who got pissy whether he listened or not. In fact, she got pissy whenever he was around. There was one time she hadn't been pissy at all, but he knew that thinking about San Francisco made her pissy all the same.

"Are you telling me how to handle my women?"

Kyle laughed. "I'm telling you that if you don't take it easy and let this heal in its own time, you'll be riding a desk for the rest of your life." Dax ignored the first part, since that was a nonoption, and focused on the second part, about him being stuck in St. Helena for longer than planned. Also a nonoption. Because in a few weeks the elite team position would need to be filled, so that was when he needed to be ready to go. "I have a new job starting and I need to be in peak shape."

"You're looking a little green to be talking about peak shape. If I were you, I'd skip shaking it for the ladies this weekend and rest," Kyle said, then burst out laughing.

"What are you talking about?"

Kyle jerked a thumb to the newspaper clipping on the community board next to the water cooler. Dax looked at the heading and that gnawing itch moved from his thigh to behind his right eye. "'St. Helena's own beefcake bodyguard to work ladies' night at Cork'd N Dipped.'"

"The article goes on to say that last week's party was crashed by a bunch of underagers. In order to keep things orderly and safe, and to please the fire marshal, management is hiring local muscle to work the door." Kyle grinned. "Nice picture, man."

Yeah, he looked like a stripper. Wearing nothing but rip-away pants and a shirt that was halfway over his head, looking like it was coming off and not going on.

"My earlier client was talking about going mainly to see if you were photoshopped. She's eighty-two and has a titanium hip."

"I was out running," Dax said, unpinning the paper from the board. He went to throw it in the trash, only to stop short when he saw the photo underneath his—and smiled. In the middle of a tsunami of pain, he actually smiled.

Then laughed, because—*best day ever*—directly below his snapshot was one of the wine bar's caterer. A hot little Greek number with auburn hair, sexy lips, wine-colored Converse, and wearing a cork-inspired costume. Big, brown, and concealing every delicious curve beneath the wire-shaped cylinder—with a corkscrew-shaped hat up top.

Dax ripped off and pocketed the photo, tossing the rest of the paper in the can. "I stopped in the wine bar on Main Street. A crazy lady snapped it." Then gave him information on Emerson in exchange for a favor. Looked like Ida was calling in her marker.

And Emerson was the resident cork bunny.

"I don't know what's worse, admitting to the one guy who stands between you and a doctor's signature that you were running or that you were in a wine bar." Kyle stopped and smiled. "So, when were you going to tell me you're the new Lady Bug leader?"

"Is anything private anymore?"

"You're kidding, right?" Kyle grabbed a towel and wiped it down his face, then tossed one to Dax. "You were wearing a hat that said Lovely while eating an ice cream cone at the community park."

"It was a popsicle," he clarified. One hundred percent real juice, no added sugar. Emerson's rules. "And Jonah said I needed to get more involved in the community."

The popsicles had been all his idea. The girls had taken to steel wool and batteries faster than most new recruits, so he'd rewarded the little pyros with a treat from the market.

"According to my earlier patient—"

"The hip replacement?"

"No, stroke survivor. She said that you were seen sharing your Cyclone pop with the food cart girl." Kyle let loose a whistle. "Emerson Blake? Gotta say I'm surprised."

"You take up coupon bingo when I was gone? Because you sound like my great-aunt Lucinda quoting the senior grapevine like it's the *Washington Post*. And for the record, I hired Emerson to cook me food that wasn't a token of gratitude for doing my damn job," Dax said and Kyle sobered. "And why are you surprised?"

"She's not your normal type."

"I have a type?" This was news to Dax. He liked women, all kinds of women. Blonde, brunette, redhead, he especially liked those. Big boobs, spinners, didn't matter. If there was an attraction, he was game. With Emerson, though, he feared he was attracted *because* they were playing a game. Although what had happened in the market earlier had felt like a whole lot more.

"Yeah, you like them easygoing, up for a good time, and not interested in breakfast the next day. Emerson is smart, straightforward, and, after her mother passed, has more ties than a parachute." Something Dax was beginning to understand. "She also isn't a booty-call kind of girl. She's the kind who leaves a mark."

Kyle was right and Dax knew it.

Clenching his jaw, Dax stood, proud when he didn't wobble. But Kyle saw through his military-grade exterior and offered him a hand up. Dax waved it off because, what the hell? "You seem to know a lot about Emerson."

Kyle stared at Dax. Dax stared back. His friend was big, but Dax was bigger.

"I treated her mom," Kyle said slowly. "Lillianna was the first patient I lost after coming home."

Not what Dax was expecting his friend to say. He'd thought his buddy was warning him off because unlike Dax, Kyle had a type.

And Emerson was it. Worse, though, that meant she'd lost her mom recently enough that the wound was still open.

"When Lillianna's condition worsened, Emerson moved home to help, came to every appointment, and was with her mom right up until the end. She's spent the past year and a half taking care of her sister and dad, and from what I hear, she pretty much is the only thing holding her family together."

"Sounds like something she'd do." Dax pictured the tough girl with the smart mouth and sad eyes putting her life on hold to come to her mother's side. A lot of things started to make sense. Including San Francisco. It was probably the first time she'd let loose, taken something for herself since her mom got sick.

That she'd chosen him was humbling, because although they could chalk it up to timing and opportunity, that night had affected him more than he'd like to admit. Then she'd left—now he knew it was to go back to her life. And damn if that didn't make him want to carry a part of her burden. Or at least not add to it.

"My suggestion is to go home, put your leg up, take one of those pills you hate so much, and get some sleep." Kyle shook his head. "I know that look and I'll tell you the same thing I tell all of the idiots who come through here. Healing takes time, and only a fool would rush that."

Being a fool was better than going crazy, he thought, and that was exactly where Dax was headed if this injury put him out longer than he'd been told. Between the surgery and recovery, he'd planned for twelve weeks total. Twelve weeks of sitting on his ass and thinking about things he'd rather forget. His twelve weeks were almost up, and if he wasn't ready at the end of them, the job would go to someone else and he'd be stuck riding a desk just like Kyle said. It was an unacceptable scenario.

Dax took a step and felt the weight of ten countries press down on his knee. By the time he dragged himself off the mat, a sharp gnawing had taken up residence in his left leg and lower back. Sweat beaded on his forehead and—*Jesus*—the only thing he could think about as he ran toward the garbage can was that the prick was right.

Dax was going to embarrass himself.

Confused and, quite honestly, concerned, Emerson tried to keep her eyes on the road, but they continued to stray to the silent passenger next to her. The sun had set, casting a tangerine hue over the valley floor, setting fire to the changing grape leaves and making for an amazing autumn sunset.

It could have been snowing for all Dax seemed to notice. He hadn't said a single word since she'd picked him up other than to tell her that PT was fine, his knee was fine. Everything was fine.

He looked fine, didn't limp when he walked to the car, even smiled. In fact, outside of the dullness behind his eyes, there was nothing outwardly pointing to the fact that he wasn't being honest. Nope, Dax was the captain of calm.

But Emerson had a gut instinct that something was off. And her instincts were rarely wrong.

"Glad your knee's fine," she said, pulling into his drive and putting a little more oomph behind hitting the brakes than necessary.

Dax didn't flinch, didn't even react other than to flash her a knowing smile. How did he remain so controlled when she knew his knee was killing him?

Emerson threw the car in park and reached across the console. She placed her hand on his knee and pressed her fingertips under the kneecap.

"Jesus," he gasped, partly out of pain and partly out of relief.

"I thought you were almost done with PT?" The way he had made it sound the other day, he was on his last few visits, but this felt like more-than-a-few-visits kind of recovery. She released her grip only to tighten again, and this time his leg jerked, but she held on. "How bad is it?"

He didn't answer, just closed his eyes as she manipulated the tissue around the knee. It was hot to the touch and, the way his breathing went shallower with every pressure point she touched, angry.

"Did you learn how to do this for your mom?" he asked quietly.

Her hand paused at the unexpected question, and so did her heart. She considered giving him her it's-no-biggie stock answer about taking a few massage therapy classes at the local JC to avoid a real conversation about what that really meant. But something about this moment, about the way he was asking, made blowing it off impossible.

"When I left for culinary school she was struggling with small things, opening jars, standing for long periods of time, but she was good at hiding it. By the time I came home her disease had progressed to the point that hiding wasn't an option. It was awful. Just walking in the yard with Violet was like hiking up the side of a mountain with hundred-pound weights tied to her ankles." Emerson took a deep breath. "She didn't want Violet to miss out and she was determined to live a lifetime in a few years. So I learned how to ease the pain afterward."

"Is that why you're the head bug?" Dax asked and she nodded.

"Lovely leader, and yeah, I had an amazing mom for twenty-seven years. Violet will never have that." Emerson's hands kept gently working his knee. It was strange, her mom had been gone almost two years and yet her fingers remembered exactly what to do. "But I am head bug, as you put it, because my sister thought it was smart to take on an army of zombies with fire sprinklers."

Dax chuckled, but it seemed strained. Then a large hand came to rest on hers. "Can I get a rain check on dinner?"

"That bad?" she asked and a swift flood of concern filled her chest.

His head rolled to the side to meet her gaze, and what she saw there floored her. It wasn't that stoic soldier she'd become so familiar with looking back. Nope, he was stripped down. Maybe he hurt too much to fake it, or maybe he felt safe enough to be open with her.

Dax without any armor was like catnip.

"It's a lot of things, so I think it would be smart for me to go inside and you to go home."

"Are you sure?" she asked, wondering when this had become so important. Yesterday she had been dreading dinner, but today, after their time at the store, she was actually looking forward to it. Looking forward to a fun night of flirting and laughing and the freedom to be a single woman. Not a nearly thirty-year-old guardian and business owner who had more responsibilities than a single mom.

Oh, who was she kidding? Emerson was looking for a fun night of flirting with Dax. Because flirting with Dax was more than fun, it was exhilarating.

"No," he said, his voice rough and his eyes—those were on her lips. So intense Emerson felt them tingle. "I'm not."

She wasn't either anymore, which was why she needed to leave. Needed to pack up and clock out, because something had shifted. The teasing banter and sexy sparring had turned deeper, and that warm hum of connection they were sharing had turned electric. Suddenly, being trapped in her little car with a man as big as life made it hard to breathe. The last time she'd felt this intoxicated had been that night in San Francisco.

"How about I get you in the house and at least make you dinner," Emerson offered. "You need to eat, right?"

Dax's eyes went hot and he cupped her face with his masculine hand. "If you go with me into that house, I'm going to want to skip dinner and go straight to dessert, sampling every piece until I decide on my favorite." His fingers dropped to the erratic pulse at her neck. "Then we'd do it again and again until our palates are completely satisfied."

Emerson's head was telling her to abort mission. A good chef knew that dessert always followed dinner—it was the hint of sweet that marked the end of the meal. The bad girl in her, the one who used to run things but went on sabbatical the day her mom got sick, reminded her that dessert was a host's way of guaranteeing that nobody left the party unsatisfied.

Emerson knew that with a man like Dax, and that wicked promise in his eyes, she'd never be left unsatisfied. He would make her sweet spot a top priority and her satisfaction his own personal mission.

"Something is warning me that it still won't be enough," he said, and Emerson's competitive side was up for the challenge. But before her sweet spot could be tended to, Dax ran his thumb over her lip and said, "And I'm leaving in a few weeks' time." He sounded almost as if the admission caused him physical pain. "So this is where I say thanks for the ride and the groceries then hobble my sorry ass up to bed. Alone."

"You just went home?" Harper asked, sliding a tray of mini spinach and dill-infused feta pastries into the fridge. She had flour on her face, phyllo dough stuck to her sweater, and her curly black hair was piled on top of her head, held there with what Emerson assumed was a half-chewed pencil or a clothespin.

Emerson knew the amount of preparation needed to pull off the farmers' market *and* Blow Your Cork in one day was going to be intense, so when her dad called early that morning saying he had an interview later that day at a high-end boutique winery down valley for a senior manager position, Emerson had no choice but to offer to take Violet for the day. Hanging with her sister at the farmers' market would be fun—she could put Violet to work selling the baklava. It was the two hours in between events that would be a problem.

Her solution? Prep for both events simultaneously before Violet arrived. Which meant she needed backup. Harper couldn't cook, but years of working with kids had taught her to be a master with directions—issuing and receiving.

She also had a velvet honesty about her that made her the perfect sounding board.

"What was I supposed to do? Force my way in and make sure he made it to bed without passing out?" Emerson dropped an apron full of plums and oranges onto the counter. Today's farmers' market special was a plum shortcake, a crowd favorite, which meant she needed to make twice the normal amount.

Harper closed the industrial-sized fridge and turned to face her. "A man who looks like that says he wants to dine on me? I'd carry him to bed, show him what's for dinner, then tuck him in. Right over me."

"Even if you knew he was leaving?" A matter that had accounted for Emerson getting exactly zero sleep last night. She wanted Dax, no question. And he made it more than clear he wanted her.

What should be a simple problem with a simple solution was complicated by the fact that in addition to wanting him, Emerson was stupidly starting to like him—and there was no simple outcome for that.

"I knew you were leaving for Paris, but that didn't mean I stopped hanging out with you." Harper crossed her arms. "In fact, I hung out with you more."

"This is different," she said. "I couldn't shake you even if I tried. Your circle of friendship is unbreakable."

Harper smiled proudly. There wasn't a soul in town she didn't know or hadn't befriended. She was the kind of person who hugged strangers and could make friends with a rabid piranha. She'd rub a fishing line in some of that sunshine she wore for perfume, tie it to an olive branch, and seduce the flesh-eating fish into embracing his inner koi. Then she'd take it home, convert it to a vegetarian, and buy it a green-powered tank.

"And Dax, well, he's—"

"Sexy, single, mysterious, and interested."

He was also so damn charming he brought up feelings that she hadn't dealt with since Liam left. And like Liam, Dax too was leaving. "He's moving to San Jose."

"Hello? Perfect situation. You need to get laid, and he looks more than equipped for the job." Harper slapped her hand over Emerson's mouth. "And before you talk yourself out of a little friends-with-benefits action and deny us this incredible opportunity, because let's be real, the last man who hit on me was Tommy Walker at last week's watercolor class when he told me I smelled like glue"—at Emerson's confused expression, Harper clarified—"Tommy *loves* glue. Anyway, I need you to really understand what you'd be saying no to."

Harper turned Emerson's head with her hands so Emerson could focus in on the front page of the *St. Helena Sentinel* and the most delectable abs and chest this town had ever seen.

"Look long and hard," Harper whispered. "Still not convinced? Then let me remind you that we live in a town of six thousand. Six thousand people we already know, Em. Every single man we will encounter from here forward will either be tourists who will leave, college kids who will think we're old, old men who will think we're desperate, or guys who knew us when we played with Barbies."

"I never played with Barbies," Emerson mumbled through Harper's fingers. "And get your hand off my mouth, you taste like crayon wax and olive brine."

Harper dropped her hands but didn't back down. "All I'm saying is that this is a chance for you to get yours. To forget about all of the stress, the demands of your family for a few hours, and have some fun."

"And maybe an orgasm or two?"

"Um, how about ten? Have you seen the man? Plus after Liam, you deserve ten." Harper's voice softened. "You deserve to be happy, Em. Really happy. You take care of everyone else and never complain, and now there is a chance for you to take care of you."

"For just a night," Emerson said softly.

"Sure, a built-in expiration date. Keeps it simple and free of expectations. I mean, everyone's going to leave at some time or another," Harper pointed out. "But this time it doesn't have to be a bad thing."

Emerson thought about that and wondered what it would be like to be free of expectations. She was a pretty private person by nature, and every relationship she had was intense, which was why she was selective of the people she let in.

This thing with Dax would be physically intense but emotionally casual, and for a girl who knew how to take her mother's vitals before she could legally drive a car, there hadn't been room in Emerson's life for anything frivolous. There also hadn't been room in her life to really live. Not solely for herself.

Emerson thought about San Francisco, about that kiss in her car, then thought about the erotic statement he'd thrown at her last night and wondered if she could go through with it. If she could put aside her need to nurture and for the first time in a long time put her needs first.

For just a night.

She looked over at the cork costume on the wall, then smiled. "Does your grandma still have that vintage '40s dress in her shop window?"

ch🍳pter
nine

"Y" ou need lunch money?" Adam asked with a grin, pulling up to the curb and making sure to park right in front of a life-sized cutout of Beefcake Bodyguard—in case Dax had somehow managed to miss the posts about it on Facebook.

"Fuck off." Dax grabbed his jacket and stepped out onto the curb, the crisp evening air filling his lungs. A few maple leaves blew down the lamp-lined sidewalk and into the street.

It was Saturday night, nearly happy hour, and he had received a half dozen calls from curious ladies inquiring about his hosting skills, a few more inquiring about his *other* skills, and enough grief from Adam on the ride over to make his right eye twitch. And unless he could talk his way out of playing Beefcake Bodyguard, his night was just getting started.

"Beefcakes aren't really my type," Adam said. "But Ms. Lambert over at the Grapevine Prune and Clip was at the bank getting a hundred bucks in ones today, just in case the rumors were true and you were taking it all off at midnight. My guess is you won't go home lonely tonight. The other guys at the firehouse have a poll going on how many teeth—"

Dax slammed the door and, finger high and loud, he waved his thanks and walked toward the bar. From the outside it looked like a typical small-town storefront. Gray clapboard siding, raised planter boxes filled with seasonal flowers, and a little red awning over the door. A couple of wrought iron tables and chairs sat in front of the street-side window, which had tasteful gold calligraphy that challenged one to INDULGE IN SECRET PLEASURES—ONE SIP AND ONE DIP AT A TIME.

Praying he wasn't expected to be the secret pleasure, he rounded the alley to enter through the side door. A red carpet ran the entire length of the alley, which was already filled with customers winding down and around the back of the building.

Not just customers, Dax groaned: ladies. Senior ladies with walkers, ginormous handbags, and saggy breasts slung up in sequins. They were all flapping their cards, the same VIP card Ida had given him, waiting for the doors to open. Excitement and impatience hung thick, and Dax knew he should run.

Too bad for Ida that she'd run an ad without consulting him first, because no way was he going to be the hired beefcake. It would take a riot squad to control this mess if it went sideways. And it was going to go sideways. There was no way all those ladies were getting in. It would be against fire code, and as soon as they realized it, shit was going to go down.

He'd only dropped by to tell Ida that he wasn't working her event, then go to the Spigot, a cash-only, manners-optional sports bar down the street where he was meeting Kyle for brews and a game.

And okay, he'd also come to see if he could catch a glimpse of Emerson in her cork costume. Maybe poke fun at her outfit, make her laugh, and charm away any residual weirdness from last night. A smart man would welcome the weirdness, embrace the distance it would create, and get out while he was ahead.

Dax was neither a quitter nor smart, because the last thing he wanted was awkwardness with the one person whose company made him feel at ease.

"Those muscles look real to me," someone said from the crowd.

"I think he needs to take it off so we can see with our own eyes," someone else said, someone who sounded a lot like ChiChi DeLuca. ChiChi, who had silver hair, wore orthopedic shoes, and married his grandpa last year.

"No inspecting the merchandise," Ida said, waddling out. She looked at Dax, took in his boots, jeans, and dark tee and shrugged. "Was hoping for dress whites, more of *An Officer and a Gentleman* look."

"Richard Gere was in the navy. I'm army," Dax said, but Ida didn't seem to be bothered by the difference, as though the two were interchangeable. "And I hoped you would have consulted me about tonight before taking out an ad in the *Sentinel*."

"It wasn't an ad, it was an editorial piece about safety in our society."

"And me shirtless on the cover addresses civilian safety how?" he asked.

"One look at those guns and any underage woman will think twice before coming in and poaching our men. But just in case, I got one of those blue light things the TSA uses to detect fake IDs."

"How many minors snuck in last week?" Because the thing about small towns was one couldn't fart without people smelling it. Dax couldn't imagine how kids could lie about their age in a place where half the patrons had, at one time or another, changed their diapers.

"Not minors, men poachers," she said, grabbing him by the arm and tugging him through the side door into the bar. "Those fresh-out-of-their-third-marriage twits who all live in that fifty-five and older community down the road. They come in here with their menopause glow and pregrandma boobs, attracting the guys with real hip joints and acting for all the world to see like they'll never need a hip replacement."

Ida paused in the entry to point to just such a woman in line. She wore sailor pants with six buttons on the front, a starched white shirt—tucked in—and gold-rimmed glasses.

"So you want me to bounce Ms. Wheeler?" Dax asked. "She was my kindergarten teacher."

"Personal histories with the patrons mean nothing. Understand?" Dax understood. More than he cared to admit.

"Good." Ida stepped close, then right up onto her toes and poked his abs with her meaty finger. "If she ain't over sixty-five, she ain't getting in. Real hips get the di—"

He held up a hand, not wanting to hear the rest. "Look, we have a problem."

But Ida wasn't listening, she was already gone, waddling her way behind the bar like a woman with a plan.

Dax blew out a breath and sank onto a stool. No point in chasing her down, she'd be back, then he'd tell her that he wanted no part of her plan. He'd repay the marker some other way. Maybe with some creative defense lessons so she could handle her own security.

It took a second for his eyes to adjust to the mood lighting, but when they did, he knew he was screwed. The entire place had been turned into an *Anchors Aweigh* set. Life preservers lined the walls, blue-and-white-striped tablecloths adorned the cocktail tables, and a big gold anchor hung behind the bar. The place was already hopping with old timers in wartime attire lining the bar, sipping sidecars and smelling like Bengay, waiting for the dance hall ladies to come swarming in.

But what had him pausing, had him rethinking his evening plans, was the dance hall honey standing at the far side of the room.

Emerson wasn't dressed like a cork tonight. Oh no, she was wearing enough body-hugging fabric to cause someone to blow theirs.

She looked soft and sexy in a vintage dress that hugged her body and went from collarbone to below the knee, only to cinch high in the waist with a tiny strip of leather. The dress was navy and white, the belt red, and the heels a blatant invitation. Her hair was down, silky auburn curls shining under the lights and flirting around her shoulders, while one side was secured with a big white flower.

She was a walking, talking, World War II dream girl.

Her eyes locked on his and instead of looking away, like any other woman would have done, she sent him an amused smile that had a bit of challenge thrown in. Challenge that when paired with those shoes was a request for trouble without consequences.

Dax loved a little trouble. Trouble without the drama was even better. But nothing about this woman said no strings.

It wasn't the dress or the bombshell body—or even the shoes. Those were giving him a green light all the way. It was that flash of vulnerability he'd seen when she was talking about her mom. About her sister.

Emerson put up a good tough-girl front, but he knew that she wasn't as bulletproof as she pretended to be.

And that slayed him. Because Dax knew all too well what a bullet to the chest felt like. So he'd take that night-of-fun challenge and raise her a partner in the short term. She could use someone on her side, and he was already more invested than just fun. So when Ida came back over with a big box of door swag and a blue light, he said, "Where do you want me?"

And that was how Dax found himself, two hours later, standing in the cold, vetting real IDs from fake ones, and passing out ladies' night swag bags that had been donated by the lingerie shop next door.

"What kind is this?" Mrs. Moberly, the town's long-standing librarian asked, pulling the red vibrator from the bag. "Oh my, it's a Go Big or Go Home."

Dax rolled his neck from side to side and mumbled, "I believe so."

Mrs. Moberly held up the device to inspect it. He could have told her that, according to the shop's owner, Clovis, the Go Big or Go Home was the preferred personal pleasure device for two out of every three women in St. Helena—three years running. He could have, but he didn't.

First, because that would be acknowledging that most of his female relatives had one or wanted one. Second, because *what the hell?* And third, because after repeating the scripted spiel to the head of the Daughters of the Prohibition board, who asked him why the overwhelming support for the device, she'd proceeded to turn it on. And watching that thing light up in the presence of someone who used to read him *James and the Giant Peach* wasn't something he wanted to experience.

Ever.

"Why don't you save this for the next person, dear?" Mrs. Moberly said, pushing her glasses farther up her nose and handing him the vibrator. Just like that, she placed a dick-shaped laser light show in his hand and smiled. "I already have one." Then she patted his cheek and even gave it a little pinch. "It's so good to see you home, Dax. Safe and in one piece. We're all real proud of you."

She said it as if he wasn't standing on Main Street holding a rubber pleasure stick in his hand and she hadn't caught him in the stacks, sneaking peeks at the boobs in *National Geographic* when he was twelve.

One last pat and she was gone, and Dax turned to the next customer.

Ah, shit. "What are you doing here?" Dax asked his brothers, only the question was rhetorical, because if one of them had been in his shoes, he'd come to laugh too.

"What did Dad tell you about standing in public with your dick in your hand?" Adam asked and Dax shoved the vibrator into one of the bags but managed to hit the on switch in the process.

A low hum shook the paper bag and vibrated off the cement and, before Dax could stop it, a bright red glow lit up the box and patriotic-themed strobe lights flickered into the inky night sky. Red, white, and blue, because when Clovis caught wind of a theme, she went all the way, which was why she hadn't just donated the standard Go Big or Go Home, she'd donated the limited edition Let Freedom Ring series.

"Wow, that can't be normal," Adam said with mock concern. "You should have that checked out."

Dax looked at Adam in his SHFD blues and hat and snorted. "Dude, you drive a red engine, play with your hose, and ring a bell for a living. And you're giving me shit? I could maim you with nothing but that vibrator."

Adam opened his mouth, most likely to say something equally as mature and constructive, when Jonah, peacemaker at his core, nudged him silent. "Giving a guy a hard time at his place of work? Grow up."

Jonah turned to Dax. He didn't laugh, didn't make a further mockery of the moment, which he totally could have, and instead put a hand on Dax's shoulder in a clear sign of support. "We just came by to check on you, see how your knee was holding up, and to ask if you were holding out on your answer about teaching the weapons class until I sweeten the deal. Because if so, I can see if the department will throw in one of those pink stocks for your rifle that all of the ladies down at the range are talking about. Maybe one that flashes lights."

"Move along, old man," Dax said, shoving his brother. "There is a strict no-asshole policy in effect tonight."

"Seriously, have you thought about the job?" Jonah asked. "Because if it's a go, then I need to process the paperwork by Wednesday."

Dax had thought about the job. A lot. The logical part of him knew that getting out with a team of guys, experiencing the kind of camaraderie that came when hanging with people who were cut from his cloth, would be good for him. Maybe even stop some of that itching in his gut.

The other part that was still somewhere over in the Middle East was telling him it was too soon. That walking into that kind of brotherhood again would be a betrayal, because he'd been a part of the best kind of team, vowed with his life to make it to the end with them, and he'd let them down.

"What job?" A honeyed voice slid over Dax's skin and settled right behind his button fly.

Trouble stood in the doorway, holding a tray of food and a cold beer, her auburn hair shimmering with fire from the twinkling lights of the awning above, well within touching distance.

"Just a temp position with the department," Dax said.

"One you should consider," Jonah added.

Adam was too busy staring at Emerson and her tray to say anything. He sniffed the air, then pulled out that easygoing smile that had gotten him laid a million times before. "Nice shoes. What's that you got under the dish cover?"

He reached for it and Emerson pulled it away. "Hands off, this is for hired muscle only, sorry," she said, not a hint of remorse in her voice. "And the shoes, they double as a weapon."

Jonah and Dax burst out laughing. Adam only grinned.

She shrugged, then smiled up at Dax. It was a little shy, a little naughty, and cute as hell. "Ida wanted to say she caught three 'illegals' who all got in using a shared fake ID and to up your game."

"Anything else?" he asked, wanting her to say why she was out here, checking on him.

"Uh-huh." Amusement lit her eyes. "She also said to tell you that Uncle Sam is slipping if one of his finest can't sniff out a soccer mom from a grandmom. Oh, and also if you could show a little more skin, she'd appreciate it."

"Was that last part Ida's request?"

She nodded at the window behind him—which had little granny faces peeking out. "Your fan club did. And they asked me to bring you a drink."

The peanut gallery gave a heartfelt sigh. Dax ignored them.

"And the food?"

Emerson opened her mouth, then looked at his brothers and smiled. Which sucked because he saw the spark in her eye indicating she was about to make some smart-ass comment, which had become their way of flirting, but she held back because of Barney Fife and Smokey the Bear. "*Ida* thought you might be hungry."

"Tell *Ida* thanks," he said, even though they both knew it was total BS. Ida might have mentioned for her to check on Dax, but feeding him was all Emerson. She couldn't help herself.

Before Dax could take the tray, Smokey slid up beside Emerson and slung his arm over her shoulder and visually perused the merchandise. "Beer and, hey, are those the famous tapas everyone's been raving about?"

"No" was all Dax said, because the grin Adam was dishing up was playful and smug—and 100 percent stupid male at its finest. And Emerson had been dealing with stupid men all night, looking their fill, making wisecracks, all while the woman was hustling to do her job. She shouldn't have to deal with SHFD's number one player. "You can't tap that or look at her tapas no matter how many times you tell yourself it sounds like *topless*. And stop breathing on my beer."

He gave Adam a gentle shove, but just like he didn't need to call Emerson on her BS, no one needed to call him on his. He wasn't getting possessive over Adam sampling his tapas, he was ticked that Adam was sweet-talking his private chef.

"He never was good at sharing," Adam said with a wink. "Cried when I borrowed his G.I. Joe doll."

"G.I. Joe is an *action figure*," Dax said slowly, "and I was five. *And* you lit him on fire with Grandpa's blowtorch."

"How else would I practice putting out a fire?" Adam said with so much *duh* in his tone Dax wanted to punch him. Then he turned to Emerson and cranked up the charm. "So rather than make him whine in front of a pretty girl, I'll place my own order for a tray."

"Too bad you don't make the age cutoff," Dax said, then held up a stamp of an anchor. "No stamp, no entry. Those are the rules." He slid Emerson a secret look. "And the lady does like her rules."

Emerson flushed, not enough that his brothers would notice, but he saw it. A faint pink tint crept up the tips of her ears. She opened her mouth to say something, something he knew by the playful spark in her eye was going to make him smile, when her phone pinged.

She set his tray on the little table he'd been using to hold the swag bags, fished her phone out of her bra, and looked at the screen. Her humor vanished—and so did the lightness she'd been carrying.

"Everything okay?" Dax asked, taking a step closer, because if he had learned anything about Emerson over the past few weeks, it was that nothing much rattled her. She took life head-on and never wavered. But she was wavering now.

"Yeah. It's just my dad," she said, and normally he would have let it go. Her smile was still there, fastened in place, right where it should be for everyone to see. But if he wasn't mistaken, it was manufactured. Just like the tough-girl posture she wore. She was upset, and something about that drew out his need to comfort her.

"Is he all right?" he asked quietly, wondering if it was Pixie.

"Sorry, I have to take this," she said, ignoring his question. "Enjoy your dinner."

The three of them watched her go back into the bar, and the way she squared her shoulders brought out this crazy instinct to follow her inside.

"Shay said you hired Emerson to do some cooking for you," Jonah said, and Dax tore his attention off Emerson and put it on his brother, whose expression was one big wagging finger. "So what the hell was that?"

"I don't know, something to do with her family," Dax said and both brothers looked at him weird. "What?"

"He meant that." Adam pointed at the tray of food, then to the doorway where Emerson had disappeared. "And that."

"Uh, my chef. Bringing me dinner."

Adam made a coughing sound that sounded a lot like *bullshit*. "As the resident fire expert of the group, I'd like to point out that what just went down was not your standard cooking heat. That was more of a slow smoldering. Harder to fight and highly susceptible to combustion."

It was also dangerous, Dax thought as he looked down at the tray. Not only had she brought him his favorite kind of beer, there wasn't a speck of green on anything.

This was confirmed by the little note that read, *No green. I promise.*

Which meant that the meal, as well as that dress, had been specially ordered. Prepared well in advance. And served specifically with him in mind.

The only way her intentions could have been made clearer was if she had scribbled her number on his forehead.

Groaning, Emerson slipped off her heels as the last pair of swing dancers cleared the floor and the bar finally quieted down. She had banked on running out of food by ten, leaving her plenty of time to find Dax before Ida let him go home, to see if he wanted to cash in that rain check. Only Harper had made enough spinach and dill-infused feta phyllo bites to keep the party going until midnight. And now Dax was gone—Ida had let him go about an hour ago—and her plan, which had taken her all day to gather enough courage to see through, was a total bust.

No need for the pinup pumps.

The story of her life. She'd been seduced by the possibility of a night of freedom, a night to let go and lose herself, and maybe, just maybe, find something fun, exciting, invigorating—a real shot at being a part of something amazing. A heady thought, one she wanted to grab on to, but life had stepped in and given her a fat smack to the forehead.

Which sucked. Big-time. She really wanted tonight to work, wanted Dax to work, because she desperately needed to have something that was just hers—even if it was temporary. Especially after that call with her dad.

Determined not to mope, because that got her exactly nowhere, she grabbed her purse and walked out of the bar. She made her way down the alley and around the back of the building, heading toward her apartment. Only when she reached the stairwell off the back of the Boulder Holder, she noticed someone waiting.

Dax sat three-quarters up the flight of stairs in a pair of black jeans and a matching leather jacket that was all biker and bad boy wrapped in alpha swagger. His elbows rested on his bent knees, a paper bag dangled from his fingertips, and two paper coffee cups sat one step behind him. He looked dark, dangerous, and so delicious her body hummed to life.

"What are you doing here?" she asked, a little breathless at the sight of him. Or maybe that was the overdose of testosterone confusing her senses.

"Waiting for you."

He stood and walked toward her, his riding boots echoing off the walkway, not letting up until he was standing close enough to touch. Close enough to smell—she sniffed again. "Is that bread pudding?" He opened the bag and held it under her nose. She breathed in the sweet almondy scent and groaned. "Not just any bread pudding. It's from the Sweet and Savory."

Only the best pastry and dessert stop in Napa Valley. And the bread pudding, made from homemade chocolate croissant bread with a heavenly amaretto sauce, was Emerson's personal favorite.

"I wanted to take you to dinner, maybe grab something after you got off, but I forgot everything in this town closes when the sun goes down. So I figured maybe some dessert."

Emerson's knees wobbled as she remembered his words from the other night. This was her chance to do something reckless, something that would lead to a night of being bad.

With the town's bad boy.

"Do you want to come up?" she asked. "To my apartment?"

Dax's eyes ran the length of her dress, paying careful attention to her neckline, hips, and bare feet. By the time he made it back to her eyes all of the air seemed to disappear.

"Yes," he said with conviction, his voice rough. "But I was given strict instructions from the chef that this dessert isn't made to go. So I had to promise not to eat it at the counter or on the couch while watching television. It's a dining experience that is deserving of the perfect setting."

Emerson knew the perfect setting.

Her bed.

"Last time some guy bribed me with an experience that required a location change, I found myself in Derek Mather's coat closet playing Seven Minutes in Heaven."

Dax let out a low whistle. "Heaven is a pretty big promise when the dude only gave himself seven minutes."

"Thirty seconds in, I figured out he thought the gateway was in his pants and I decked him."

Dax laughed. It was a good laugh that was real and transformed his entire face. The stress lines bracketing his mouth softened and that shell-shocked expression disappeared. And a hum vibrated through her entire body.

"I hope your offer is better," she said. She hoped his offer was for seven hours of heaven—or as many hours as they could fit in before dawn.

"How about we start with dessert?" When she lifted a questioning brow, he shook the bag. "A real dessert. With a view to die for."

"You know Lexi's bread pudding has raisins," she pointed out and Dax looked at her like he could handle a few raisins—or at least pick them out. "Raisins made from green grapes."

"I'm open to trying new things," he said but she could tell green food wouldn't have been his first choice. Fair, since it wouldn't have been hers either. But he seemed to have a plan, which was great since her plan hadn't extended past the dress and shoes. "And I know a little spot that would pair perfectly with bread pudding and new adventures."

That was all Emerson needed to hear.

She took in his jacket, which made her mouth water because it took him from dangerous to lethal. "Are you cleared to ride your bike?"

"Nope," he said, sounding a little unsure.

"So you're taking me to dessert, after sixteen hours on my feet, and *I* get to drive?" She snatched the bag. "Man, you know how to charm a girl."

Truth was, he did. After an entire night of his eyes on her, hers on him, thinking over his promise, her body had gone into hyperdrive. But finding him on her stoop, holding her favorite dessert, had taken this to a totally different level—one she wasn't quite sure how to interpret. A clear sign that she was out of her element.

"No ride. And I can't promise heaven because there are green raisins involved. But I can promise you a little slice of it." He closed the distance between them, his big body taking up all of her personal space, then took off his jacket and slipped it over her shoulders—his warmth surrounding her. "Come have a seat and I promise it will be exactly what you need after tonight."

"Big words," Emerson said, snuggling deeper into the leather. It was buttery soft, smelled like new car and wild nights. But felt like an invitation. Not an invitation to forever, but something sincere and honest.

Beneath all that flirting and swagger, Dax was struggling with demons of his own, a history of loss and guilt that kept him from what he desperately needed. Genuine connection.

"I'm a big guy."

No kidding, she thought as he dropped his hands to her hips, spanning them around her back and making her feel petite and incredibly feminine. Then he flashed her one hell of a smile that let her know he came through on his promises.

No. Matter. What.

ch💍pter
ten

"Y ou were right," Emerson said, polishing off the bread pudding and leaning back to rest her elbows on the steps behind them. "That was exactly what I needed."

Although Dax loved to hear her admit that he was right, because he knew just how hard that must have been for her, he had to admit, silently to himself, of course, that he hadn't come here with the purest of intentions.

Okay, he'd totally come here to take her dress and shoes up on that offer they'd been sending him all night. Only he'd seen her walking home in the freezing cold, her shoes in her hand, a lifetime of worry in her eyes, and he'd changed his plan. Gone from thinking with his dick to thinking like a friend.

Then she sat on the step, with only a few inches separating them, and her dress shifted up her thighs, showing him enough silky skin that "friend" became the last thing he was feeling.

"It's crazy. I didn't realize you could see so far from here," Emerson said, taking a sip of her hot cocoa and staring out past downtown at the faint glow in the distance. "Is that Oakville?"

"Yup," Dax said, leaning back too. "If you go up a step the trees block your view, and if you go down a step the buildings on Main Street do." He knew this because, embarrassingly enough, he'd tested out each step for the perfect inspiring view, hoping it would lead to an inspiring view of her bedroom.

Instead of a hot game of Let's Tangle the Sheets, though, Dax was sitting on a cold concrete step eating bread pudding with raisins, which weren't as bad as he'd thought—they were worse—and he was enjoying himself.

How crazy was that?

She smiled up at him, and man, she was gorgeous. Calm, relaxed, in the moment, and so unbelievably gorgeous it was hard not to stare. "I can't believe I have never noticed that."

"If you stop moving long enough, you start to see things you never noticed were there before," he said, knowing how true that statement was. Until tonight he'd never noticed just how hard Emerson worked to keep her world moving. And just how tiring it must be to have all those people counting on her.

She laughed. "If I slow down, everything crumbles."

"In my job, it's imperative to slow down, see all the options. That's when everything comes into perfect view. Things that seemed impossible are suddenly crystal clear, and avenues you thought were a waste of time end up being golden opportunities."

"Like what?" she asked, nudging his shoulder with hers. "Like handing out vibrators to a bunch of grandmas?"

He nudged back until she was smiling. "You could have warned me."

"And take away that golden opportunity? Nah."

"Make fun if you want, but look." He leaned forward and pointed between the buildings. When she bent down to see what he was pointing at, he put his arm around her shoulder to help guide her. And yeah, it was a total kid move, a way to get his hands on her, but she didn't seem to mind, so he went with it. "Right there through the alley you can see town hall, and where you park your cart on Mondays. But if you move up . . . see that flashing light there."

She straightened to look where he was pointing over the rooftops, nibbling that lower lip of hers and squinting. "That cluster of stars?"

"No."

He drew her closer, until his lips were next to her ear and her hair was brushing his jaw. "There," he whispered. "The blinking lights past Oakville. That's the airport in Napa, and a plane getting ready to land."

"Really?" she whispered. "I would have just passed it off as a star or something. What else do you see?"

She turned her head and aimed those long lashes his way and *bam*—he saw more than he'd anticipated. Her normal sharp edges were frayed, her mascara was slightly smudged, her eyes bruised, and she looked adorable. Soft, messy, and completely vulnerable.

No, he thought, looking deeper. She looked lost, as if she was asking *him* for clarity. The most independent woman in the history of the world. And didn't that make his heart show its soft underside.

"Want to tell me what that call was about?" he asked.

"Not really," she said, but he held firm, didn't give her a way out, which had her eyes sparking. "You want to tell me what Jonah was talking about earlier?"

That would be a big, fat negative. Talking about the job would require talking about why he couldn't take the job. And that was not a conversation he wanted to get into with someone who couldn't understand.

But she was looking at him, smug now, as if to say touché, and those walls of hers were going back up.

"Fine," he relented because he knew he wasn't the only one out of his comfort zone. They were both extremely private and ridiculously stubborn, so if someone didn't back down, this conversation would end before it got started. And for whatever reason, he wanted to talk. To her. See what could have rattled her so badly tonight. "I'll answer your question, then it's your turn."

"Is that the adult version of Show Me Yours and I'll Show You Mine?"

"Let me guess, Derek Mather tried that game too?" he asked and she laughed. It was a great sound, a movement that lit her whole face. Dax considered it a small victory since she'd seemed so down when he'd seen her walking toward the stairwell.

"No, lucky for him," she said. "But you're supposed to be telling me about the job. So get to it."

Damn, she was a bossy thing.

"Jonah offered me a job working for Napa County," he said, proving he knew how to share. "Running the weapons and combat training for the sheriff's department."

"I thought you had a job in San Jose."

"I do. This would be temporary, just to help out Jonah until he can hire the real deal."

She lifted a brow and Dax knew what she was thinking. Jonah had asked him for a favor and he was going to say no? Say no to the guy who had stepped in and picked up the pieces when their dad died?

"I don't think Jonah would have asked you if he didn't think you were the real deal," she said quietly. "That isn't his style."

No it wasn't. And walking away from a job before it was done wasn't Dax's. "I've never really trained recruits," he admitted and then, because he couldn't seem to shut up, he added, "I don't know, it might be fun. I mean, I was a squad leader. But teaching classes? Not really my strength. I don't want to leave Jonah hanging, though."

"Ah," she said as if it made so much sense now, and he wanted to ask her to explain it to him, because he was still confused. But she shrugged and in her most diplomatic tone said, "Well, it sounds like

Jonah thinks differently, and it would give you the opportunity to get your feet wet with a team before you take the other job."

That was exactly what Jonah had said, which made him feel worse for keeping his brother on the line. Maybe he needed to man up and move on.

"Problem is," she said softly, leaning in closer, "you don't seem like a dip-your-feet-in kind of guy to me. Which means you either go in half-assed or you walk away leaving a team hanging."

"It's not like I'm leaving them," he defended. "They don't even have me yet."

"You asked my opinion." She rested her hand on his knee. "I gave it to you. Don't act like I burnt your G.I. Joe doll."

"Jesus Christ! He's an action figure! And okay, fine, if I took the job, I would serve as a temporary solution to a long-term problem, and if Jonah couldn't fill the spot before I left, then, you're right, the department would be short a leader again. Or I'd have to see if I can postpone my position in San Jose." He already knew the answer to that. "And stick it out here until they find someone."

"You, Dax Baudouin"—she poked his thigh—"have a God complex."

He went to argue but there was no censure to her statement, just a sense of deep understanding, Empathy that shook him to the core.

"I've been called worse," he said quietly, then placed his hand on top of hers, offering a gentle squeeze. "Tell me about your dad."

She sighed. "This is harder than Show Me Yours and I'll Show You Mine," she said, moving to take her hand back, but he tightened his hold, trapping it there. "My dad went on an interview today. It was the exact kind of position he was looking for. A boutique vineyard, small and family run. They offered him the exact position he had before my mom got sick. It was the perfect setup."

"And?"

"It doesn't matter, he didn't get the job."

"It matters to me," he said, lacing their fingers. "And it obviously matters to you. So tell me, why didn't he get the job?"

"Because he gave them a list of every Lady Bug event, every school holiday, every special occasion, including National Fairy Day, that he'd need time off for. At the interview." She huffed, full of fury and frustration. "Who does that?" She held up a silencing hand. "My dad, that's who. He is the only guy in this recession who will walk away from a dozen amazing job offers and claim National Fairy Day as a legit reason."

"Maybe he's just not ready," Dax said. "Maybe for him, going back to work, doing the same kinds of things he used to do when your mom was around, means accepting that she's gone."

"But she is gone," Emerson said and he could hear the emotion in her throat. "She has been gone for almost two years. And standing still, wishing it wasn't so, doesn't change reality. It just makes life that much harder."

It made everything harder for Emerson. That was for sure. Dax could see the weight she carried for her family, understood her need to keep moving forward for fear that if she slowed down, even for a moment, she'd slip back to that place.

"Not everyone grieves the same," he explained gently. "For some people, picking up the pieces and moving on only serves as a harsh reminder of what's missing. And with every step forward, you become more aware of what you lost, like trying to fit into a life that no longer fits you."

"You think my dad is blowing these interviews because he doesn't want to get back to what he loved for thirty-five years?"

"He loved your mom too, and from what it seems like, she was his life. Maybe it would be easier for him to start over fresh. A new direction that allows him to remember your mom and what they had, but something that gives him the chance to reinvent the next part of his life. Kind of like what you're trying to do with the food truck."

"My food truck is a step forward," she pointed out, the challenge in her voice strong.

"Your dad is making progress too. He's figuring out what he doesn't want."

Dax watched as she let that settle. Then with a small nod she asked, "Is that what you're doing? Why you're going to San Jose instead of staying here or going back in the army? Because you didn't bring home all your teammates?"

Dax felt the unfamiliar jolt of unease at her question. Since he'd come home, no one had openly asked him about the men he'd lost—good men, friends who'd deserved to come home but wouldn't because life wasn't fair.

"I don't know what I'm doing," he admitted. "I came home, some of the best guys I know didn't, and I'm not sure what that even means. Or what it even feels like yet." And then because he'd already started spilling his guts like a little girl, he added, "All I know is that being here, surrounded by my family and childhood, reminds me of how different my world is and how everyone else's seems the same."

She didn't laugh or point out that everyone had problems, and that everyone suffered from loss. She moved her fingers around his knee, as though sensing his pain and needing to soothe him somehow. "So you're looking for a place that doesn't know you?"

"I don't know what I'm looking for. But I know it's not here, in a department filled with guys I knew when I was a punk with a motorcycle and tattoos." A squad where he would be responsible for his brother and his friends. People who were his world.

"You're still a punk with tattoos. Bummer about your bike, though," she said, her fingers dancing up and down his leg, getting higher and higher and so incredibly high he sucked in a breath.

"If I was still that same punk, I wouldn't tell you that's my right knee."

She kept rubbing—a little deeper and, *holy hell*, higher. "I know."

"As in my injury is on my left knee." And she was two inches from a touchdown.

"Oh, I know," she said and Dax felt his eyes roll to the back of his head. "Just like I know that any department you decide to go to will be lucky. Just make sure that you aren't so busy focusing on this new life of yours that you lose sight of the life you need."

"And who's going to look out for what you need, Emi?" Dax asked because he was tired of talking about things that made his head hurt and his chest ache. He wanted to feel more of that pleasure she was dishing out. And he could tell by the direction she was headed, she was all talked out too.

"I don't know, Ranger." Her hand stopped a scant inch from his flagpole, then she scooted that tight body of hers closer, so he could smell the amaretto from the bread pudding and turned-on female. Which was fine with him, because the motion caused her dress to ride up even higher, showing off a good three inches of leg and a little red garter belt attached to the sexiest pair of fishnets he'd ever seen. "Are you applying for the job?"

Normally he'd be a *hell yeah* kind of guy. He'd apply with the garter on or off or, hell, he'd wear it if it made her smile. In fact, he was applying for whatever position would bring them both back to that night in San Francisco and the way she'd moaned his name. The only thing he wasn't applying for was forever, because he wasn't the kind to offer that to anyone. He knew that life was tenuous at best, so unpredictable and ever-changing that he couldn't promise something he didn't believe in.

Nothing about Emerson was predictable—or easy. Normally she was cloaked in Converse, a leather skirt, and that hands-off attitude. Occasionally she dressed up like a giant cork. But tonight she'd shown up at the bar looking soft and sweet in a dress that a wife would have worn to greet her man at base. A part of him wondered what it would be like to have a woman like her waiting for him, but the other part knew better—he wasn't that guy. Would never be that guy.

"I'm not a long-term bet, Emi."

"I have enough long-term in my life, Dax. Tonight I'm just looking for some fun." There was a playfulness to her voice that went straight through him.

"Then it looks like I'm your guy," he said, sliding his hand around the nape of her neck and pulling her in. "Because babe, I am going to have you smiling so hard you'll feel it straight through next week."

"Big words again," she said against his lips, then her hand slid that extra millimeter higher and she smiled. "Oh. Right. You brought backup."

Her hands had him groaning in pleasure, but her making the first move was so incredibly hot, he reined in his focus so he could turn up the heat and make a move of his own. And this wasn't a move from his standard playbook, because when it came to Emi the rules didn't apply.

So he lowered his head and took her mouth without warning.

And that kiss packed more heat than a nuclear missile. It wasn't the usual hot-and-heavy kiss or even the I-missed-this kiss that one might expect between two people who had a steamy but brief history. Nope, it was a tongue-down-her-throat, hands-on-her-ass, real lightning-worthy and let's-get-it-on kind of kiss that a man gave a woman when he wanted to be clear about just how hard he was going to rock her world.

Only she moaned into his mouth, a sweet mewling sound that was as sexy as it was unexpected, and Dax admitted right then, with his ass frozen to the concrete step and Emerson's hands giving him the massage of his life, that he might just be the one to have his world rocked.

This, Emerson decided, was the best interview she'd had in years. Maybe ever.

Dax kissed like a man who knew what he wanted and wouldn't hesitate in the follow-through. It was a wicked promise and an erotic threat all wrapped up into one hot ball of yummy man. And he was right, this was just what she needed.

A night of adult fun that didn't have to grow into strings.

He nipped at her lower lip, taking this show straight past slow and into confident demand. His fingers, they were confident too—teasing the edge of her dress, tracing back and forth over the edge of her thigh-highs to fiddle with the clip on the garter belt. Then his thumb did a little one-two action and the clip unfastened and a fishnet was released.

"Inside," he mumbled against her mouth. "We need to take this inside."

She didn't want to go inside. Not yet. She was just getting used to the erotic feel of his hot lips on her chilled skin. "Later."

His hands came around her wrist and stilled her fingers—right as she was about to get the last button of his jeans undone. "There won't be much of a later if you keep that up." She wrapped her free hand around his neck and bit his ear. "Okay," he said. "We go inside and you get to pick the first location."

She thought that over and smiled. "We go inside and I get to pick the first location and the first position."

"God, you drive me crazy." He kissed her hard and fast, letting her know it was the right kind of crazy. Or at least she hoped. Then he took her by the hand and led her to the apartment door.

Emerson rummaged through her backpack for her keys, which she found under the still-unmailed Street Eats envelope, then slid them in the door. She had tempting and tattooed trouble incarnate standing behind her, and everything she'd been working toward right in front of her. Could she really afford this distraction right now?

"Second thoughts, Emi?" he teased, tracing her spine—with his lips. "Because if we go in there, you won't be sneaking out in the middle of the night. This is going to last from now until we both can't move."

Emerson's bones liquefied. She turned around and found herself pinned between the door and Dax, who at the moment was a tower of temptation in yesterday's scruff, a battered ball cap, and button-fly jeans—with the top buttons already undone.

"One night," she clarified. "And then everything goes back to normal."

He leaned a hand on the frame of the door, boxing her in. "If you say so."

"I need to hear you say it." She held her ground, because there was so much riding on the next few weeks and maintaining this job with him. "Nothing gets weird between us?"

"What do you think I'll do?" he asked. "Sleep with you now and fire you Monday?"

"It's been known to happen."

He studied her for a long moment, then his eyes softened, along with his voice. "Nothing gets weird, Emi. I promise. And I might not be the kind of guy you'd bring home to Dad, but I never go back on my word."

"Then no second thoughts." And no ditching out before she had her fun. "I was just wondering if I should pick the wall next to the fireplace or the shower, then I remembered my body soap is green, so maybe wall?"

"Smart-ass," he said, his hands skimming down her dress as he walked her back a few inches and the door gave way. Suddenly they were inside, the door kicked shut, and even though it was completely dark, she could feel the fire of Dax's gaze, his warm breath as he ate up the remaining distance.

"You like it when I'm a smart-ass," she challenged.

"I like it better when you're a naked smart-ass," he said, slipping his jacket off her shoulders and continuing to guide her backward, past the couch, the table, and into the kitchen.

"Admit it, you're just a fan of my ass."

"I need to do a thorough investigation before I can make that endorsement." His hands slid up her thighs, slowly over her tush, giving it a little squeeze, then all the way up her back. Her body tingled with every inch his fingers rose. When he got to her shoulders, he lowered his hands back down, only she heard the whisper of her zipper going with them. Felt his world-roughened fingertips following the long descent of the dress.

Then her dress pooled to the floor and his hands palmed her ass, molding and shaping it, even tracing the seam of her silk panties from the back, then—*oh, sweet baby Jesus*—the front.

"Still not sure?" she asked, a millimeter away from a complete meltdown.

"Oh, I'm sure," he said, taking a cheek in each hand and scooping her up and setting her on the really cold wood surface of the kitchen table. She squeaked and then he flicked on the light. "I just needed a moment to really compare."

His gaze raked over her, taking her all in as she sat on the table, splayed out for his viewing pleasure. He paused on her garter belt, then flashed her a grin that was all trouble, causing her pulse to skyrocket and her mouth to go dry. Everything else went wet, because that was all it took. A single flash of his teeth and that slow burn deep in her belly was lit.

"The shower's that way." She pointed down the hall, wondering how this had already spiraled out of her control.

"I can't appreciate you fully in the shower." She reached over to flip the light switch and he caught her hand. "Or with the lights off."

She imagined he used that commanding tone when he was giving out orders. It sure made her want to take direction. "You can't appreciate anything because I'm sitting."

He laughed low and gravelly, sounding very male and very amused. "I wouldn't be so sure about that, Emi." To prove it, he rested his palms on either side of her and leaned forward. Her lips parted in anticipation, desperate for his touch. But at the last minute he dipped his head to run his tongue over the lace trim of her bra, then sucked her aching bud into his mouth.

"Dax," she moaned, her head falling back to give him better access. Access that he took full advantage of, teasing and nipping until she forgot what they were arguing about.

A fact she was certain he knew, because she felt him smile against her skin, and he kissed his way down her belly, making it quiver the farther south he journeyed. "A man can't enjoy dessert in the shower," he said and she felt his words vibrate against her skin. "He wants to feast slowly, take his time to savor and enjoy."

His statement was as alpha as they came. Confident and assured, with enough cockiness that she had no doubt he would deliver on his promise. And then some. Plus, his teeth were nipping at the lace along the upper edge of her garter belt, causing that slow burn to turn into a wildfire.

Then, without warning, he planted one final kiss, so close to home she wanted to weep with relief, until he pulled away.

Emerson's eyes flew open, and it took her a moment to gain her wits and realize that he was sitting on a kitchen chair, making himself comfortable.

"What are you doing?"

"What I've wanted to do since I woke up in San Francisco and found you gone." He gently took her ankle and placed it on his thigh. Then the other, giving them both a little squeeze, telling her to leave them there. As if she could possibly move.

Her mind went fuzzy when, with a masterful flick of the fingers, he let the clip open on her fishnets, hooked his thumbs in them, and slowly slid them over her knees, down her calves, and finally off. "Actually I've wanted to do that since I saw you walk out in this dress tonight. But this," he said, eyeing her barely there silk panties. "This I have been dreaming about for months."

Emerson watched breathlessly as he lowered his head to brush his mouth along the inside of her thigh, sliding ever so slowly up to the lower edge of her panties, where he gave a sexy tug with his teeth, then a more deliberate one with his fingers. As he pulled the silk down, his lips followed, kissing every inch of skin he exposed.

Dropping her panties to the floor, he looked up at her through his lashes. "Ready, Emi?"

He didn't wait for her to answer, instead sliding his hands beneath her bottom and dragging her forward until she was teetering on the edge of the table. Then, without breaking eye contact, Dax slid his soft tongue all the way up her center.

And his mouth? His mouth was everything he'd promised: diligent, skilled, deadly accurate—and equipped with teeth that had her worked up in a complete frenzy in an embarrassingly short amount of time.

Dax was also the ultimate tease, keeping the pace slow and purposeful, taking her higher and higher without letting her crash. But there was something reverent about the way he held her hip, the way his thumb slid back and forth over her stomach, offering her comfort and connection.

His big, calloused fingers slid up her leg, then one slipped between, while he thoroughly took her apart, stroke by stroke, slowly driving her out of her mind until her heart was pounding against her rib cage and her need was so intense it ached. The harder she reached, the further away she seemed to be. Then she heard herself begging.

"Dax, please."

"Please what, Emi?"

"Please," she breathed. "Now."

She could have sworn he said, "Now what?" Or maybe that was him chuckling, but the big jerk didn't please her anything. He just kept feasting and teasing as if he had no intention of ever letting her come.

"Now," she said, tightening her legs. "No more foreplay. I need you in me now."

"You can boss me around all you want, Emi," he said against her burning flesh, and yup, he was chuckling—and slowing down. "But in my world, it's ladies first. Always."

And true to his word, he slid in a second finger, his sniper skills coming in handy, allowing him to hit the target.

"Do that again," she said, realizing she was bossy.

"That?" Another bull's-eye and her body tightened.

"Oh yeah, just like that." Because bossy be damned, she was so close to an orgasm. When he did it again, her core coiled to ride that fine line between pain and pleasure. He gave a final pass, and her body arched up against his mouth and she exploded around him, her hips jerking with sweet release.

She had no clue how long she lay there, but when the aftershocks faded she fluttered her eyes open to find herself flat on her back and Dax standing over her, a forearm on either side of her head. His tattoos were taut and flexed as he held himself above her, and he was wearing a slow, sexy smile.

And nothing else.

Dax was naked. Completely and gloriously naked.

"Are we going to the shower now?" she asked when she was able to breathe.

"Oh, no. That's dessert. We still have the main course." He pinned her to the table with his deliciously hard body, running his hands down her sides, molding them to her butt.

He smelled good, felt even better, and when he leaned down and whispered, "Wrap your legs around me, Emi," she did as she was told, because even though he could be bossy too, she wasn't rude enough to point it out.

He gave her a devastating kiss, thorough and slow, building the heat, and she decided she liked him bossy. Because he rose in one fluid motion with her in his arms, and when they settled he was sitting on the chair and she was straddling his lap. She slid forward, rolling her hips so his hard ridge pressed against her sensitive flesh.

"A man has to sit to feast?" she guessed, then remembered his injury. "Or is it your knee?"

He laughed. "It's not my knee that's the problem, trust me." At her confused expression, he took her face in his hands and whispered, "Baby, I have to sit because with you I have a hard time finding my footing."

The honesty in his statement shook her. So did the undertone of affection she heard in his voice. Lust, fun, passion. Those emotions she could handle. They were basic and singular in nature. That's what she'd signed up for. Not this weird fluttering that was happening in her chest.

She opened her mouth to say something light, something flippant to get them back on the same page—the page that ended come morning—but he was kissing her again, long, intoxicating kisses that scattered every last thought from her mind. And reminded her of why she'd chosen him.

Dax was a temporary kind of guy. Perfect, since she was temporary's newest best friend. So when he leaned to reach for the condom he'd set on the table, she took it from his hands and, acting like a girl who did this all the time, ripped the foil.

"The rule at my house is—"

"There's a rule?"

"Oh, you'll like this one. I promise." She moved enough to slide the condom over him, giving a little stroke and squeeze in the process. Then she laced her arms around his neck and tightened her legs until she was pressed up against him. "No one leaves the table until everyone is finished."

"Best rule I've ever heard," he said, running his hands up each rib to caress the underside of her breasts. With a little tug the lace came down, propping them up on display. "Almost as good as this look on you."

His arms went around her, tight and unyielding, pulling her to him as he kissed her. Hard and all-consuming, he devoured her mouth. His hands roamed her body, his tongue traced the seam of her lip, her neck, even her breast as his grip tightened around her waist and lifted her to his mouth.

He had her on the brink and shuddering in less than two seconds. She was so caught up in the feel of his stubble rasping against her flesh that she gasped when he entered her in one slick, long thrust.

Dax groaned and held still as if savoring the moment. Emerson was savoring it too. Savoring how full she felt, how free.

Then she opened her eyes and saw him watching her, and she knew what else she felt. Connected. He must have felt it too because he didn't move for a long moment.

Eyes on her, he guided her up, then back down, setting the pace. Taking them to exactly where they both wanted to be, and her further and further away from the soul-deep exhaustion that had become her life, until her grief and responsibilities melted away and all she could do was feel.

Feel Dax and their insane sexual connection.

Wanting more, she slid her arms around his neck and they moved together, skin to skin; the friction of their bodies was what she was seeking. Even then she needed more—more connection, more contact, more Dax.

She buried her face in his neck and breathed him in.

As if he could read her body, he deepened the thrusts, one hand sliding up to cradle her head to him, the other slipping under to stroke her swollen flesh. And she was gone.

The orgasm took her over and she clenched around him, screaming out his name, blissfully floating toward heaven. With one last thrust, Dax let out a rough groan and came with her.

His cheek rested on her head and they both sat there for a moment, breathing hard and holding on tight, as though if they let go it would all be over. Things would go back to the way they were before they'd entered her house.

Except that was what they'd agreed on.

Dax's hands slowly ran up and down her spine, making her want to snuggle in closer. But that might be mistaken for being in this for the long haul, so she gave him a nudge and pushed back. "I still have my bra on."

"Not for long." He reached out and, poof, her bra fell to the floor. He looked at his handiwork and smiled. "Wouldn't want it to get ruined in the shower."

ch💗pter
eleven

Monday morning, Dax slept through his alarm clock for the first time since basic training. He woke feeling relaxed, rested, and nightmare-free. Great sex seemed to be the cure his doctors had been looking for. He'd see if Kyle could write him up a prescription. Maybe it would change Emerson's whole one-night stance. He hoped so, because it had been twenty-four hours since Emerson pointed out the sun was up and their night over, then kicked him out—and he could still taste her on his lips.

Pulling on his running shoes and a pair of sweats, he headed toward the Silverado Trail, where he was meeting Adam for a "therapeutic" jog. Last night a cold front had moved through and the early morning frost had yet to burn off, but the thick scent of harvested grapes hung in the air.

Adam was at their meeting spot in some matching name-brand ensemble, stretching like a playboy, when Dax sprinted up.

"I thought the point to this morning was to ease into things," Adam said, shifting back and forth on his feet. "So that you don't blow all the hard work the surgeon did in San Diego."

"Are we talking easing in army terms or fire department? Because I'm not doing any of that prissy shit." Dax waved a hand in Adam's direction.

"You mean like handing out dildos with built-in laser pointers?"

Point taken. "I'm just saying you run with empty hoses, we run with telephone poles. Just want to make sure you can keep up."

"I would have thought you'd be nicer after Saturday. You were actually making headway with the cute cart girl." Adam turned his ball cap backward and studied him. "Unless you didn't get any."

Dax ignored this and took off in a hard jog, because that wasn't the problem. He'd gotten plenty. It was a steaming, mouthwatering, three-course affair. Only just like the first time, come daybreak it wasn't enough.

Adam easily caught up, which meant Dax was in worse shape than he'd thought. They jogged in silence, following the same route they'd done when they were kids and he was training for the day he could enlist. Only the farther they went, the more he thought about the other night.

"You're pouting," Adam said, then stopped and laughed, resting his hands on his knees. And just when Dax thought he was laughing at him, Adam laughed some more. "No way, you *like* Cute Cart Girl."

He did. He liked the crazy cart cutie. She was funny, quirky, sexy, and tough. Her entire world had been buried with her mother, yet she kept pushing forward, even carrying the added weight of her family without complaint. Never once allowing the extra baggage or unfairness of it all to take her under.

Then the other night, she'd dropped the tough-girl act and showed him her soft edges, and man, soft looked good on her. Almost as good as Emerson looked on him.

"I'm not pouting," Dax said.

He was strategizing.

Dax was doing his daily PT in the gym off the kitchen when he heard a knock at the door. It was prickly and impatient, which meant Emerson was early. He glanced out the window but didn't see her car.

The knock sounded again, followed by a text on his phone. He grabbed his phone, read the screen, and laughed.

I know you're home.

He texted back.

Are you stalking me?

His phone buzzed immediately.

That would be weird. And we promised no weirdness. Remember?

Oh, he remembered. And nothing about it felt weird to him. He texted back.

Knock knock . . . You say "who's there?"

To which she replied:

Seriously? Just open the door.

Dax found himself smiling.

It's unlocked.

He gave a few rapid curls to make the tats stand out, then set down the weights and, ignoring his shirt, grabbed a rag off the bench to at least clean the sweat off his face when he saw the front door burst open.

Emerson stormed inside, her flame-covered Converse squeaking on the wood floors as she stalked the length of the house and right up to him. She was sporting another one of those fantasy-inspiring leather skirts, a black tank that did nothing to hide her curves, and enough anger to singe his nuts off. She also had a canvas grocery bag in hand.

"My dad just called me," she said, her eyes sparking with fury. "Do you know why?"

He had an idea. Not that she gave him time to answer.

"It seems *someone*"—she set down the bag to throw up jabby air quotes—"from Baudouin Vineyard called him and asked him to come in for an interview tomorrow."

"Good for him." Dax crossed his arms and leaned a shoulder against the door frame, waiting for the bad part of her story. Because he knew if Roger was interested, the job would be his. He knew this because he'd called his grandpa that morning and asked him for a favor.

"It's for a tasting room manager position," she said dramatically. "My dad has never even gone wine tasting!"

Dax still didn't see the problem. Most women would be thanking him, and even though he knew Emerson wasn't most women—hell, she was unlike any woman he'd ever met—he still hadn't anticipated this kind of response. "Well, he lucked out then, Baudouin wines are the best in the valley."

Her eyes narrowed into two pissed-off slits. "Cut the shit, Dax. You're that someone." Then the strangest thing happened: her anger turned to agitation. She was nervous. "I thought there wasn't going to be any weirdness."

He pushed off the wall, approached her, and rested his hands on her hips. "There isn't."

She batted at his hands but didn't back away. "The guy who I just saw naked is finding my dad a job. That's weird."

When put like that, yeah, it was. Even weirder than his asking his grandpa for a favor—something he never did.

"For the record, I saw you naked too," he said, and she didn't laugh as he'd hoped. "And even though it sounds weird, it's not. You said he needed a job, I knew that my grandpa was hiring. I might have mentioned your dad's name."

There. Simple. Very normal. Nothing to be upset about.

But she was still upset.

"That wasn't your place." She poked him in the chest. Hard. "It was supposed to be one night, no strings, and now you've just gone and . . . well, you've . . ." she sputtered, made a few exasperated huffs, then poked him again. Right in the pec. "You tied us together."

"I made a call."

She turned and paced, and he could see her mind processing the information. Emerson was independent, liked to stand on her own two feet. He got that. He wasn't called Wolf for nothing. But Dax knew when he needed backup. And Emerson needed some in a bad way.

"What if my dad gets the job?" She spun around. "Or what if he gets the job and they fire him because he isn't qualified? Then he'll be unemployed and a failure."

"It's talking about wine," he said. "I doubt that a guy who's worked with grapes for thirty-five years can't talk about wine to some customers."

She blew out a breath. "Why did you recommend him?"

This time he paced the room, until he was standing back in front of her. "Because your dad needed a job, my grandpa had one, and that's what friends do. You're helping me out with rehab. What's the difference?"

"I'm cooking for you because you're paying me, and because you're helping out with my sister's Lovelies." *Yeah, it was still a pussy title.* "We were even. This makes it . . ." She took another breath, and when she looked up at him, all he saw was exhaustion. Bone-deep exhaustion that rubbed him the wrong way. "It's just easier to manage expectations when I handle everything myself."

He wanted to argue that she couldn't balance the load she'd been carrying forever. At some point she was going to break, and he didn't want to see that happen. Then again, he wouldn't be around when it finally did.

"You, Emerson Blake"—he poked her shoulder—"have a God complex."

And he meant that in the best possible way. Not in the same way as his, staring down the scope, deciding who lived and who died. Emerson was a nurturer, feeding and caring for everyone in her life, doing whatever it took to make their lives better.

Fuller.

"Takes one to know one," she finally said, gifting him a small smile. She was still frustrated, that much was clear, but most of her defensiveness had faded. "No more weirdness. You are my client, I am your Lovely co-leader. That's it. Got it?"

He gave her a slow, thorough study until her face was as red as the flames on her shoes. "Something we can talk about tonight, over dinner."

"Oh no." Hands out, she took a big step back. "I will cook you dinner, then leave."

"That's not the deal."

"The deal was a meal a week. Over three weeks would equal three meals. We had three meals Saturday." She held up three fingers to demonstrate.

"I had three." And because he loved to see her squirm, he took her other hand, which was jabbed into her hip, and pushed up four more fingers. "You had seven."

She snatched her hands back and picked up the grocery bag. "No one likes a bragger, Dax. No one."

A few days later, Emerson stood in front of the post office on Main Street, her jacket pulled around her ears. The office was clearly closed, and according to the sign, it wouldn't open for another two hours. Two hours was a long time to wait.

She could go for a run, eat an entire pan of bread pudding, pick the lint off her couch.

"I should come back," she said to no one in particular.

Or you could drop it in the mailbox. Because she knew if she walked away, come tomorrow that envelope would still be in her backpack, and then it would be too late.

She pulled out the envelope and looked at it in her hand, then at the mailbox, even touching the little handle to see how easy it was. Open, insert, and snap, it would be mailed.

Then she would be one of the fifty official contestants in Street Eats, and all she'd need was a truck. Which, if everything went perfectly between now and next week, she'd have. It wouldn't be the fancy one she'd imagined, but it would be enough to get started.

If everything went perfectly. She wanted to laugh because lately her luck had been fairly crappy. Perfect had become such a foreign concept, wishing for it made her palms sweat.

Last night she'd made up her mind: she was going to go for it. She even set her alarm for the crack of dawn and came down in her Converse and yesterday's makeup. But now, standing here in her pj's hidden under her coat, knowing that if she mailed this letter and something went wrong and she *didn't* get the food truck . . .

Wouldn't that be a mess?

She would miss out on her only chance. By nature, golden opportunities came around once in a lifetime, and the rule was you had to take them. She knew the committee would be unlikely to choose her again if she never responded or wasted their time by applying, then saying no thanks. But if she sent it in and then was a no-show?

Emerson closed her eyes and took a slow breath, trying to get a handle on every possibility. When that didn't work, she changed tactics and tried to think of what her mom would want her to do.

If ever in doubt, eat the whole tray.

Lillianna Petridis-Blake would rather risk a tummy ache than settle for a nibble of crumbs any day. Kissing the envelope, Emerson reached for the handle, and her phone buzzed. She dug it out of her coat pocket and read the screen.

If you need help putting it in the box, just ask.

Emerson paused, then slowly turned around to see if Dax was behind her and, "Holy hell," her throat closed in on itself, making her battle cry more of a squeak. She clutched the envelope protectively to her, as if the act alone would stop her heart from exploding out of her chest.

Dax stood *right* behind her, towering over her, actually, pulling in air as if he'd just run a marathon. It didn't seem to matter that there was frost on the ground, he stood confidently in a pair of low-slung shorts that fell midway down his impressive thighs, a black shirt that clung to his biceps and abs, and a pair of mirrored wraparound sunglasses that said *Make my day*.

He looked sweaty, sexy, and like the kind of man who *could* make her day. Only that day—and night—had come and gone and they were back to being client and chef.

"What are you doing here?" she asked, irritated that her heart was still racing and it had nothing to do with the scare.

"Out for a run." And as if planned, a single bead of sweat rolled down his temple, which he wiped on his shoulder. He took in her ponytail, winter coat, and flannel pajama bottoms peeking out beneath, and grinned. "You?"

"Mailing a letter," she said.

He lowered his glasses to look at her. Or maybe it was so he could see just how amusing she was. "You know you actually have to put the envelope in the mailbox for the magic of the postal service to work."

"I am." But she was still clutching it to her chest.

"Is that why you've been doing recon and collecting intel in your pajamas for the past fifteen minutes?"

"'Recon,'" she said, mimicking his voice. "Oooh. Is that official army jargon?" He actually smiled. "And why are you stalking me?"

"I'm a Ranger," he said, lowering his voice and stepping closer— if that was possible. "If I was stalking you, you'd never know it until you felt my hot breath on your neck. And even then you'd wonder if I'd been there."

"Your hot breath is everywhere now." She waved a hand in his face and the envelope slipped out of her fingers.

She bent to pick it up, but he was quicker. He was also a snoop.

"Street Eats," he read, then those steel-blue eyes met hers and she felt a whole lot more than her palms sweat. "Is that what you need the money for?"

She snatched it back. "Why is it any of my client's business what I need the money for?"

"A question with a question. Why am I not surprised?"

"Says Mr. Open Book." She tucked the envelope in her coat pocket with a pat. "You're always sneaking around and snooping in my business, yet you've never once told me, well, anything. I drive you to PT and I don't even know what happened to your knee."

He looked at her for a long moment and Emerson considered taking it back. Telling him she didn't want to know, because knowing meant sharing, and sharing, as Violet would tell her, meant caring. She had too many people in her life to care about. She didn't need to add another.

"My knee . . . I got distracted," he said, his eyes never leaving hers. "Long enough to give up my location and put my teammates in a shitstorm that ended in two casualties. The knee is nothing compared to what could have happened, though."

Emerson stilled in horror over what he must have gone through. What he'd seen and what he'd lost. A tough, stoic soldier who'd probably visited every corner of the earth but carried few, if any, happy memories from his travels. "Did you lose someone important there?"

"Everyone there lost a lot of someones," he said, the guilt and pain still clear in his voice. "But that day?" He shook his head. "Thankfully, we all made it out."

Emerson wondered if he really had. Or if, like her, he was going through the motions so fast there was no time for a real life. No time to reflect and take stock. If he was moving forward, he'd never have to go back.

"Not because of me and my elite training," he said bitterly. "We got lucky. And since Lady Luck can be temperamental at best, I don't want anyone standing near me when she decides to go hormonal again."

Emerson could have said something encouraging, some little tidbit on life to tie up what must have been an incredibly difficult and gut-wrenching time with a pretty bow. But shit happened, she knew this, and quoting motivational posters didn't take away the stench of guilt. Or the pain. It just diminished the importance of the loss.

"To Lady Luck," Emerson said, holding up a double birdie, and Dax laughed. "And now for the show-you-mine moment I owe you, I was waffling because once I mail this envelope I have three weeks to find a truck, get it ready, come up with a winning menu, and find a crew to man it."

He shrugged as if that was no biggie. When in fact it was the biggest biggie of her entire career. "Then why not just drop it in the box?"

"Because I haven't decided if a bellyache is worse than crumbs," she said and felt an irritating burn start behind her eyes. Blaming the early hour and lack of sleep, she blinked, but it only got worse.

Allergies. It had to be some allergic reaction to all the weirdness in the air. It was throwing her off, because surely they couldn't be tears.

She cleared her throat. "My mom and I were supposed to do this together. I would do the cooking and she would help with the prep and work the window, since we were afraid my intensity would scare off customers."

He chuckled. "And now you are short a team member?"

She was short so much more than that. She was short her mom's laughs, and hugs, and endless love and support. Such a deficit was created when her mom passed that Emerson wasn't sure if her dream held any real value anymore.

Emerson didn't even know what she was going to serve. There hadn't been enough time to put together a concrete menu plan. They'd made a list of possibilities, a backup list just in case, but nothing had been decided, and making that decision now, without her mom, made her feel empty.

"Yeah, and Harper and Shay have a Kitten Therapy for Kids conference that weekend, so I'd be flying solo. And solo doesn't work in a food truck."

Unlike her cart, a successful food truck required a team effort. Which was why they'd planned on hiring an employee or two. But to find someone she could spend twelve hours in a pressure cooker with and not want to stab them in the throat would be difficult. To find that perfect someone before Street Eats?

Impossible.

Dax shrugged, different than his normal *I've got this* shrug. It was almost shy in nature and self-conscious in its delivery. "I'm not much help in the cooking department, but I am lethal with a knife and excel at giving and taking orders."

Emerson blinked, certain she was having a negative reaction to the weirdness, because she must have misunderstood him. "Are you offering to be my sous chef?"

Dax opened his mouth, then closed it as if he too were confused by his offer. Then he grinned—all charm and swagger. "Why, Emi, are you offering me a job?"

She took a step back. "Negative, Ranger. I need to be able to work with a sous chef and I don't even know if I like you, let alone if we could work together."

"Oh, you like me, Emi." He grinned and came at her. "And we work together just fine. The other night proved that." She swallowed—hard. "It also proved that I know how to bring in a crowd."

This was true. With Dax working the window every woman at the event would flock to her truck. And as of now she didn't have a better plan. Her dad would be more of a distraction than a help, her friends were out of town, and her mom was gone.

Which left Violet or Dax. Violet couldn't reach the window. But Dax had hesitated—she'd seen it in his eyes—and that, more than the flutters in her belly, made her nervous. "Why are you offering to help?"

"I don't know, maybe I can pick up some basic cooking skills and learn to make more than toast and steaks." He fiddled with the yarn ball at the end of her hat. "Or maybe I feel like I cornered you into taking the job with me and now that I see how busy you are I want to help you out."

"I'll figure something out, but thanks." She was fine, absolutely fine. *Fine, fine, fine.* And if she said it in threes it would magically become true.

"Never play poker," he said with a laugh. "And before you tell another lie, think about it. It's one event, then you hire someone else, and we both move on."

It sounded so easy. Just like one night, no strings, which didn't seem to be working out all that well.

"I'll think about it." He looked at her like her pants were on fire, so she added, "All right, Tough Guy, have you told Jonah your decision about the weapons training position?" His expression said no, that he too was a big fat chicken, and Emerson made the appropriate sound.

"Did you just cluck?" he asked, and she did it again—this time flapping her arms. "Fine, if I go across the street and talk to Jonah, will you put the damn envelope in the box and hire me for the day?"

She looked at the box, then back to the man who had given her one of the best nights she'd had in years. If she had settled for crumbs with Dax, she would have missed out on what it felt like to be carefree again.

Decision made, Emerson pulled the letter out, sent up a silent prayer to her mom, and dropped it in the box.

"Good decision," Dax said softly, and she felt a secret thrill from his approval.

"What are you going to tell Jonah?" she asked, telling herself that it didn't matter.

He leaned in, and she felt that hot breath on her neck like he'd promised, and in a conspiratorial voice he whispered, "I said I'd talk to him, not tell you what I decided. Why? Do you want to know?"

"Nope." She pulled back, tightening her coat. "No weirdness."

Which brought her to the next topic of conversation she hadn't wanted to address. "My dad went on the interview. And he seems to be excited about the job." She cleared the humble pie from her throat. "He liked how flexible the hours were and is excited about working with tourists."

Roger was more than excited. He'd talked nonstop all through dinner. Apparently, before he landed in wine he had wanted to be a cruise director, which in retrospect shouldn't have been as surprising as it was. Living on a floating daydream on the high seas was right up her dad's alley. And working in a warehouse with the same people, day in and day out, had become taxing, he'd said.

"He still hasn't gotten an official offer, but it was the first time he seemed open to going back to work," Emerson finished. "So thank you."

"I'm happy it worked out" was all he said. No "I told you so," no rubbing her nose in it, like she would have done. Just sincere happiness that maybe her dad had found something he could take an interest in again.

"I want it to work out," Emerson said, surprised at how her voice caught. In fact, thinking about her dad finding his place irritated her eyes and her chest. Thinking about him finally finding happiness, well, that about took her out at the knees.

Emerson wasn't sure what overcame her, but one minute she was staring up at Dax and wondering why his eyes looked so soft, and the next she was stepping into him and wrapping her arms around his middle. Without hesitation, his big arms came around her, until she was completely engulfed in 250 pounds of bad-boy brawn and gentle steel.

Emerson allowed herself to lean into him for just a second to collect herself, to absorb how amazing it felt. Her life had become some abstract equation of love and duty, balancing her own needs against those of her family. Yet a guy who professed to be allergic to obligation had the emotional awareness to give her what no else in her world took the time to understand.

Unwavering support.

"This doesn't change anything," she said into his strong chest. "And I'm still mad at you."

She felt him chuckle. "I figured as much when I saw the pureed broccoli in my breakfast. The bits were too small to pick out but big enough to make my eggs green."

"It was a quiche and broccoli is the supervegetable. All the big-boy soldiers eat it because it makes them grow up tall and strong."

His pecs danced under her cheek. "I think I'm good."

ch*p*ter
twelve

"It doesn't look like Elsa's castle?"

Dax looked out at the five pint-sized survivalists in training, all sitting knee to knee, crisscross at his feet in a "Bug Huddle," as Pixie had called it. He was at the head of the huddle, as crisscross as his leg would let him. "Which one of you is Elsa?"

Giggles erupted among the troops. When no one spoke up, he asked again and the girls looked at each other like *Who is this guy?* And just when Dax was about to tell them to run until they were too tired to giggle, because Lord knew he was too tired to hear any more giggling, Violet raised her hand.

She was in jeans and her Lady Bug uniform, but unlike last time, she had on hiking boots, a red knit cap, and matching mittens—and no wings. "Hey, what happened to your wi—"

Emerson jumped up from the picnic table behind Violet and started slicing her hand frantically across her throat, a clear indication that she needed him to cease his interrogation immediately. Distress call heard and understood, he coughed and finished, "Your Converse?"

Violet looked down. "These are my hiking boots. See?" He did. And he wasn't impressed. They were pink, with pink sparkly laces—and not a speck of dirt on them. As if she'd never been hiking a day in her life. "And Elsa's not a Lady Bug, she's the princess from *Frozen*, Lovely Co-leader Mister."

Dax scrubbed a hand down his face. And here he'd thought today would be easy. Because, surely, how difficult could it be, hiking in the park and teaching a couple of capable kids to build a shelter using limited supplies? They could walk, talk, read, and giggle—surely they could follow simple instructions. Making it through Ranger selection and his sixty-one days of spec-op training at Fort Benning had been easier.

"Well, according to the official Loveliest Survivalist Campout rules," he said and could imagine his brothers laughing. A big military badass like him quoting Lovely rules.

But he was already sitting on the ground, crisscross applesauce, as Violet had instructed, and wearing a stupid-ass hat. Might as well commit.

He held up the book as proof. He felt like he'd been pretty clear, and the troops had been nodding, but now that he was done explaining, they were looking at him as if he were an alien with three heads. Who was slow in the three heads. And perhaps had cooties. "To qualify, the shelter needs to be constructed from a single eight-by-ten tarp and things found in nature."

He pointed to the pine boughs he'd collected and tossed in the center of the Bug Huddle. Then he smiled, because he'd learned that when he didn't make a conscious effort to look friendly, the little brunette with freckles would duck her head to avoid eye contact and try not to cry. And she was disappearing behind her curtain of hair.

Next to her sat the blonde with curly hair who came with a note explaining that she couldn't eat dairy, gluten, peanuts, soy nuts, corn nuts, nuts of any kind, refined sugar, imitation sweeteners, soda, or food coloring. Dax couldn't remember if air was on that list but ignored the food coloring and sugar part since he was certain those Astro Pops were not made with real fruit juice. The poor kid was so buttoned up Dax could barely see her face peeking out from beneath her jacket.

"Well, Elsa made hers out of ice, isn't that nature?" This came from the one with the Coke-bottle glasses.

He leaned down and squinted at her name badge. "Kenzie, right?" She nodded. "Why don't we make one out of a tarp like the rulebook says?"

At his suggestion all of the girls' faces fell. Except for Kenzie's—hers went combative. "Is that because you can't make one from ice or because the rules say we can't use ice?"

He looked at his co-leader for some help, but she was too busy pretending to organize the handouts on indigenous plants for the Fun Forest Foods portion of this survival training class. She was also grinning behind the handouts, he could see it in her big green eyes. Sure, they'd had a plan coming into today—divide and conquer—so he'd taken shelter and she'd taken food sources in the wilderness. But a little backup would have been nice.

"Since it needs to be less than thirty-two degrees for ice to form"—Dax licked his finger and put it in the air as a cool breeze blew by, scattering the pine needles and carrying the fresh scent of Christmas and rich earth, but his finger didn't freeze—"and it's clearly not below thirty-two, it would not be a naturally occurring element in the wilderness we are going to enter." And since they still didn't look like they believed him—*him*, the guy who had survived being stranded in the desert with only his rifle, his blade, and his ruck—he added, "It will be insulated, so it will keep you warm even if it did snow."

"I thought you said it wasn't going to be cold enough to snow," Violet said to the glee of Glasses.

"I did. It's not." Dax cupped the bill of his hat and curled it for a moment. "Look, making a shelter out of ice is stupid."

The girls all sucked in a scandalized breath and almost—almost—drowned out the single chuckle. From Emerson. Who, if she weren't looking so damn good in those snug Carhartts and a snugger thermal top with the top two buttons undone, would be on his list.

The undone buttons, though, put her on an entirely different list.

"The first rule in survival?" he said.

"Stay calm!" they said in unison.

"Great. And the second rule?"

"Work smart!"

Now they were getting somewhere. "Right. And working smart is finding the easiest path to the best solution. And making a castle out of ice when you are in a survival situation isn't as smart as making a shelter out of branches or a downed tree, things you can find easily."

The girls all shared a look. He wasn't sure what it meant, but then Violet reached over and patted his hand. "It's okay that you haven't built an ice castle, Lovely Co-leader Mister, you could have just said so. We'll make a regular old shelter from your tarp." She turned to the rest of her troop. "Right, Bugs?"

"Right," the girls mumbled disappointedly.

Maybe this was one of those pie dish moments and Emerson was right. Maybe he knew zip about females. Obviously even less about princesses and ice castles. But he knew how to survive so they'd do it his way—plus he was bigger. "This shelter I'm going to teach you about. This is what Rangers would build if they found themselves in trouble. So if there are no more questions—"

Kenzie's hand shot up and he ignored it. "Let's work smart. We'll use that downed tree behind you as the main support and then find more wood to fill it in. So let's break up into two teams." He put an arm through the middle of the girls. "Shirley Temple. Glasses. You two go collect as many branches as you can," he said to the blonde one and Kenzie. "They don't have to be thick, but they need to be tall. At least as tall as you are. And you two," Dax said, then smiled because he was addressing Freckles. "I need you and Violet to gather as much fern and moss and as many pine needles as you can carry. The greener the pine needles the better because the smell will ward off bugs."

"But we are bugs," Violet said, concern lacing her face.

"Bugs that bite." He eyed Kenzie, who he was pretty certain had sharp teeth, and clarified, "Mosquitoes." The girls nodded so he pushed himself to a stand—which took more energy and maneuvering than he'd have liked. "Dismissed." No one moved. "First team done gets to pick the popsicle flavor."

They took off running, their little pigtails bouncing.

"Ice shelters are stupid?" Emerson said, coming up behind him, her official red-and-black polka-dotted binder pressed to her chest. "That's the best you can come up with?"

"I was ambushed," he said. "For a minute there I thought there was a fifth, missing member named Elsa."

"I would have helped," she said, her eyes sparkling with humor. "But you assured me you had it. In fact, I believe your exact words were 'My legs weigh more than all of them put together, Emi. I've got this.' Then you gave that constipated look you've got going on now."

"Admit it," he said, stepping closer. "You just wanted to watch a group of six-year-olds hand me my ass."

"I was going to intervene, but then I started reading this list of dangerous and edible plants found in nature. Which I was supposed to go over *before* you sent them off into the wild alone." She held up photocopied pages from a book he'd lent her about surviving off the land. "Funny thing, Ranger, did you know that nearly everything survivalists eat in the wilderness, outside of catching small prey, is green?"

She smacked a stapled packet to his chest, so he trapped her hand there and stepped even closer. He couldn't help it. When she was all bossy and sassy, he was like a moth to her flame. "I've eaten a lot of things I don't like. Even had crickets on occasion when I was desperate, but that doesn't mean I want to stir-fry some up tonight."

Rangers were experts at making something out of nothing—the way to survive was to adapt and overcome—but even when he'd been forced to eat nature's salad, he'd gagged. Not that he'd let his men see, but it had happened.

"If we are going to get the girls to try clover and dandelion salad, then you have to eat clover and dandelion salad. The X-tremely Edible category is our best shot at winning a trophy."

According to the handbook he'd breezed through last night, the X-tremely Edible division of the campout challenged each team to find nutrients in nature and creative ways to trap or locate food sources.

"And you have to pretend to like it." She didn't move her hand but extended her pointer finger to poke his pec. "One gag and the whole class is over. Got it?"

Another poke.

"Yes, ma'am."

"So put on your Ranger face and man up. Clover is your new best friend."

He wanted to point out that he was already one step ahead of her. Manning up wouldn't be a problem. She wasn't touching him anywhere sensual, just her hand poking into his pec with purpose, but it was as if he could feel her everywhere. She could feel him too, because her eyes went heavy and she looked a little lost, a little dazed, and a whole lot like she wanted him.

"What's up with Pixie and the no wings?" he asked quietly.

Her face lit with excitement. "We're trying something new, so don't make a big deal out of it. But her teacher thought it would be best if the wings stayed home, and she started answering to Violet." He could tell that she agreed with the teacher, but reinforcing the rules fell completely to Emerson. "So I promised Violet that I would do the twilight walk with her before dinner, like my mom used to, but only if she left the wings in her closet during the week." She leaned in. "And it's working!"

"You're a good sister." He moved his arms so that their knuckles lightly brushed. "The way you take care of your family is . . ." He searched for the right word. "Sweet."

She dropped her gaze to his chest and shrugged. "Most people would argue about me being sweet."

A few weeks ago he would have been one of those people. But he knew better now, knew that her hands-off thing was all for show. It was her armor. What kept her safe from all of the disappointments life had thrown her way.

Dax slipped his finger under her chin and lifted it until she met his gaze. "Most people would be wrong then, Emi, because everything about you is sweet."

Their gazes held, hers so uncertain and lost he wanted to pull her to him like he had the other day. "It's getting weird again," she said quietly, and he could see the pulse beat in the base of her neck.

"I think you meant to say, it's getting good." He stepped closer and her breath caught. If this was weird, then he was officially a fan.

"You should probably go find that wood," she said but he noticed she didn't move.

"The wood—"

Her eyes went wide and she pressed her hand over his mouth, shaking her head. "No, please don't say it's in your pants."

"Okay." He kissed the palm of her hand and she jerked it back. And yeah, he might have given her a gentle nip. And then, because he didn't want to be another one of life's disappointments, he gave her what she needed right then. Laughter. "I also won't tell you where the party is then."

She threw her head back and laughed, then stuck the papers in the neck of his shirt. "Read up, Ranger. I want you prepared for lunch."

Dax watched her go, her hips swaying as she walked to the picnic table. That sway was the kind of sexy sway a woman gave when she knew a man was watching—and wanted him to watch.

Yup. She was feeling it. Fighting it, but feeling it all the same.

He didn't bother to tell her he wasn't eating her lunch, that he'd stopped by Stan's earlier and enjoyed two bowls of chili and some corn bread—and an hour of chopping. He pulled out the papers and went to hand them back when he noticed red markings in the margins. Phone numbers, notes, big red *X*s through parts.

He looked closer. It wasn't pages from his book—she'd accidently handed him her list of trucks for sale. Commercial food trucks, to be exact. There must have been ten pages, containing the details on over thirty food trucks for sale in the area. The first several trucks were either untouched or marked out. In fact, there were only three that he could find in the packet that were circled as though possibilities.

"Why is the truck on page two crossed out?" he asked because he didn't know a lot about food trucks, even less about cooking in one, but he knew cars. He'd also seen Emerson work in his kitchen enough to understand that the few trucks she had circled weren't big enough. "Or these circled ones smaller than twenty-nine feet?"

She looked up and he knew the second recognition hit. Her eyes went wide and she was on him in seconds, reaching for the paper. He wasn't sure what came over him, maybe it was the expression she wore, the same one she'd worn when doing the mailbox shuffle the other day, but instead of giving it back, he flipped the page and pointed to the twenty-nine-foot semicustom truck that would be perfect. "I like this one."

"Then you should buy it," she said, successfully snatching the papers back and sticking them in her binder. "It's only thirty grand more than the others."

He followed her over to the table and leaned a hip against the corner. "That much of a difference?"

She sat down and pretended to reshuffle the handouts, not saying a word. Fine with him, he was used to waiting people out—it was what made him such a good sniper. He could wait for hours, days if he had to. Most people lived to fill the silence. Emerson held on longer than he expected, but after about three minutes of the birds chirping and leaves rustling, she broke.

"It's frustrating," she said. "The difference between a renovated roach coach and a renovated food truck is like twenty grand, then with upgrades and equipment it goes up from there."

"Is this the only commercial truck warehouse in the area?"

"For financing reasons and my timeline, this place seems to be my best option." She shrugged, then reached under the table and pulled out two bowls filled with weeds and flowers that the girls had collected at the beginning of the day. She picked up a clover and nibbled it. Dax's throat constricted a little. "I was thinking I could get a bigger truck that needs a little TLC and clean it up. But with Street Eats not that far off, I don't think that's a smart option."

Dax considered pointing out that he was great with TLC, both with cars and women, but since both would break her weirdness rule, he offered, "I know a guy who runs car auctions for Sonoma County. Repos and stuff for the police department. If you'd like, I can give him a call and see if he has any better options." Her eyes went cautious, so he raised a hand. "No pressure. No weirdness. No marker. I want to barter for the intel."

She crossed her arms, which did amazing things for those two undone buttons. "I'm listening."

"After I'm done teaching the girls to make a shelter, I will go call my buddy. And you explain to the girls that I couldn't stay for the forest feast."

"You're that scared of a little clover salad?"

"Yup."

"Fine, deal."

Dax was about to lean in and kiss on it when what sounded like a small herd of antelope frolicked up behind him. "We got the needles and leaves, Lovely Co-leader Mister," Violet said.

All four girls stood there panting, muddy, and with needles stuck in their hair. They were smiling proudly, their cheeks and noses red from the cold, as they held out their bounty for appraisal.

It wasn't enough to make a complete shelter, but it was enough to get them started. "Good job, troops. Drop it over by the big log."

"All Elsa did was wave her hands and dance and her ice castle was done," Kenzie pointed out. "This is way harder."

Another chuckle from Miss Helpful.

He silenced Emerson with a look, then addressed Kenzie. "Well, it will be warmer and maybe we'll even win the Resourcefulness Under Pressure Award." So there.

"Lovely Co-leader Mister," Violet said, holding up a familiar-looking three-leaved plant. It was waxy and red and—ah, shit. "What's this?"

"That's poison oak," Kenzie pointed out. "It is a climbing shrub that is native to North America and related to the cashew plant."

Shirley Temple's eyes went wide as she dropped her bundle and jumped back. "Isn't a cashew a nut?" Her words were frantic, but her voice came out a strangle of tears. "If I have nuts I need to use my EpiPen, which is a needle and it hurts. And I don't like to hurt."

Freckles looked as though she was about to burst into tears at the idea of seeing a needle, and Violet started picking up dirt and throwing it in the air like it was magic dust.

"It doesn't have nuts on it," Kenzie explained, her tone heavy on the know-it-all. "It just has a poisonous oil that causes an itchy rash wherever it comes into contact with your skin." She looked at Dax. "Did you know that poison oak can't grow in freezing temperatures?"

Friday afternoon, Emerson closed up her cart early and rushed down Main Street. The sun shone bright overhead, painting the orange and red maple leaves with a golden glow. She was meeting her dad and Violet at Stan's Soup and Service Station. Violet had made it through a whole week without wearing her wings to school—something to celebrate.

Her sister was finally moving past this confusing stage, finding her footing in the world, and Emerson wanted to make sure Violet understood how proud she was of her. Which explained the Tupperware box filled with baklava she'd stayed up late last night making.

Emerson stepped into the service station and was greeted by the seasonal scents of roasting pumpkin and nutmeg. Roger and Violet were already sitting at the counter, smiling and sucking down a root beer float.

"Sorry I'm late," Emerson said, kissing her dad on the cheek, then Violet. "Wow, root beer float before dinner? Must be a special occasion."

"No," Violet said, confused. "Dad and I have a float every morning before scho—"

"Drink up, honey." Roger put the straw to Violet's lips, then smiled at Emerson. Sheepishly, she noticed. "Have a seat. We're about to order."

Emerson let it go and pulled out the stool next to Violet. Hooking her coat on the hanger under the countertop, she sat, springing back up immediately when something poked her butt.

"Ow!" she said, rubbing her backside. "What is that?"

"My trap," Violet cried, leaping to her feet to come and rescue the sticks held together by twine. "Did it break?"

"I don't think so." Emerson took a closer look at the work. It was circular, smaller on one end and bigger on the other, like a megaphone. It was also more Dad-work than student inspired. "Is that a cornucopia for school?"

"No, it's a fairy trap. Dad and I made it," Violet said, using her napkin to brush it off. "It's not done yet, though. I need to make a door so once a fairy goes in she has to wait for me to let her out. I caught one last night but she got out and only left behind some fairy dust."

"Fairy dust?" Emerson said, her heart sinking as she met Roger's eyes over Violet's head and gave him a long, steady look. He held up his palm as if saying *It isn't wings.*

"I wanted to show it to you." Violet looked up, her eyes big and proud.

"It's, uh . . . wow! I don't know what to say." Only that it negated everything she'd worked so hard on all week. The walks, the long talks, the special dessert she'd made. This entire celebration dinner.

"It's a perfect survival trap," the waiter said, and Emerson's heart did that funny flutter. Scratch that. It was more of a roundhouse kick to the ribs because it wasn't a waiter at all.

It was Dax.

He towered behind the counter in a pair of battered jeans, his signature soft-looking T-shirt, and a ball cap pulled low, but today he had on an apron that stretched across his chiseled chest. A white line cook's apron with soup splattered down the front, and he had a half-cut squash in his hand. His lips curled up at the edges as he pinned her with his gaze.

"What are you doing here?" she asked, but her eyes clearly pointed out that he was being a stalker.

He pulled out a notebook and in his most professional voice, informed her, "Letting you know that our soup of the day is roasted pumpkin with basil."

"Roasted pumpkin." Roger tapped a contemplative finger to his chin. "You like pumpkin, Violet?"

"You work here?" she asked quietly.

"Today I do. Tomorrow I'm at the county public training center. A few weeks from now, I'm sous cheffing at Street Eats." He smiled. "I am a man of many, many talents."

She had the memories to prove it.

"You're running the training class?"

A hum of something dangerous coursed through her veins. Not only had he followed through on his part, he'd told Jonah yes. She told herself not to read too much into it. Just because he was teaching a class didn't mean he'd sign on to stay.

She wanted to tell him he'd done the right thing, helping Jonah. And that it would help him too, but he was already taking the trap from Violet to examine. "Good work."

Violet beamed. "It's to catch fairies."

Emerson placed a hand to her head—it was the only thing to do other than banging it against the counter.

"Or you can use it for something useful, like catching fish at the Loveliest Survivalist Campout." Emerson looked up and Dax's gaze was on her, warm and unwavering. "Isn't there some kind of competition for that, Lovely Co-leader Emi?"

Her face heated at the use of her nickname in front of her family. "The, uh, X-tremely Edible competition?"

"The X-tremely Edible competition?" His lips curled up and she knew he was thinking about their night together. She was too.

"The Calistoga Lovelies Nine-Eight-Three win that one every year," Violet explained.

"Maybe this is St. Helena Lady Bug Lovelies Six-Six-Two's year," he said, grabbing a paper placemat. He tore it into several strips, then laid them out and began weaving them together. "Imagine this is wet manzanita bark that's been cut into strips. You can weave it together like this and then place it in the middle of your trap." His hands worked at lightning speed to demonstrate a way for Violet to make something non-fairy-centric out of her trap. When he was done, he put the funnel-shaped cone into the center of the cornucopia. "Like this. Then when the fish swim in, they can't easily swim out."

"Cool." Violet took the trap and studied it intently. Dax just smiled at his handiwork. And Emerson smiled at Dax.

"She likes those pumpkin cookies from the store," Roger mumbled, completely oblivious to the goings-on around him. "The ones with the candy black kitties on top. Will it taste like those?"

"Not sure," Dax said. "Never tried it. Not a big basil fan."

"Basil, huh?" Roger said. "That doesn't sound very celebratory, does it?"

Before Dax could answer, Violet was back in the game. "Do you think fairies could get out?"

"I'm not sure when fairy season is," he said, following like a champ the tennis-match pace that her family was notorious for keeping. "I do know that bass are everywhere. And that trap there is a perfect shape for a winning bass trap."

"Winning trap, huh?" Violet clapped her hands at the excitement of winning something. "Would you help me?"

Emerson felt her stomach bottom out as Dax considered the question. She could see the word *no* forming on his lips, knew how it would crush Violet, but couldn't blame him. In her family, offering to help was the equivalent of devoting your life to the cause. And the Blake family was a never-ending cause.

Not that Emerson was complaining, but it was her cause. Not his to deal with.

"Violet, Dax has a lot—"

"Of experience with these kinds of traps," he interrupted, shocking the hell out of her. She'd given him the out and he'd stuck around. "In fact, I've used ones similar to these in survival situations. Maybe you can teach your troop how to build the trap, and I can teach them how to make the funnel."

"Like partners?" Violet asked, all eyes. "Dad, did you hear that?"

"I sure did," Roger said, putting the menu down and smiling. There was a twinkle in his expression that Emerson hadn't seen in a long time. He was happy. "I think this calls for a round of floats."

"But you haven't finished the float you ordered," Emerson pointed out. Violet grabbed the straw and sucked it down, licking her lips in a *problem solved* way.

"Three floats," Roger said to Dax, then smiled as if the lights, after a long two years, had finally flicked back on. "Bring one for yourself, too."

"Oh," Emerson said, stacking the menus. "I'm sure Dax is busy. I mean, he's working."

"Well, he can take a short break, right?" Roger asked.

Dax looked at Emerson as though deferring to her, then said, "As long as it isn't weird."

A stab of guilt hit her so hard she had to force herself to swallow. He had done nothing but help her family and she'd accused him of being a stalker. Of being weird.

"No, of course. It's on me," she said and a wicked twinkle filled his eyes. "I meant I'll buy you a drink." She remembered that first night at the VFW hall, when he'd offered to buy her a drink and she'd shot him down. The irony wasn't lost on her—or him, since he was grinning.

"I'll accept."

"Great," Roger said, smacking the countertop with his palm. "Because we are celebrating. Big news."

Oh boy, last time Roger had "big news" it was a multilevel marketing scheme that one of the guys at the local sports bar swindled him into. It involved fish hooks and bobbers and Roger had lost a bunch of money. Something that never would have happened before he lost Lillianna.

When her mom had been alive, Roger had been funny and focused and driven and so incredibly meticulous he could juggle several projects at once. It was what had made him such a great vineyard manager. Then he'd lost his true love and it was as if he couldn't concentrate through the loss.

"What's the news, Dad?"

"I officially got the job at the tasting room," Roger said, and it took everything Emerson had not to cry. She felt her eyes burn and her throat close up, but she held strong. If she started crying now, she might not stop. And wouldn't that be embarrassing. "I start Saturday. I know it's your crazy day, but they want to train me and—"

"We'll work it out." Emerson leaned in and kissed his jaw. "Whatever the schedule is, we'll work it out. I am so proud of you."

"It's just a job," Roger said but everyone there knew it was more than that. It was his first real attempt to move on. To put the loss behind him and find a new start—just like Dax had promised.

"Congrats, Mr. Blake," Dax said as though he had nothing to do with making this moment possible. "I'll go make those floats now."

He sent Emerson a wink, and before she could thank him properly, he disappeared behind the swinging doors and into the kitchen. Emerson pulled out her phone and swiped a text.

Thank you for everything.

It was just four little words, but they seemed to mean so much more. Simple, and from the heart. Her cell immediately buzzed back. She looked at the screen and laughed.

Stop being weird.

Emerson had promised herself nothing would change after their night, but that had been before today. Before Dax made her sister feel special and helped her dad find his way. Before the hug by the mailbox and before Emerson realized that, in fact, everything had changed.

And it wasn't weird at all.

ch🍳pter
thirteen

"Were you aiming for my nuts or was it a lucky shot?" Dax said after the initial body-jolting impact and feeling of WTF? passed. Grimacing through the shooting pain in his inner thigh, and knowing it was going to last days, he looked at the casing on the floor. Had it been an inch higher Dax would be singing soprano instead of chewing off Fucking New Guy's head.

Assuming, of course, that each deputy was carrying real ammo instead of Simunition, a nonlethal training ammunition that all of the guns had been loaded with for today's CQB training.

"No, sir, I saw the shot and took it," FNG's voice came through the headset seconds after his team had gotten in position and were awaiting their superior's command.

"And shot the hostage in the dick?"

"I didn't know you were the hostage, sir," he said, breaking what was supposed to be radio silence.

Dax wasn't the hostage. In this training scenario he was the kidnapper, but in real life, it wasn't always clear who was who, which was why waiting for orders was imperative. Instead, the kid had taken an unsanctioned shot, ignored a direct order, and was too busy playing hero to play by the rules.

Dax looked out the window of the one-story, nondescript house that sat in the middle of the Napa Valley Public Safety Training Center and pinpointed the little shit's location on a rooftop a few buildings away. "Why, because I wasn't tied up and was holding a gun?"

"At the sheriff's head, sir. You were holding a gun at the sheriff's head."

"He isn't the sheriff today, now is he? This is a drill." Dax looked over his shoulder at Jonah, who was tied to the chair and wearing a bright-ass hostage shirt. He gave a *Who is this guy?* look, to which Jonah responded, *FNG. What do you expect?*

Uh, not to be shot.

Jonah gave a *Sorry, bro* shrug. That was it. His nuts were nearly shot off and all he got was a *Sorry, bro?* And yeah, the kid was an FNG, so it was expected that he'd be a little jumpy and a lot hyped on his first training—everyone was. But to shoot the possible hostage ten minutes into the exercise?

"That's a pretty big misshot, Gomer," Dax said into his headset. His name wasn't Gomer, but it would do until the kid learned how to control his premature trigger problem. "Your hostage is dead."

"Dead, sir?"

Dax pointed dramatically to his package, knowing the kid could see him through the rifle's scope. "Yeah, you shot his goods off, so I imagine he won't be of much value to the captors, who now know your location, by the way. And your team? They're pissed because it's game over. So want to come down here and bring me an ice pack so you can tell me what you're going to do to ensure you never misshoot again, and I can make sure I don't swell up to the size of a grapefruit?" There was a long pause, just static on the line. "Gomer?"

"Uh, yes, sir?"

"I can see your mirror of a forehead puckered at my two o'clock. Did you misunderstand my command?"

"No, sir." But he still didn't move.

"Just making sure because 'We need the hostage alive' seemed like a pretty clear order to me. Almost as clear as 'Bring me a damn ice pack,' yet I still don't see your freckles moving toward me." Another moment of hesitation and Dax allowed himself to smile—a little. Maybe the kid wasn't as stupid as he thought. "We were playing Rescue the Hostage and you killed the hostage," he lied, seeing how the kid would respond. "Game over. Now be a man and bring me ice."

Dax watched as Gomer stood and slung his rifle over his shoulder. "On my way, sir."

"Aw, Jesus. Is he serious?" Jonah mumbled and Dax muted their headpiece so Gomer wouldn't hear.

"I can't believe this." Jonah saw the kid tackle the external ladder, and he jerked back and forth in the chair, because the only thing that had been made clearer than that the hostage was to be rescued alive was that the game was not over until the commanding officer said so.

And Dax, although their training officer, was not their commanding officer. Jonah was, and that kid had just made a tactical error that in a real-life situation could have cost him his life.

Today, it might cost him his job. This training op was a mix of deputies and rookies, a way to increase training skills while creating an environment to see who would move up the ranks. Gomer started out with a strong showing at the range, then went lone wolf the second he saw the shot.

Dax would be lying if he said he hadn't considered the same thing a hundred times before, only he knew that when in a situation where the information was constantly changing, deferring to the person with the widest vantage point was critical.

"Just cut me loose," Jonah said, tugging on his hands. "Can't make him piss his pants if I'm yelling while zip-tied to a chair."

"As far as I'm concerned the game is still on." Dax gave him the *Sorry, bro* shrug and Jonah liked it about as much as Dax liked getting shot in the goods. "And don't count Gomer out just yet." Jonah stopped rocking in the chair long enough to lift a brow. "What? The kid's got something. That shot was impressive, a hundred yards with Simunition is a damn fine shot. Had I not stood when I did he would have caught me in the chest."

Dax patted his Kevlar vest.

"But he didn't," Jonah said. "He shot without having clearance or a clear shot."

"But he saw a shot and didn't hesitate." Something that Dax couldn't say.

He'd had a shot, was given clearance, then looked through the scope . . . and knew the target. It was more recognition, really, a familiar face Dax had seen in the neighboring village walking with his kid, holding his hand. And surely a guy who loved his kid that much couldn't be the right target.

That was it. A simple thread of connection and Dax had hesitated long enough to give away his position and put a group of guys he considered family, who were counting on him to have their backs, in the middle of a seriously screwed-up situation. And the guy who swung hands with his kid had launched the mortar that took out Dax's knee.

"He took the shot," Dax repeated.

"And hit the hostage."

"I'm not the hostage," Dax reminded Jonah, loving to see his older brother squirm. "I'm the captor."

"Yeah, I'm tied to a chair with hostage written across my chest in neon yellow, you had a gun at my head. All it took was saying to him, 'Hey, man, I'm the good guy,' and he buys it," Jonah said, and Dax could hear the frustration in his voice.

He could also hear the regret. Jonah didn't want to let this kid go. He saw in him the same potential Dax did, but overlooking a mistake this epic would be difficult. Because as team leader, Jonah decided who made the cut and who worked the desk. And if he put his faith in the wrong person, someone would die—and he'd have to live with that.

"Trust your gut," Dax said.

"My gut says he ignored direct orders and broke radio silence and, *Jesus*," Jonah said. "There he is all sweaty and winded, running with his rifle and a freaking ice pack."

"The rest of your guys are still in position," Dax pointed out. "And yeah, he messed up. But he did it in a training situation. In front of his team. He won't make that mistake again."

Once upon a time, he'd been that same pumped-up, high-strung soldier jonesing for his first real combat situation to prove he was a hero. Then he'd met Sergeant Conley, who corralled all of that anger and energy and turned Dax into an elite soldier who knew that heroes were saved for comic books and action flicks, and he was being trained to do a job. "The kid just needs a mentor."

"You're applying," Jonah said and Dax couldn't help but notice that the question mark at the end was missing.

He shook his head. "Not happening."

"What I meant was that you already applied," Jonah said, smiling. "I wrote your résumé last week and sent it in. Congratulations, the job is yours. Now untie me before I kick you in the nuts."

Dax wasn't going to untie his brother, just like he wasn't going to take that job. If someone had to make the hard calls, it wasn't going to be him. Ever again. Although the thought of staying in St. Helena didn't make his chest itch as badly anymore, the idea of playing judge and jury for another fifteen years was enough to take him under—and he'd just remembered how to breathe again.

"Until I hear you say 'game over,' this training is still a go." When Jonah just smiled, Dax cleared his throat. "And thanks for the endorsement," he said truthfully, because a guy like Jonah having enough faith in Dax to send in his résumé meant a lot. "But I heard back from Fallon. The job is mine. I can start as soon as Kyle gives me the all-clear."

Something he needed to talk to the doc about at his post-op appointment that Adam was taking him to tomorrow.

"Congrats," Jonah said with equal emotion. "Fallon runs a tight ship and they'll be lucky to have you." Jonah smiled, but his tone was dead serious. "Any team would be lucky to have you, Dax. Including mine."

Dax wasn't so sure about that. In San Jose he would be hired muscle with some serious skills behind him. No connections, no shared history, just a former sniper with a reputation and a job to do. Here, surrounded by family and friends, he was afraid he'd hesitate. Connections did that to a person, screwed with their head and contributed to making crap decisions.

He thought of Emerson and the way she'd leaned into him the other day, as if he were the only thing keeping her standing. How good it had felt to be the sole grounding force in her vortex of chaos. And how instead of pulling back like he should have, he'd pulled her closer, encouraged her to lean on him as if he was applying to be her own personal hero—then agreed to do the CQB training knowing he was going to leave.

Yeah, crap decisions.

"This one is delish," Harper moaned around bits of homemade pita. "It's so juicy and spicy."

"It's my Greek twist on a slider. I use ground lamb and short ribs for the patty, like my mom did, but then put my secret roasted red pepper and caviar aioli on top," Emerson said, knowing it was a front-runner. The dish was complex and rich without being snooty, and walked that fine line between sophistication and street food.

"This is a definite menu must-have," Harper said, shoving the rest of her slider in her mouth, then licking her fingers clean. "I could eat this every day."

That was exactly what Emerson was going for. A menu that could win over the judges but remain approachable to the locals. Delectable without pretentiousness. And if she was being honest, it had heart too.

Smiling, she took a sip of wine and leaned back on the lounge chair, content to just sit by and watch the trees blow in the breeze.

It was Sunday afternoon and Emerson had a rare day off, so she'd decided to spend it sharing a bottle of wine with Harper on her balcony, sampling a few ideas she had for Street Eats. They were also celebrating Emerson's Blow Your Cork earnings—which after the last event put her just two grand shy of her goal. She still hadn't found a truck, but with her menu taking shape and the RSVP in the hands of the committee, she was feeling hopeful.

Something she hadn't felt in years.

"Speaking of delish," Harper said with a secret smile. "What's up with you and the beefcake?"

"Nothing," Emerson said.

Harper snorted. "Nothing, huh? Then why are you flushed?"

"I am not." She touched her cheek and—this was becoming ridiculous.

First the flutters, then the hoping, and now flushing? It was like she was turning into one of *those* girls. And she had worked her entire life not to be one of *those* girls. "It's because he hugged me."

Harper froze, second slider halfway to her lips. "Hugged? You let him hug you? As in putting his arms around you and sharing an embrace?"

"I hugged him back." And it was a fantastic hug too, all sweet and gentle and warm and—*oh God*, there went the flutters.

"Is he okay?" Harper leaned forward, shock and a little smart-ass lacing her features. "Are you okay?"

"I hug people."

"Like who? Name one person since Liam, no, wait, your mom, who you hugged. And Violet doesn't count."

Emerson thought long and hard on that one, wanting to prove Harper wrong. Had it really been that long since she'd hugged someone? Wait, yes. "I hugged you. That night Shay got her shop for the pet rescue."

"That was over a year ago and I hugged you. You merely tolerated it, just like you tolerated the celebratory Street Eats hug," Harper clarified, and Emerson wondered if Harper remembered every hug of her life. "To qualify as a hug, it needs to be reciprocal. So this hug with Dax—"

"Dax and I had sex last weekend, against nearly every horizontal and vertical surface of my apartment, and you didn't ask all these questions. But we hug and it's a matter of national security?"

Harper waved a dismissive hand. "That was sex. This," she whispered, leaning closer as though imparting the meaning of life. "This is different. He's different."

He was different, and so was Emerson. She could feel it and she feared that people could see it, so she strategically avoided her friend's glare, instead paying particular attention to the arrangement of mouthwatering mini cupcakes she'd prepared—which were spongy and light with a rich liqueur frosting—to detract from the fact she was grinning. Like an idiot.

"We're friends," she said, knowing it was true. Only half the truth, but true all the same.

"Yeah, hot, vertical sex and hugging with a supersexy guy. Totally friend zone. I don't know what I was thinking."

Exactly what Emerson had concluded the other day at Stan's—she was in deep. It didn't matter when he left, she'd feel the loss, because when she was with Dax everything in her world tilted right. And when she wasn't with him all she could think about was what it felt like being with him.

Dax was funny and easy to be around and so incredibly kind to her family. And he'd called her sweet. No one had called her that before, but when he said it she felt sweet. Like she could be the kind of woman who got the great guy.

"I don't know what to do," she admitted.

"Are you kidding me?" Harper laughed. "Hearing about that night was hotter than my last nine dates combined. My entire dating history combined." Harper released a breath and took in Emerson's expression. She wasn't sure what she looked like, but it must have been bad, because suddenly Harper went superserious. "It's more than sex, Em, he's crazy about you."

"How would you know? The man cut out of town the day he could enlist, then was MIA for the past fifteen years."

"Because I pay attention," Harper said with a laugh. "And if you would, you'd see that the man is as allergic to human interaction as you are, yet he hires you to cook for him. In his house, thank you. Helps your sister's Lady Bug troop, finds your dad a job, and just happens to jog past your cart twice a day and pretend he isn't checking up on you."

"He's checking me out," Emerson corrected.

"No, he's checking up on you. There's a difference."

There was. Emerson knew. It was the same reason she'd agreed to pick him up from PT every week. To make sure he was feeling better. "I coerced him into helping with the Lady Bugs."

Harper rolled her eyes. "The only way a man like Dax could ever be coerced was if he allowed himself to be. Look at the guy, he's built like the Hulk." Emerson always thought more Captain America, but whatever. "He agreed to help because he wanted to help *you*, Em. And that's as real as it gets."

It was that real side of Dax that made Emerson so nervous. It wasn't just that he helped her dad for no reason, or that he hugged her when she needed it most. It was how he made her feel when he did those things. As if she meant something to him.

Something that went beyond one night. Something that might be worth hanging around for. He'd met her family, seen her crazy life, and yet he was still there. Not for always, but for now. And that should be enough.

But what if it wasn't?

"I mailed the letter Wednesday," Emerson admitted.

"I know. And I'm really proud of you." Harper leaned over and patted her hand like she'd just received a gold star for effort.

"What do you mean, you know?" She hadn't told anyone except Dax. And he only knew because he'd caught her—then hugged her. And yeah, she'd hugged him back. But she hadn't said a word since then, to him or anyone else, because if for some reason she didn't get the truck, she didn't want anyone to give her those *Poor Emerson* looks she hated so much.

"I peeked in your purse on accident." Harper sat back. "Okay, it wasn't an accident, I was going to mail it if it was still there Wednesday afternoon so you wouldn't miss the deadline. Thanks for mailing it, though, it saved me from infringing on your privacy."

"You already infringed by going into my purse."

Harper cocked her head, looking deep in thought and perplexed. With a nod she said, "I can see how it would look that way to you." Emerson wanted to point out that it would look that way to anyone. "And if it bothers you that much, then I promise not to stick my nose in your business."

"That's like you saying you're going to give up breathing."

Harper lifted the lid off the dessert tray and snagged a Metaxa-and-orange cupcake. "I won't do it again," she promised and made a big show out of popping the cupcake in her mouth, her cheeks puffed.

Emerson reached for a cupcake too when the roar of a motorcycle barreled down Main Street. Both women froze, neither moving an inch. Then the engine revved closer and it sounded as though it was right below her balcony, and her good parts did a little revving of their own.

Harper's eyes got big and she hopped up on her knees to look over the railing. She let loose one excited giggle, then calmly took her seat. Crossing her legs demurely.

"Is it him?" Emerson whispered, ignoring the fluttering and the flushing. And the bead of hope.

Harper pointed to her mouth, still full of cupcake, and shrugged.

"Oh, for God's sake, I give you permission to stick your nose in my business."

Harper swallowed and peeked back over the rail. "Yup, it's him."

"Is he parked in front of our building?"

"Can't tell," she said. "He's in a pair of camo pants, though, and his legs are wrapped around a big, black motorcycle. God, he looks like Dirty Harry meets Magic Mike." Harper sighed. "Even from this distance I can see the outline of his tattoo."

Distance? That meant he wasn't close enough to notice if she took a peek? "There is no way you could see his muscles through his jacket." Dax would never ride without his jacket or helmet. That was a fact.

"Oh." Harper looked over her shoulder and grinned. "Not that tat. The one that peeks out from beneath his shirt and jacket, only to disappear below the belt."

Emerson knew the tattoo well, so well she felt her mouth go dry at the memory. Unable to resist, Emerson leaned over the railing and looked down—only to find Dax looking up. Right at her. Smiling.

He was on his bike all right, but the only distance separating them was one story. Straight up.

"What are you doing here?" she asked.

"I wanted to check on Shirley Temple," he called up, that cool timbre rolling over her. "See if the poison oak had gone down any."

"Megan's mom called yesterday and said that most of the swelling and itching was gone, and she should be ready to go to the campout this weekend," she explained, and he made a universal gesture for *close call* by wiping off his forehead.

She was relieved by the news too, because in order to compete for the Loveliest Survivalist, a Loveliness needed a minimum of four Lady Bugs.

"Hey, I thought you weren't allowed to ride your bike."

"Just got cleared," he said. "I was going to go for a ride to blow off some steam, maybe find some trouble to get into." He released those dimples and Harper gave Emerson a giddy *Oh my* look. "You up for a little trouble?"

She was up for trouble, all right. So much it hurt. But if he was cleared to ride, then it wouldn't be long until he was cleared to leave. "How was the training yesterday?"

"Come for a ride and I'll tell you all about it."

Said the fox to the hen. "I'm testing out my food truck menu. There is a lot of green stuff or I'd invite you up."

"You know you look slightly to the right when you tell a lie," he said. "Not to mention when I stopped by earlier, your friend said you were planning on a low-key afternoon. Just sipping wine and tasting cupcakes."

Emerson shot a dirty look at her *friend*, who lifted her hands in surrender. "I talked to him before I promised to butt out. And I'd like to remind you that you gave me permission to butt back in a moment ago."

"The doctor said I can't ride alone. See," he hollered and she looked back over the railing. Dax held up a white piece of paper, which may or may not have been a prescription, but it looked convincing.

When she didn't move, he shoved it back in his pocket and ran his fingers through his hair. "Come on, Emi."

That was all it took. Him saying her name that way. Tired and rough around the edges, so exempt of the normal BS and charm that she found herself caving. He didn't want to go for a ride, he needed to disappear for a while. That he needed her to go with him spoke to a part of her that she couldn't shut off.

"You're glowing, Em," Harper said quietly. "Glowing. Tell me you still don't know what to do."

Oh, she knew. She'd known since San Francisco, she'd just been too stubborn to admit it. "You like cupcakes, Ranger?"

"Depends," he said with a rare boyish smile. "What's the color of the frosting?"

Emerson squeezed tight, a mix of thrill and terror pumping through her body as Dax sped along the winding mountain road. Thrill because the bike was going fast enough that it felt as if they were free-falling in tandem, their bodies pressed tight together from the force of the wind.

There wasn't an inch of her front that wasn't in full, bone-melting contact with his back, and shoulders, and thighs, and butt. Oh my, that butt. It matched the God complex he wore so well. In fact, every time he zigged the bike their bodies zagged in the best way possible.

The terror part came from the overwhelming sense of being out of control. Every hard turn Dax leaned into, her body screamed for her to go the opposite direction. Because leaning into what felt like falling went against everything she knew.

A firm hand pressed down on her knee, which was nestled tightly against his thigh. "Emerson," Dax hollered over the wind roaring around her mask. "Do you trust me?"

Emerson didn't do trust so well. Life had taught her better. But there was something about Dax and that take-anything-life-throws vibe he wore like a cape that made her want to trust. Made her want to let go and experience every terrifying thrill that came with it.

"Yes," she hollered back.

With a quick squeeze to the thigh, he yelled, "Then close your eyes and hang on."

And she did. Without hesitation. She squeezed her eyes shut and grabbed tighter, her hands resting low on his stomach, loving how safe she felt wrapped around his broad, strong body. Because even though she was holding on with everything she had, it somehow felt as if she was finally letting go.

Free.

Alive.

The bike rumbled under them moments before it surged forward, and she laughed over the rich, throaty roar of the engine. As Dax leaned she followed, quickly learning the subtle cues to read his body. The way his midback muscles flexed before he dropped into a higher gear or how one side of his abs would tighten moments before he steered into a sharp turn. It was as if their bodies were communicating, talking back and forth without words, working together in the most elemental way.

It was intimate.

Almost like a hug-spoon combo where Emerson got to play the big spoon. It seemed to go on for hours and had the power to wipe away her worries. Her dad's new job, finding Violet sleeping in her wings last night with a new fairy trap Roger had made under her bed, nothing mattered. Her mind went peacefully, pleasantly blank—lulled into a calm state by the sound of the ride.

Dax must have felt it too, because the more road they covered the more relaxed he became—and the more connected she felt.

Emerson had a deeper understanding of the stoic soldier. His wild ways were nothing more than a way to release all of the emotions that had no place else to go in his tightly controlled world. Dax kept everything carefully contained until there was time to blow steam—and blowing steam in a town with ties would be hard for a guy like him.

"How are you doing?" he yelled.

"Perfect." Absolutely perfect.

She felt him chuckle. "We're almost there."

She opened her eyes, surprised to see that the Mayacamas Mountains, which separated Napa Valley from Sonoma, were behind them. And in front of them sat rows of fire-colored vineyards with metallic strips that marked the harvested vines shimmering in the afternoon sun. Off in the distance, there appeared to be a big landing strip.

Dax slowed the bike down as they turned into the private airport. He pulled up to the hangar and cut the engine. Emerson loosened her grip slightly, but Dax's hand came to cover her linked fingers. He didn't say anything, just held her there. Fine with her since she was pretty sure her legs would buckle the second she tried to stand.

She felt him take a deep, meaningful breath and release it. He released her hand too, and she guessed that was her cue to slide off the bike. Which she did with minimal issues.

Although when Dax slid off the bike he looked as though he were a Scottish warrior dismounting his horse after a month-long battle. Smooth moves, rippling muscles, and dangerous swagger.

He pulled off her helmet, then his, and she could see that he was a few days behind on shaving, leaving a sexy shadow of stubble. But it was the shadow of exhaustion lining his face that had her taking his hand in hers.

"Want to tell me about yesterday?" she asked.

It was obvious something was bothering him. He seemed more relaxed than he had earlier, but there were more questions than answers in his eyes. And the only thing that came to mind was the training.

He set his helmet next to hers on the seat, freeing up those manly hands of his, which he wrapped around her. "I'd rather do this."

The heat of his lips covering hers carried enough torque to rev her engines past the point of a throaty purr. The man kissed like he rode, hard and wild, and took her to the edge in no time flat. Or maybe it was that an hour of having that much horsepower and testosterone-laced man between her legs was like an afternoon of serious foreplay.

One kiss and Emerson's body went haywire.

She wrapped her arms around him, finding the perfect place so quickly it was scary, then pressed herself up against him like they were still on the bike. A low, husky groan that was all lust and male appreciation sounded, right before he deepened the kiss.

"God, you taste good." He nipped her lower lip, his hands sliding up and down her spine as though he liked the feel of her under his palms. Then they slid into her back pockets, cupping her butt through the denim. "You feel even better."

Emerson wanted to say she could make him feel better, but with one last kiss he pulled back, slowly releasing her lower lip. His eyes were heavy lidded and his body hard and ready against her stomach. And his bike? It was just a few steps away.

Dax pressed his forehead to hers and released several rough breaths. "I want nothing more than to finish this right now. But we have an appointment."

The sexual haze faded. "Appointment?" That made today sound like more of a planned outing than the spontaneous *let's see where this road takes us* ride she'd signed on for. "What would you have done if I hadn't come with you?"

"I have a bag of bread pudding in the leather saddlebag just in case I needed to play hardball." He took her hand. "Ready?"

She kept pace with him as he led her toward the massive metal hangar doors. She noticed that their hands were swinging. She'd never taken Dax for a hand-holding kind of guy, and she sure as hell wasn't a hands-swinging kind of girl, but after that ride it felt natural.

Sweet.

Emerson rolled her eyes, because there went the flutters.

"You going to tell me about yesterday?" she asked.

He slid her a sidelong look and shook his head, but when he spoke his voice was surprisingly gentle. "Later. Today's about you."

The concept was so foreign, Emerson stumbled. It was as though her body were rejecting the word because nothing has been about her in years. And she'd agreed to come because she thought he needed her, she'd seen it in his eyes, but suddenly he was turning the tables and it made her uneasy.

"What do you mean, about me?"

"It's a surprise."

She dropped his hand. "I don't like surprises." She hated them, in fact. They ranked right up there with clown-themed kids' parties and root canals. And days about her.

He looked at her defiant expression and laughed. "God, you are the most suspicious person I have ever met. And you aren't going to go in there until I tell you what I have planned, are you?"

She crossed her arms.

"Even if I promise you that it's not going to make things weird?"

"Nope."

Dax looked at the sky and sighed. "Fine. I told you I'd call my buddy with the police department. I did and found out that the DEA confiscated a twenty-nine-foot gourmet food truck with all the Sub-Zero bells and twelve-thousand-watt whistles in a drug raid a few months back. Seems they were selling more than po'boys. It's scheduled to be auctioned off next month."

She let out an unsteady breath. "Dax."

"Before you rip me a new one, I only came along because I wanted to check under the hood for you, make sure it is as cherry as he said it was, because Ray's a stand-up guy but he's also a SEAL, which means he tends to embellish. A lot. So when he said he could sell it to you for the minimum bid, I wanted to make sure it was a good deal."

He threw out some number that was right under her budget and Emerson found speaking difficult. "Why?" she asked.

"I wanted to be here to check it out. If it isn't what you're looking for, then we bounce."

"No. Why did you do this?"

He gave her an unfamiliar look that had an odd feeling filling her chest. "Because you needed it."

And weren't those the heaviest few words she'd ever heard. Not only had he come through for her, he wasn't asking for anything in return. And he said it as if it were that easy. No conditions, no expectations attached to his intentions. She asked and he came through. He didn't take over like most people would, tell her what she should think or do, just offered his help. For no other reason than to make her life easier.

She wasn't sure how she felt about that. But the way he was looking at her, with a secret smile that had her insides turning, it didn't seem so scary, and if it meant a little more time with him, feeling like this, then she'd give it a try.

"I don't know what to say," she admitted.

He took her hand and pressed it to his lips. "There is nothing to say." Then with another kiss, this time to her lips, he tugged her toward their appointment.

They walked in silence, not suffocating uncomfortable silence, but the nice kind. Where no words were needed to fill the space. But plenty of information was being shared. It was just like being on the motorcycle.

A few feet from the hangar, she released a breath. Behind those doors was the start of everything, and she was almost afraid to look. Standing out here, thinking about the possibilities, gave her a sense of anticipation—that anything was possible. But once she opened that door it would be real, no turning back.

"Tell me one thing about yesterday," she said, needing a distraction.

"The new guy shot me in the nuts," he said, and mission accomplished. It was such an unexpected statement it explained the mortifying snort, followed by so much laughter her eyes watered.

She glanced at his package and dropped his hand. "Is that something you'll have to disclose on first dates now?"

"I'm not really a dating guy," he said, and if he meant for it to be a warning, then he blew it by taking her hand back and threading their fingers.

"You going to head up another exercise?" she asked, holding her breath for his answer.

"I'm heading up a weapons training in a few weeks," he said. "It was the only way Jonah would agree to give the new guy a second shot."

Emerson didn't know what made her melt more. That he had committed to a time past his hometown-stay expiration date. Or that he'd stuck it out to mentor some new recruit. "I'll buy you a steel cup," she joked.

"Smart-ass," he said with a smile.

"We've played that game before too," she said and, *whoa*, look at that, their hands were swinging even higher. She felt like skipping.

All the way into her fresh start.

ch🍳pter
fourteen

Usually when a woman showed up to Dax's house with frosting and a blindfold, spending the night chopping vegetables at the kitchen counter wasn't what he had in mind. Yet there he was, sporting a hard-on and bare feet while Emerson skirted around his kitchen, green things covering every inch of his counter.

Not that he could see the counter anymore, since she'd pulled out the blindfold a few minutes ago, but he could feel their presence. Just like he could feel Emerson walking toward him.

She was trying to be stealthy, probably holding some of those asparagus by their freaky tips, but he could hear her bare feet on the wood floor, smell the orange cupcake batter she had dropped on her apron earlier.

There wasn't anything about her that he couldn't sense—including the fact that she felt more for him than she let on. And Dax was terrified that the feelings situation was quickly becoming a two-way problem. She wasn't just in awe over her new truck, with its top-of-the-line appliances, double-wide serving window, and industrial range—she had taken one look at her dream machine and, man, those green eyes had locked on his as if he was her own personal hero. And in that moment, as Emerson ran her hands over the stainless steel countertops, Dax had felt like her hero, even found himself wondering what it would take to be the kind of man who made her smile like that every day.

Who made *her* every day.

Then he reminded himself that in order to do that, he'd have to be there every day.

Not wanting to go there right then, he waited until Emerson passed behind him on her way to the sink and reached back to grab her leg.

"Dax," she squeaked, then swatted his hand. "You aren't Lethal Weapon Ranger right now. You are a judge."

"Does the judge get to sample your cupcakes?" He heard her smile. It was the wrinkled nose smile combo she gave when she thought he was being cute. The little snort gave it away. "If not, then I want to change my character. To Lethal Weapon Ranger. He sounds like a cool guy who gets all sorts of cupcakes thrown his way."

"The judge gets to lick frosting off my finger," she said and walked back around the counter. He tracked her from the fridge to the sink, then finally she was standing behind him again.

"Now, open up and tell me what you think."

"Fine." He spun in his chair to face her. "I'll play judge for a while, but"—he sniffed the air, which was rich and spicy, with a hint of brine—"that doesn't smell like cupcakes. Game over."

He reached for his blindfold to take it off, but her cool hands settled on his. "Cupcakes are last. I have to take you on the complete culinary journey so you can see how the flavors build and play off each other. Now stop being fussy and smell this."

Since fussy was one letter off from a fighting word, Dax did as told. Fragrant steam moved across his lips and his mouth watered. He inhaled deeply, shook his head, and fussy be damned, sat back.

"Sorry, baby, I hear words like *culinary journey* and all I smell is green." He took another tentative sniff. "Is there green stuff in that? Because green always comes in last place for this judge. It comes in last for Lethal Weapon Ranger too, in case that was your next question."

A sigh escaped and he could picture her blowing the little wisps of hair off her face. "Then stop being a judge and stop being a Ranger," she said quietly, her hand resting on his knee, rubbing the right spot to release the pressure. "Today, right now, just be Dax, the guy who turns everything into an innuendo and hates all things green. And let me be the chef, who convinces you my food is incredible." Another little squeeze to his kneecap. "Can you do that?"

"I don't know," he said honestly.

His mother had died because she'd forgone cancer treatment so that Dax could live, something he remembered every time he looked at his brothers. Then he'd become a soldier, spent fifteen years in the army, the past nine of those as a Ranger sniper, making him some people's last judge and jury. His entire career had been a balancing act between life and loss, a Sunday school lesson of the Lord giveth and the Lord taketh, and Dax wanted to know who the hell decided he was the guy for the job.

Someone had, though, and guess what? He didn't want the damn job anymore, but he couldn't just stop who he was. Being a Ranger was his whole life, the good and the bad. Some parts were easy to walk away from . . . the rest left him feeling more isolated than a five-day stalk in the middle of BFE. How did someone just turn that off?

"I do," she said, her hands coming to rest on his cheek, and *that* was how to turn it off, he thought. One touch from her and it was as if everything vanished. "Now open up."

He could feel the soft breeze of her breath against his face as she spoke, the ends of her hair brushing his arm, and everything in the air shifting to something much more intimate. Vulnerable. He had shared a part of himself with her yesterday, and now she was offering him a chance to experience an important part of her.

He opened wide, and she slipped something salty and crunchy inside.

"This is my take on a Greek nacho. I was going for approachable with voice. Loud but not entitled."

Just like her, he thought as he closed his lips around it and the bold collection of flavors exploded in his mouth. It was vivid and complex and damn good. Intense power packed into a tiny body, with plenty of originality and attitude, followed by a nice kick of heat at the end.

"Well?" she asked and he could hear the hopeful uncertainty in her voice.

"It doesn't taste green," he said and she went to smack his chest, but he caught her midair. Not a hard task for a guy who held the platoon record for disassembling and reassembling a service weapon blindfolded. "It's really good, Emi."

"Like another-bite good?" She bounced on her toes while she talked. "Or I'd-have-to-eat-the-entire-plate good?"

"Like I'd lick the crumbs off the plate." And to prove it, he brought her hand to his mouth and licked each and every finger, spending a little extra time on the last.

He heard her breath catch, felt her pulse pick up, and knew he was in trouble.

Dax had convinced himself that his interest and attraction stemmed from their unfinished business at the wedding—a bad case of the whole one-that-walked-away syndrome. The cure was as simple as one more night.

Emerson was on the same page. Or so she told him. A no-strings, wall-banging event was all she was looking for. But there was nothing no-strings about her. She was selfless, nurturing, and the kind of woman who couldn't see past always. She put up a good front, distracted him with her tough-girl shoes and one-night 'tude, but the more time he spent with her the more he realized that she had a big heart and an even bigger capacity to love than anyone he'd ever met.

Being around that kind of intense focus and emotional connection was addicting. Made him crave things he couldn't have. Do things he shouldn't do. Like slip his hands around her hips to slowly draw her between his parted knees.

"Next bite, Emi." He skimmed his thumbs over the waistband of her skirt—he couldn't help it—while he slowly opened his mouth and patiently waited for the entrée course. But instead of a bite of lamb burger he got something a whole lot better.

A kiss. A sweet and gentle brush of the lips that was meant to soothe. And he needed soothing, so completely that he couldn't help but kiss her back. And of course, when it came to Emerson, kissing her led to touching her, and touching led to sex.

Only she'd come here for help with her menu. Sadly, not sex. Otherwise she would have walked in the door naked with a box of extra-large, ribbed-for-her-pleasure condoms instead of an insanely short skirt that left no room for underwear and carrying a bag of groceries. Not that he needed the ribs—he knew how to operate his equipment.

Her breathy little moans were proof of that. So was the way she snuggled closer when he glided his palms down her thighs and around the back of her skirt to tease under the lower hem and the silky skin that lay just beneath. Not that he was checking to see if her evening's preference was commando, thong, or a simple string, because he had promised to be just Dax.

Not Judge Show Me the Cupcakes. Or even Lethal Weapon Ranger. But Dax, the guy who made her world easier.

Except that, *oh holy shit*, she wasn't wearing any underwear. That much was obvious by his single, solo flyby. But lack of lace didn't equate to an offer. Just like a kiss didn't mean sex. Especially this kiss.

Emerson came at him soft and pliant and so damn welcoming that the right thing to do would be pull back, clarify intentions, and make sure no one misunderstood.

Make sure they didn't get distracted and walk into dangerous territory.

"What was that for?" he asked against her lips.

They were both breathing hard, but when he asked her the question, she began to sway gently back and forth on her feet. And he felt her head tilt down so that intent gaze of hers was on his chest, no longer his face. She was nervous, and he wished like hell he could see her so he could understand why. Because one look in her eyes and he'd know what she was feeling. He hoped to God it wasn't what he was. Which was a whole lot of something.

The not knowing was killing him, so Dax reached for the blindfold. Once again she stopped him.

"Wait, not yet." The shyness in her voice had him rerouting that hand to her cheek. She melted into it. "The kiss was my way of saying I like this Dax and thank you. For the ride on Sunday, helping me get my truck, which is perfect." Her lashes moved against his palm as if she'd closed her eyes. The swaying slowed and her hands came to cover his. "And also for liking my Greek nachos even though there was green stuff all over it."

"If that's what happens when I eat green stuff, then green is my new favorite flavor," he said and she smiled against his hand.

"Wait until you taste my cupcakes." Palms flat against his pecs, she leaned closer, her cupcakes coming into complete contact with his chest.

His hands? Those went to her ass. "Is that your way of saying you want to skip right to dessert?"

She didn't answer, but moments later he smelled the bitter sweetness of chocolate and some kind of liqueur.

"This is option one," she said, teasing his lips with the frosting. "My double chocolate cupcake with ouzo-infused fudge frosting. It will make you go *mmm*."

It made him go *mmm* all right. He wasn't sure if it was the rich, silky flavor of the cupcake or the way she nestled herself between his legs when she fed it to him. But he'd give it a ten on the sexy-as-hell scale. It went to a solid fifteen when her thumb brushed his lower lip, then he heard her suck the frosting off.

"And this one." Again with the reaching and brushing, and fun fact, being just Dax was fucking great. Although Lethal Weapon Ranger had all sorts of cupcakes thrown his way, Regular Old Dax, the guy whose new favorite flavor was green, had the best two cupcakes on the planet pressed against him. Teaching him that he was a quality over quantity guy. Something he'd always assumed, but Emerson confirmed.

"This is my orange zest cupcake with a Greek Metaxa frosting. And," she said, smearing the frosting on his lips, "it's my favorite."

Funny, that! It was his new favorite too. Even better than green. In fact, when her mouth came down on his to help him with the tasting, he decided then and there that he didn't want this flavor on the menu. He wanted this one all to himself.

Bright and deliciously tart, the cupcake and its creator were a breath of fresh air in his war-torn world. He needed her like he needed his next breath. And breathing ranked pretty damn high on his list of survival skills. But this went beyond surviving, and she was nearly straddling him, negative the panties, and Rangers always led the way, but he wasn't a Ranger right then, or else he'd lead them right into his bedroom.

The way she licked and nibbled off every speck of frosting from his lips made him want to return the favor. With every flavor of cupcake. And maybe they could even come up with a few new ones.

"Emi," he said against her lips. "Are you sure?"

She mumbled something, but it was too hard to understand with her tongue down his throat, too much nipping and hands in the hair to be considered sweet and warm, but it was as big of a welcome as a guy could expect. And in case *that* wasn't crystal fucking clear enough, she slid onto his lap, straddling each one of those toned legs on either side of his thighs and locking round the back.

Question answered.

Always a gentleman, Dax did his part to ensure her comfort and safety, helping her slide even farther up on his body. Lucky guy that he was, helping led to touching, which had her doing those little moans and shimmying closer, and well, *hallelujah*, look at that! His hands were back on her ass, like a heat-seeking missile locked on its target, and all of that situational awareness preparation Uncle Sam paid so much for came shining through, because, just like he'd predicted, she was completely commando under there.

Silky, soft, and totally bare.

A situation that required a flat surface.

Mouths fused together, cupcakes front and center, he turned the chair toward the counter and went to lift her when she shook her head.

"No."

Dax paused. "Was that a no to sex on the table? Or more of a no, sex is off the table and that was just a bold thanks for being my friend? Because if it was the former I'd like to point out that this is a different counter, so we're good. But if it was the latter, more of a caught up in the moment and already feeling regret, then I get it. Second thoughts happen."

He might cry later, but he'd understand.

She didn't answer right away and he couldn't tell what that meant. Then her cool fingers touched his cheek and slid up to remove the blindfold. It took a moment for his eyes to adjust, but when they did he found himself staring into the deepest green pools, which were filled with hunger and need, and so much raw compassion his lungs stopped working. "No second thoughts. In fact, everything just got a whole lot clearer."

She held up a condom and he nearly wept. This wasn't some spontaneous, caught-up-in-the-moment, cupcake-inspired sex. This was premeditated. She'd thought about this, knowing Emerson, long and hard, sure to weigh the risk with reward, and she'd still decided she wanted to be with him.

Without a word, Emerson slipped off his lap and took his hand. She also took charge. Leading him through the house. No questions asked, he just watched the sway of her hips and let her tug him farther and farther down that hallway, making him guess where she wanted tonight to take place. At first he thought the garage, pull Lola inside and go for a different kind of ride. Or maybe the hot tub on the back porch—there were a few of those water noodles they could get creative with. But when she reached his bedroom, the same bedroom he couldn't seem to get comfortable in, he stopped.

She offered up a sweet smile and squeezed his hand. It was small and dainty as squeezes went, but there was a gentle understanding behind it that had his insides stilling. She met his gaze. "I could never regret you, Dax."

And wasn't that the most incredible and terrifying thing she could say. Even worse, she meant it. The truth was right there, staring back at him. She was feeling the same crazy pull he was. It should have made him want to pack his ruck and pop smoke. In theory this had just become one of those math equations where two steam engines were speeding down the same track toward each other, and it didn't take a genius to figure out that they were a train wreck waiting to happen.

She looked at his bed, seemingly untouched since he hadn't slept in there in weeks, then back to him. "Trust me?"

At her words, calm stillness took over, radiating from her fingertips on his jawline and moving out until everything inside him downshifted and all he felt was peace. Nightmares, emotional strings, regrets, disappointing Jonah, her—himself—it all disappeared as he became hyperaware of the woman in front of him. Her scent, her confidence, the way her fingers gently slid down his jaw. It was all he could focus on.

Not like earlier, not from the trained soldier, but from somewhere deeper. Somewhere that he had no business visiting. But with her he couldn't help it. Found that he didn't want to change direction, not yet. The impending collision felt exciting.

He felt alive.

"Absolutely," he said with a certainty that shook his core, then he took her mouth.

She took his right back, reminding him of exactly why he couldn't stop thinking about her. The first kiss had them stumbling backward into his room until they crashed up against the nightstand next to his bed. The second kiss had her spinning them backward and him going down on the bed.

"Your knee," she said, her hair a mess of tangles, her skirt slightly askew. The moonlight came through the window and reflected off her wet lips and bedroom eyes. She looked hot, horny, and incredibly beautiful.

"Can't even feel it." In a second he was on her, grabbing her arm and yanking her down—right on top of him. She giggled at first, then he rolled her over and under him, and when they settled he'd managed to rid her of her top and make her laugh. It was so contagious he found himself laughing back, until those talented hands of hers slid down his chest and into his pants.

"I can," she said and gave an eye-rolling-to-the-back-of-the-head squeeze. "But I want to feel more."

"I want to finish that tasting," he said, sliding a hand under her to, *voilà*, free her cupcakes for their tasting. "I'm pretty sure these will be my favorite."

"They're not frosted," she teased but arched so he could look his fill. And he did.

Dax looked and tasted his fill until she was quivering beneath him and he was certain that, one, her cupcakes had the power to end world hunger, global warming, and all future wars, and, two, she might moan like the kind of woman who could rock his carefully crafted world, but she tasted like home.

And he'd never wanted to come home more than right then.

But before he could think too much about what that meant, her hands were on the move, teasing and stroking and distracting, effortlessly so, taking him out of his head and back into his bed—with her. Which was a hell of a lot less scary, so when she nudged him over, bossy as ever, he rolled onto his back to give her all the room she needed to feel.

"Too many clothes," she said, yanking his shirt up, over, and off. The zipper of her skirt went down and quickly followed. Hooking her fingers in the waist of his sweats, she looked up at him through her lashes. "Your turn."

Dax wanted to point out he didn't get to finish giving her *her* turn, but lifted his hips as told and watched as Emerson freed him and—

"Holy hell" was all he got out before she covered him.

With. Her. Mouth.

That sexy mouth that could be so sharp and oh so sweet. And Dax considered himself one lucky SOB, because his pants were around his knees, his legs hanging off the bed, and Emerson was kneeling in front of him, driving him right out of his head with her gentle licks and not-so-gentle sucks. The perfect mix of give and take that was destined to end the party before it started.

Which would be a shame since she'd brought her cupcakes.

"Emi," he said, sitting up and tugging her into his lap, facing her so her back was to his front. "I want to do this right."

More like he needed to get it right. With her. Tonight.

"Those moans told me I was doing it right," she teased, moving her ass so it was nestled perfectly against him.

"You mean moans like these?" He ran his hand up her stomach to cup her breast, his thumb brushing back and forth across her nipple with featherlight pressure. She bit her lip to hold back the moan. He did it again—she closed her eyes.

But still no moan.

"Stubborn," he whispered, bringing both hands up to cup her breasts, his thumbs pressing over the puckered surface, then pinching down, ever so gently.

"Oh Dax," she groaned, her head falling back against his chest, giving him enough primo real estate to nibble along the curve of her neck.

"There's my girl," he said, running one hand down her stomach and between her legs. His fingers teased around the edges until he felt her breaths come in short gasps, then up the middle, and finally sank into pure heaven.

First one, quickly adding a second because she was already so wet and ready that a few twists was all it took to feel her tighten—he could also feel her hips pushing against him, straining for control and desperate for more pressure.

He gave it to her, then backed off. Not a lot, but enough so that when he added the third finger she jerked forward and yelled, "Oh hell."

Really loud, but he still didn't let her come.

"I do love it when you swear at me," he whispered against her ear, giving it a little bite. "But 'Oh Dax' would make my day."

She didn't laugh or give him the "Oh Dax" that he was looking for. Instead she spun around until she was straddling him, hands on his chest, looking him in the eyes. And man, feisty looked good on her—almost as good as she looked on him, with all that sensual challenge flickering in her eyes.

"How about you stop talking and bring me my O, Dax?"

It was an order he was happy to comply with, one that had him going combat ready.

With a salute, he said, "Yes, ma'am," and together they had that condom on—no ribbed for her pleasure because she knew better—in no time flat. Then she was lifting up, his hands on her hips, and he was entering her in one thrust.

And together they both sighed a hearty "Oh God."

Dax might have said it again, because she felt that good. That right. So right he didn't just want to have her in his bed, he wanted her to stay there. Past breakfast, and maybe through lunch, so that when dinner came she could prance around his kitchen in just her tank top, no panties, cooking him up green stuff that was good for him because she was good for him.

Too damn good.

So good that when she started moving he was pretty sure his heart lodged itself in his chest, and when she wrapped her arms around his neck and he buried his face in her hair, he felt as if he were going to explode out of his body. His skin was tight, his lungs pissed off, and everything that was going on inside was too much for his body to contain. It couldn't all fit, yet with her he did.

He fit so perfectly.

"Dax," she said and he realized she was doing all the work because he was doing all the feeling, so he rolled them over, tucking her beneath him so he could look into her eyes as it all happened.

"Right here," he said, moving inside of her with deep, strong strokes. She was strung tight, so close to the edge that he moved faster, never looking away. She met him with every thrust, her eyes boring into his in a way that he couldn't hide. Anything.

For once it was all out there in the open, and she wasn't running, closing her eyes, she was taking him as he was, demanding more. Not someone else, just more.

"Right," he breathed as he withdrew all the way. "Here." He slid all the way back in, to the hilt, and she cried out his name. And when he felt her first tremor of release, he gave her everything he had and she took it, giving him even more in return.

"Right here," he groaned as she shattered around him, squeezing so erotically tight that it was too much and not enough all at the same time. All the exhaustion, the pain, and the past coiled into a tight ball in his chest and then exploded, and he came so hard his arms buckled and he managed to pull them onto their sides right as he collapsed.

Pressing his face into her hair, he pulled her close and breathed her in. All the way in. She didn't move, just melted into his chest, and Dax knew that right here was exactly where he wanted to be.

Much later, Emerson opened her eyes, surprised to find that the sun was shining—and Dax was still asleep. Well, part of him was awake, but she was pretty sure that was because he'd fallen asleep cupping her backside as if he owned it.

And he did own it. He was wrapped around her like a military-grade bubble of awesome, keeping all of the worries at bay. She was sure that once she left Planet Dax, she would admit that he owned her heart too. That somewhere between no strings and sharing secrets Emerson had fallen.

And she'd fallen hard.

She may have even started down that slope in San Francisco, which would explain a lot of her recent behaviors. Seeing him that first night at the VFW hall, she had felt giddy, reckless, scared. All ginormous signs that she should have run. But she'd also felt a sparkle of hope that maybe she could have something of her own, something that was all hers, and it had made her brave enough to go after her dreams and enter Street Eats.

Not content to settle for crumbs any longer.

Only now that wasn't all she wanted. Which was a mistake on her part, because he was leaving, and just the thought of starting over again, trying to figure out her life with one more person missing, brought on the flutters.

Not the good kind, but that destined-for-a-meltdown variety she hoped to never feel again. Needing some air to gather herself, she carefully untangled herself from Dax. Only his arms tightened around her and his eyes slid open.

"Hey," he said, his voice gravelly with sleep. "Where are you going?"

To hide. "To make some breakfast."

"What I want isn't in the kitchen," he said, his hands kneading her butt. "It's right here."

"But I have to get ready for work."

He looked over his shoulder at the clock, then plopped his head back down and wrapped his arms around her in a way that was slightly possessive. "Not for another hour." He gave her a gentle kiss on the lips, then closed his eyes, cuddling into her like she was his lifeline.

And that was when the panic set in. As far as she knew his plans were still the same. But then there were moments like this, confusing, wonderful, magical moments, when he held her as if he was promising to never let go. Which gave her hope.

False hope or real, she wasn't sure. And she was too scared to ask.

"What's wrong?" he asked quietly, his hand stroking down her spine and back up.

"Why do you think something's wrong?"

He chuckled. "Because I can practically feel your stress pressing into me."

She wanted to point out that it was her flapping, because she was a big fat chicken. "Nothing's wrong."

He scooted up to lean against the headboard, then positioned her so she was lying on his chest, her face tilted up to meet his gaze. "Now tell me what's wrong."

She opened her mouth and he tucked a strand of hair behind her ear. "Before you tell that lie on your tongue, remember the thing you do with your eyes. Dead giveaway." So she closed them and dropped her head. "Emi?"

She took a deep breath and looked up past his flat stomach, his rippling abs, and impressive pecs, into those deep blue eyes that melted her heart. "Last night was"—*amazing, life altering, epically intense*—"nice and I just don't want it to end."

His expression softened and he said, "It doesn't have to. Just decide to stay."

She opened her mouth to ask him the same thing, but all she heard in her head was a loud, patronizing *cluck, cluck.* So Emerson did something she hadn't done in years—she snuggled into his arms and closed her eyes.

And wished with all the fairy dust in the world that he would stay, right here, with her. For always.

ch🧑‍🍳pter
fifteen

Bothe State Park was over 1,900 acres of untouched nature at its finest, located a few short miles north of St. Helena in the foothills of the Napa Valley. With its year-round hiking, spring-filled pools, and wide variety of indigenous trees and plants, it was the perfect place for the annual Lady Bug Loveliest Survivalist Campout. It was also the place that St. Helena Lady Bug Lovelies 662 was going to win its first Loveliest Survivalist trophy.

Emerson had packed everything they'd need—and a few extra things, like a batch of unsanctioned brownies and cupcakes, just in case their X-tremely Edible plans didn't work out so well. Dax spent some time before their Lady Bug meeting on Thursday helping Violet perfect her bass trap. He could have just made it for her—it would have been easier.

But Dax didn't do easy. He did things right. So he stood by patiently while Violet explained to the girls how to make the exterior, not even interrupting when Violet made every mistake possible with the trap, and a few that seemed impossible.

Then it was his turn to show them how to make the funnel. The girls giggled when he said a weave was kind of like a braid, made a big deal out of the fact that he carried a knife in his pocket, and made gagging noises when he said they had to clean the fish. He never raised his voice or lost his cool but took the time to encourage and instruct in a way that boosted all of the girls' confidence. Not to mention made Emerson's heart a few sizes bigger.

"Do you have your tarp?" the regional queen bug asked, a sash of badges and ribbons twinkling in the afternoon sun as she searched through Lovely 662's survival pack.

"It should be in there," Emerson said, helping search the pack. But it was nowhere to be found. "Violet, did you take out the tarp?"

Emerson looked down at her group of girls, with their wrinkled sashes and mismatched boots, staring in awe as a Loveliness from Sacramento marched by in slick-looking mountain climbing boots and matching ponytails—all twenty-seven of them.

"Violet?" she prompted and when her sister turned to look at her she felt her heart sink. Making shelter in the community park at home had not prepared them to take on teams that looked like they built log cabins for fun. "Did you take the tarp?"

"No, Lovely Leader Emerson," she said, her eyes back on the Sacramento Lovelies.

"Oh dear," Queen Bug said, all fret and worry.

"If you forgot your tarp, our Lovely is selling regulation-sized ones by our tent," Liza Miner said, coming up to the table with her entitled smile and starched Calistoga Lovelies 983 uniform. "You can't miss it. It's the tent with the nine-time Loveliest Survivalist Champion flag above it. Just tell them I sent you and they'll give you a deal."

"Yeah, thanks, we're good," Emerson said, tipping the bill of her nonregulation camo-colored ball cap that said #LOVELIEST-LOVELINESS.

"Are you sure?" Queen Bug asked, her eyes firmly on her clipboard. "Because we are all out. Not a single tarp left."

"Can't compete without a tarp," Liza said sweetly, then leaned in. "Or is this your way of saving your girls from embarrassment?"

This time all of her girls looked over—and they looked defeated before they'd even been given the chance to compete. It was Kenzie who spoke. "Are we disqualified?"

"No way," a sexy and confident voice said from behind them. "We're just getting started."

The girls cheered and raced over to their co-leader, who was walking up the trail looking like he belonged on the cover of *Hot Survivalist* magazine with his ruck, two tents strapped to his back, a cooler filled with stuff heavy enough to make those arms flex, and a bright blue tarp.

Emerson felt like kissing him square on the mouth—except that would break the *no PDA by unmarried Lovely leaders on Bug Time* rule. And it would send inquisitive Violet into a tailspin of unanswerable questions. So when he got to the registration table, she took the tarp and gave him her biggest smile. "Thank you."

His lips curled up into a slow smile. "Later you can sneak into the boys' tent and thank me properly."

Her knees went weak, but she covered it well.

"You're a Lovely leader?" Liza asked, no doubt taking in his 250 pounds of spec-ops badass. Dax didn't have to wear his uniform for people to get that he was highly skilled, specially trained, and extremely lethal. And his matching #LOVELIESTLOVELINESS cap said he was Emerson's.

At least for the weekend.

"Co-leader, and yes, ma'am. St. Helena Lady Bug Lovelies Six-Six-Two," he said as if he were giving his rank and file. "Right, troop?"

"Right," the girls screamed. Liza blanched. Emerson chuckled.

There were survivalists and there were Survivalists.

Then there were men like Dax. And no matter what happened this weekend, she knew that he would make sure those girls had fun, walked away with their heads held high and smiles on their little faces.

"Now, if you'll sign us in, I will go supervise while the girls set up camp." He gave Emerson a wink that had her knees going weak, then he whispered, "I'll make sure the boys' tent goes up first."

Emerson watched as he headed down the trail toward their campsite, a gaggle of little girls on his tail. Kenzie was telling him the proper procedure for constructing a tent, Megan was showing him her anti–poison oak gloves, which were nothing more than glorified dish mitts, Lana silently carried a tent pole, and Violet was content to skip next to Dax.

Something Emerson could relate to.

"Cut the crap, short fry."

Dax caught Violet by the back of her wings as she snuck out of the girls' tent. The kid had gone all week without those things and suddenly, right after the competition was finished and the team was awaiting the judges' decision, she'd cut out and disappeared into the woods.

Only instead of reemerging with her bass trap, she transformed herself into Tinkerbell, complete with wings, bows in her hair, and a handful of glitter. Yet *she* was scandalized, looking at him as though he were the one staring down two to five days of Emerson-enforced hard time.

"It's Pixie Girl," she informed him primly.

"You're AWOL, kid. You broke rule number nine, always stay with the group."

"That's rule number seven," she corrected.

"Whatever, you disappeared and left your team standing to face the judges alone. Not cool," he said in his scariest team-leader tone.

"Well, you said a bad word." She pinched a finger full of glitter and tossed it at him. "Bad word begone."

Eyes on the culprit, Dax brushed the glitter bomb off his pants. "I've got an idea. How about you do one of those chants with the glitter and transport yourself back to the competition so you can hand in that trap?" She didn't move. "Better yet, transport your sister over here so you can tell her I said 'crap' and I can tell her that you are full of it. How does that sound?"

"I don't want to make Sissy mad," Violet said to the dirt on the ground. "And I don't want to let my Bugs down or be full of that bad word."

Resisting the urge to explain that although it was technically a four-letter word, as far as offenses went, it ranked as a pathetic one on the foul chart, he pointed to her wings. "Then why are you skipping out on everything you worked so hard for to put on that getup?"

"Because I'm a fairy!"

Glitter hit him in the chest this time. Dax ignored it. Instead, he kept his laser-lock glare on the little fibber in front of him, whose poker face was almost as pathetic as her sister's. "Try again." She reached for the glitter. "Without the flashbang of sparkles."

Violet dropped her hand and sighed. Big and weighted, and Dax knew he was finally getting somewhere. The kid wanted to tell someone her secret. It had probably grown so big in her little head that she felt as if she were going to explode with admissions.

Worrying her lip, she glanced around and leaned in at the waist with a cupped hand over her mouth. "My dad's here. He watched me and my team. And I think we're going to win."

"I think you're going to win too."

His girls had decimated the other teams. Fastest fire, most creative and effective shelter, and, more importantly, they'd stayed calm and worked smart. And as a team. Until Violet disappeared.

"But even if you don't, you should be up there with your team, facing the music together. Not down here playing dress-up," he said, then realized his hands were on his hips like he was some kind of helicopter parent. He dropped his arms. "What does your dad have to do with this whole I've Got Wings game you're playing?"

Dax knew all about playing the part—he'd done it a hundred times before. Hell, his entire life was about putting on a game face, even if he wasn't sure of the outcome. When things got squirrely, his men would look to him for leadership and direction—and even the slight hint of doubt could cost lives. So yeah, he knew all about playing the part.

"He still believes," she said, barely above a whisper.

This time it was Dax who exhaled. Because everything suddenly clicked. The wings, the ridiculous name, the fairy trap she made with Roger. "Are you dressing up because your dad thinks you're a fairy?"

Her shoulders sank and a cool breeze blew past, catching the ends of her wings and giving the illusion that they were flapping. "I don't want to make him sad, like when I found out Santa was really Emerson." There were so many sad things about what she'd just said, Dax had a hard time swallowing. Santa wasn't Dad, it was Emerson. "So I have to be Pixie Girl when we win, so he'll still believe. He smiles when I'm Pixie Girl."

"Have you ever thought that maybe he smiles because he loves you, Violet? Or that he's pretending too because he thinks it will make *you* smile?"

Her big green eyes went wide and she shook her head.

Dax crouched down low and put a hand on her slim shoulder. "You don't need to pretend to be something you're not to make your dad happy. You make him smile just the way you are."

"You sure?" she asked and he was pretty sure he heard a sniffle.

"That's an affirmative," he said and before he knew what happened, little arms were wrapped around his neck and pink glittery wings were jabbing him in the ribs, but he didn't care. Violet might not be a fairy, but her hugs were pretty magical.

"Now, get running, because according to Bug Time, you've got less than five minutes before the judges come around, and that bass trap of yours will lock down this competition."

She gave him a big smile and a salute, then took off.

"Hold up." He grabbed her by the wings again before she got too far. "I'll take these."

"Thanks, Lovely Co-leader Mister." She shrugged out of them, reached into her pocket, and came out with a handful of glitter. "Can you hold this too?" she asked but didn't wait for an answer, dropping the glitter on—and inside of—his boots, then racing up the hill.

"Thanks, Lovely Co-leader Mister," a sexy and amused voice said from behind him.

Dax turned around and his breath caught in his lungs. Emerson stood in the shadows of an oak tree behind the girls' tent. Dressed in a uniform of khakis, starched white shirt, and a red sweater vest, she should have looked like a soccer mom but managed to look sexy as hell. She also looked a little vulnerable at that moment, her expression a potent combination of awe, admiration, and adoration.

The first two he knew what to do with. Had received those looks a lot. They came with his rank and Ranger tab. The last one, though, he didn't see that often with regard to him. And never from someone as amazing as Emerson.

"I thought you were with the girls."

"I was." She stepped out from the shadow. "But then Liza Miner saw our shelter, which is beyond impressive, and started googling how we did it. When she realized that we didn't cheat, she started yelling instructions to her Lovelies to add pine needles for bedding.

The Sacramento leader called foul, took Liza's phone, and dropped it in the fire." She grinned. "Our fire, because it's the biggest, and the situation went bad fast, so Queen Bug banished anyone over ten wearing a Lady Bug patch until the winner is announced." She looked at her watch. "Which should be in a few minutes."

"How long have you been standing there?" he asked.

She walked over to him, not stopping until her arms were wrapped around his middle and her head pressed against his chest. "Long enough to know you make me smile just the way you are too."

As Dax drew Emerson in close, he decided that he'd do just about anything to make her smile. When he'd first agreed to be a Lovely co-leader, he'd done it to get into Emerson's pants. Now, after a few weeks of working with the girls and his co-leader, he decided he'd rather be right here, with her. Standing beneath a canopy of oaks and pines, miles from town, her looking up at him as if she liked what she saw.

Not that he didn't want to see if she went camo or commando under those PTA pants, but he was also interested in seeing more of what lay beneath that Kevlar exterior.

"Are you admitting that you like me, Emi?" he asked.

She pulled back and gifted him the most amazing smile. "Ask me after we win."

A faint chanting in the distance caught his attention. He looked past Emerson's shoulder at the trail ahead. "Looks like you're going to have to answer that question sooner than you thought."

Emerson turned around right as a cluster of three-foot-talls tore down the trail toward them. Violet was leading the pack, a big red Loveliest Survivalist flag flapping as she ran.

"Loveliest Loveliness! Six-Six-Two!" they chanted.

"We won?" Emerson asked, bouncing up on her toes. And the sheer amount of joy radiating off her was enough to bring a man to his knees.

"Looks that way."

"Oh my God. We won." She kissed his cheek, then spun around and started jumping up and down, chanting along, "Loveliest Loveliness! Six-Six-Two!"

Dax took a step back as the chanting and flag got closer, knowing that they would want to wave it all the way to the campsite. But instead, they bypassed their tents and kept going—straight at him.

Four sets of ear-piercing giggles and sparkly boots surrounded him, and before he could brace himself, they were all jumping up and down, their dainty arms latching on to him in a group hug that was pretty incredible.

And Dax felt like he'd won too.

Dax's heart pounded hard exactly once.

Coming completely alert, he forced his heart rate to slow, kept his eyes closed and his body stock-still so he could hear everything. Process the threat.

The night air, thick with the scent of damp soil and fresh pine, stirred the trees outside his tent. But something was stirring the air inside. *More like someone*, he thought, relaxing his body, as he caught the aroma of milk chocolate and sneaky woman.

Releasing a calming breath, Dax cracked open one eye to see Emerson waving a hand in front of his face. She was wearing a giant Bed Bug T-shirt that hung to her knees, her mascara was slightly smudged, and her hair was a disaster, falling down her back in bed-rumpled corkscrews.

"Are you awake?" she whispered.

He was now. That was the thing with Rangers, they were trained to grab sleep when they could. Dax could reach REM mode in seconds, and be in full combat mode even quicker.

Not giving her time to process, he moved fast, hooking an arm around her waist and, before she could release the scream he felt building, he pulled her down, rolling her under his body. She was curvy and soft and all things warm woman. "You tell me."

She blinked up at him. "Jesus, Dax. You scared the crap out of me."

"*Crap* is a bad word," he said, then ran a hand down her leg to find nothing but body-hugging leggings. "And this is the boys' tent."

She slid her fingers into his hair. "I know."

"Girlie parts in the boys' tent." He nuzzled her throat, pressing little kisses to her exposed skin and making her gasp. "My twelve-year-old self would be jealous."

"You seem so surprised," she said, wrapping those elegant hands behind his neck and skimming them under his shirt. "You invited me to the boys' tent to give you a proper thank-you. Remember?"

"Oh, I remember." He kissed her neck, her breathing going erratic when he reached the little hollow area in the curve she loved. "Full disclosure. I invited you to the boys' tent to get you in my sleeping bag."

"I know," she said, all kinds of sexy lacing her words.

He lifted his head. "Why, Emerson Blake, are you breaking one of those rules you're so fond of?"

"You like it when I break the rules." She wrapped those lush legs around his, turning him inside out—and breaking more than a few Lady Bug official chaperone rules. "The question is, what rule do you want to break tonight?"

All of the erotic possibilities that came to mind set him on fire: two lone survivors stranded in the wild with only their body heat to keep them warm. No, sexy bombshell from the neighboring campsite jumps into his tent, naked and terrified of passing bears. Or, better yet, Lady Bug Lovely leader is so hot for her co-leader she sneaks into his tent to seduce him under the stars.

"Why are you smiling?"

How could he not, with her looking at him like that? All warm and open, her edges softer than usual. Happier too.

"Just thinking."

She snuggled closer. "About?"

"You."

Then he kissed her. Slow and steady, taking his time to explore every inch of her mouth, to coax out those breathy little moans that he'd become addicted to. He wasn't in a hurry—not tonight. Not with her holding on to him as though she was content to stay right there, in his arms, and do just this until the sun came up.

"You taste amazing," he said.

"I taste like brownie contraband," she admitted. "I brought a bag with me but lost them in the scuffle. I'm pretty sure they're all mushed by now."

"Let me see," he said as if that was the excuse he needed to get his hands on her. The truth was he'd been waiting to get his hands on her since that hug in the forest. Hell, since San Francisco. It was all he could think about at times. But tonight, surrounded by a bunch of girls, he'd have to settle for an old-fashioned make-out session—pj's required.

That didn't mean he couldn't feel his fill, which he did, making her giggle, then slid his hands down her bottom. When he could see her eyes heavy with need, he said, "Can't find them."

With one hand in her hair, the other on her delectable ass, he slanted his head and covered her mouth completely. She turned up the heat and everything seemed to shift to perfect, so damn perfect and right, he wanted more. More of this. More time. More Emerson.

So much more that he heard warning sirens blaring for him to slow down. Take a step back and assess the situation like a trained soldier should. Unfortunately, the only situation that mattered right then was what was going on beneath the T-shirt, and it seemed that road was dead ahead.

Silencing those sirens, he slid his hands down to the bottom of the worn cotton shirt and gripped the hem. His fingers dipped beneath to play with the strip of silky skin above her waistband.

"They're not under there," she whispered but lifted her hands above her head in surrender and gave a wicked smile.

"Then I guess I'll just have you for dessert." He tugged the hem past her belly button and pressed a kiss there. Her flat stomach rippled under his touch, the moonlight reflecting off of her very bare, very silky skin. "Much better than brownies."

"Did he say *brownies*?" a tiny voice whispered.

Dax froze. His lips a scant inch from heaven.

"I like brownies." Hushed agreements, and a few not-so-hushed agreements, followed. "Especially ones that don't got nuts."

Emerson smothered a laugh and Dax closed his eyes. Outside a flashlight clicked on, illuminating four shadows on the other side of the tent flap. They were small, with braided hair, and carrying stuffed animals of some kind—and pillows.

"Are you freaking kidding me?" he whispered.

Or at least he thought he whispered.

"That's a bad word, Lovely Co-leader Mister."

Lovely Co-leader Mister dropped his head to his Lovely co-leader's stomach and closed his eyes and wished for them to go away. Her hands came up to thread through his hair, gently running her nails down his neck, and Dax had a hard time focusing. "They won't leave now that they know you're awake."

On cue, there was a loud tap at the tent as though they were being polite and checking to see if it was okay to disturb the family of the house. "Can we come in?"

With a small tear for all that was lost, Dax lifted his head and said good-bye to dessert, then sadly lowered the shirt.

"Lovely Co-leader Mist—"

"Yup," he said, sitting up. "Come on in."

A flurry of whispers echoed off the hills behind them and the tent flap opened. Four heads peeked in. Flashlight beams went in every direction, forcing Dax to squint against the blinding glare. A short scuffle, a few giggles, and lots of slippers on sleeping bags later, they were all sitting crisscross applesauce in his tent.

Even Emerson, who was looking way too amused for his liking.

He ran a hand down his face and sighed. He heard a small gasp, located Freckles, who was sitting right next to him, and forced a grin. And damn if the girl didn't grin back. Bright white teeth cutting though the dark quarters.

"Why are you in here, Lovely Co-leader Emerson?" Shirley Temple asked, and Dax raised a brow. *Yeah, explain that one, Lovely.*

"She was talking to him about going in the castle," Violet said and, *huh*, Dax had never heard it called *that* before.

"Yup, I sure was," Emerson said, sending him a reprimanding glance when he chuckled.

"So are you going to take us?" Glasses asked. She was vibrating with so much excitement she looked like one of those jumping beans. "Are you going to take us to see the castle?"

"If I say yes, will you all go back to bed?" So that he could get back to Emerson's castle.

After several head movements that he took to mean affirmative, he agreed. Only the girls didn't leave. In fact, they all scooted closer, grabbed hands, and started squealing.

"Shhh," Emerson said, placing a finger to her lips, but she was smiling too. "We're supposed to be asleep." Then she looked at Dax. "Are you serious, you want to go?"

Okay, obviously this was another example of just how little he understood women. Even Freckles was on the same page and the kid didn't speak. "Go where?"

"Disneyland, silly," Violet said.

Emerson rested a hand on his knee, but it didn't help his heart—which was racing so hard he thought he was going to pass out. "Disneyland?"

With four kiddos, a flag, and built-in troop mom?

"Since our team won the Loveliest Survivalist we get to represent our region at the state level. This year it's at Big Bear, which is only a few hours from Disneyland," Emerson explained, and the excitement in her eyes had something pinching tight in his chest. "I told the girls I'd look into maybe staying an extra day or two and taking them to Disneyland. We'd love it if you could make it."

All this talk of *we* and *our* had his head pounding and his chest itching.

Dax twisted his neck to the side to relieve the growing pressure. It didn't help. Neither did the anticipation and expectation staring up at him. He looked at Emerson, and it only made it worse. "When is it?"

"Next month."

Next month he'd be in San Jose, playing hired gun to some bank account in a suit. And Emerson would be here, with her family, in St. Helena, moving on with her life and making a go at her new career. That was the deal. Because once he went back to work, he wasn't sure how to keep up this life.

No matter which way he looked at it, or how many different scenarios he ran through his head, their two directives didn't align.

And that was the core issue. He didn't want to be Ranger Dax anymore, but he didn't seem to know how to stop. Or understand who he was and what he offered without his rank and Ranger tab.

Except for when he was with Emerson. His gaze met her warm one and he took a breath. A deep breath, because with her none of that seemed to matter. He could just be whatever he needed to be in that moment. No strategies or hard decisions or thoughts about the future.

Until now. Now there was Disneyland, with *we* and *our* and a readymade family—as if an extension had suddenly been applied to their expiration date.

Actually, that wasn't true. Dax had been extending their expiration date since day one. In fact, at times, when he allowed himself, in the quiet moments when they were together, he could almost see a future. Maybe even a home base.

It was small, like looking at it through the scope, but it was there, which made zero sense.

Dax knew everything about life on a base and jack shit about building a home. He'd made a career out of jumping from one theater of operations to another, always playing the role of team leader.

Problem was, Emerson was looking for a partner. And he was leaving.

chapter
sixteen

Monday morning Emerson dropped Violet off at school, then ran by the market to grab some turkey bacon and eggs. She was going to teach Dax how to make a healthy breakfast burrito.

She wanted to thank him for an incredible and successful weekend, and what guy didn't love bacon. He didn't need to know it was fake-n-bacon. And if he figured it out, she was hoping to distract him with her cupcakes—which were frosted with a new flag-inspired bra from the Boulder Holder.

Parking her car, she grabbed the bag off the passenger seat and stepped out into the pouring rain. Another storm had blown in, bringing with it two inches of water and the fresh smell of wet grass and winter.

Grinning, something that she hadn't been able to stop since she'd dropped him off at his house yesterday, after a weekend to end all weekends, she knocked on Dax's door. It was funny that the best weekend she'd had in years took place with a bunch of Bugs and the town's bad boy. Only Dax wasn't bad and he sure wasn't a boy. He was strong and gentle, reliable without being smothering, and so incredibly perfect.

For her.

And she was perfect for him. He hadn't said as much, but she could feel it in the way he held her, watched her when he thought she wasn't looking, and how he came through. In every single way.

Her heart warmed at the memory of him and the girls in the tent. How he listened patiently as each one told him what ride she wanted to go on first, what princess she wanted a picture with, and how, with him on their team, they could be the best survivalists in the whole state.

Rain splattered her shoes and the outside of the paper bag, so she knocked again. When no one answered, she let herself inside. After putting the groceries in the fridge, she headed toward the back of the house where she found Dax—bent over the bed looking sexy and delicious in nothing but a low-slung towel.

"I should have set my alarm earlier," she said, stepping farther into the room. "Looks like I'm two minutes too late to wash your back." She let her fingers glide up his back, to rub his shoulder. He felt tense, so she peeked around him and her hands froze. So did her heart.

His bed was covered with clothes, all of his clothes. Clean and folded into perfect squares, and being placed into a duffel bag that sat in front of him.

He was leaving.

"Or maybe I got here two minutes too early," she joked, but something inside of her went cold.

"I talked to Fallon last night," he said to the suitcase, not even turning to look at her. "I can finish up PT in San Jose while I get brought up to speed on my new job."

Emerson's heart slowed down until everything felt painfully surreal. "That's great," she managed to get out, but found herself looking to the right. She dropped her hands and took a step back. "Did, uh, Kyle give you the okay?"

"Yup."

One word, cut-and-dry, and that grin of hers didn't just fade. It died. And she had no idea what was up with her stomach and her chest and all that pinching. "Did you call Fallon or did he call you?"

Dax stopped packing and turned to finally face her. "He called me."

"Oh." Emerson let loose the breath that she'd been holding, felt some of the pressure release at his answer.

"They wanted to see if I was open to starting early." He looked at her and his face went carefully blank. "I told them I could start tomorrow."

"Tomorrow?" The pressure was back and she was certain it would kill her, because this wasn't a requirement of the job. It was a voluntary enlistment. "But what about helping Jonah next weekend with the weapons training? What about Street Eats? And the other night . . ."

You asked me to stay.

"The other night was amazing," he said gently, taking her hand. "All of it has been. And I won't leave you hanging, I made a promise to help and I always live up to my promises. So I'll just drive back for the day."

Not the words she'd been hoping to hear. In fact, it was the opposite of what she needed right then. Emerson knew what it felt like to do something out of duty and obligation, and she didn't want to be that kind of burden. Not for Dax.

She wanted to be the one who made him laugh and feel good. Lighter. Freer. Special. Because that was what he'd done for her.

"Was it just sex?" she asked, remembering that the key to survival was to stay calm. "For you, was it just amazing sex?"

"No, Emi, it wasn't."

"But," she said, knowing that there was an exception to his statement. A condition to his feelings. "It wasn't enough to stick around, right?"

Dax blew out a breath and looked at the ceiling. "You knew I was going to leave, knew that it would come to an end. You were the one who said no ties."

"I know," she whispered, feeling like an idiot with all those *you*s being thrown at her. "I did, but something changed."

Everything had changed. Emerson had started thinking past the job, past the distance, past the problems, and toward the future. With him.

And she'd thought that maybe he'd been thinking the same. That regardless of what he decided, what job he took, they could make it work. Or at least give it a real chance. It was only two hours to San Jose and his family lived here and—*Oh. My. God.*

No.

No no no no no!

Emerson covered her face. She was stupid, and a fool, and so incredibly and completely in love it hurt.

"Are you crying?" Dax said, tipping her face up. There was so much guilt and sheer terror over the fact that he'd made the tough girl cry that she willed her tears back and dropped her hands.

"I'm not a crier, Dax," she argued through the tears.

"Then why do you have water—"

He paused, his face going pale. He knew. Of course he knew. Dax could uncover a single terrorist hiding inside of a mountain in the middle of the desert by sticking a fork in the air. Here she was, the worst poker player in history, her eyes darting right, right, right to the truth. And he knew.

"I never wanted to make things harder on you," he said gently, brushing away a stray drop of rainwater from her cheek with his thumb.

"Then don't," Emerson argued. "Don't look at me like you're going to pack up, give me a peck on the cheek, and then never think about this again. Because I won't ever stop thinking what if, and I don't think you will either."

"This was supposed to be simple," he whispered with so much terrifying finality, her stomach sank. She had one last shot to get him to listen, to get him to hear her, gather all the facts before he made his decision.

"Love is never simple, Dax," she said, confident in that truth.

He stood there staring at her as if she'd handed him a death sentence. A small sob rose in her chest because saying that word aloud, finally admitting the truth for what it was, she felt as if she was giving them a new chance at a real life.

"And since we're two of the most complicated and stubborn people I know, I imagine it will be crazier for us to get it right. But I am willing to try, willing to put my heart out there and see if you're man enough to pick it up. And I hope to God you are, because I might not know how to date or handle no-strings affairs, but I know how to love. I have been doing it my whole life, and it is terrifying and intense, but it can also be safe and freeing if you allow it to be." She took his hand in hers and looked up at him with all of the fear and nerves and love she had to give. "I don't want the crumbs with you, Dax, I want the entire tray."

"Emi." He opened his mouth to say more, then he hesitated. It was subtle, but she saw it, felt it ricochet around her soul.

Shaken, she dropped her hands and stepped way back. "Oh God. This is the condition." She was so familiar with conditions she should have seen it the second she walked into his room and spotted the duffel bag. "This is where you say, 'hey, I showed you a fun time, helped you out, and now can you be a champ and pull it together and go back to your regularly scheduled life?'"

"It wasn't like that," he said but she knew he was lying. "I don't want to go back to how things were, but my life is in San Jose and yours is here."

"Bullshit. Your life is here, Ranger." He winced at the mention of his title. "You have family, friends, a whole lot of people who love you. Right here. Why would you want to leave all that behind to start over somewhere else?"

He let out a mirthless laugh.

"You know what, I don't think you have a God complex, I think you're a chicken," she argued. "I don't even think you want that job, I think you're taking it because it's easy."

"Is it so bad that I want easy?"

Emerson stopped breathing. It was a direct hit. Nothing about her, or her life, was easy. She knew that, but there was nothing she could do to change it. "Sometimes the good things take a little extra work."

"I'm tired of hard, so damn tired of trying . . ." He raised a palm up but didn't finish, didn't tell her why he was willing to walk away. Then an absolute determination overtook his expression. Emerson saw Regular Old Dax disappear and the stoic soldier take his place. "I took the job. End of story. The longer we drag this out, the harder it will be in the end. For both of us."

If she thought she was in pain a second ago, it was nothing compared to the deep ache inside her chest, which burned so cold her body felt like it would shatter. One sob and she would break into a million pieces.

She knew how to embrace loss, even knew how to put the pieces back together. This time, though, there would be no way to repair her heart.

Reminding herself that the key to survival was to stay calm, Emerson straightened her shoulders, back to the carry-the-world place they'd been her whole life—only this time it felt heavier, as if she would crumple the second she walked through that front door.

"You're right," she said, proud that she was sticking with she wasn't a crier. "This entire thing has been one long drawn-out ending. I just had the ending wrong. Again."

"Emerson," he said but she didn't wait for him to finish.

She was tired of fighting for things she loved only to have them leave. For once she wanted someone to fight for her, to come to her side. To tell her she was worth the crazy.

But he wasn't going to say any of those things, so she turned and headed for the door.

The pressure built in her chest and she knew it was about to rain hard in her soul. So she clutched her hands over her heart to make sure it stayed in one piece until she made it home. In a daze, she slid into her car and went on autopilot until she found herself pulling into her parents' drive.

She raced through the pouring rain, up the lawn and to the front door, where she banged until it opened. Only instead of finding her mom on the other side waiting with baklava and a hug that could cure anything—except for ALS—she found her dad. Dressed in a Hawaiian shirt, shorts, and Birkenstocks.

"It's raining," she said, looking at his shoes.

"What's wrong?" Concern laced his face as he stepped onto the porch and into a puddle, which sloshed into his sandals. Emerson watched the water flow in but it never came out, instead being absorbed into the sole. "Fairy Bug?"

At the sound of her childhood nickname, Emerson looked up right as the first sob rolled through her chest and broke free. Followed closely by another, and by the time the third one racked her body she was in her dad's arms, pouring herself into him until they were both sitting on the wet brick.

"I need Mom," she begged, and Roger's face went into panic mode, as if trying to figure out how to gently remind his grown daughter that her mother was dead. She was gone and never coming back. "I need her so much right now and she's not here."

"I need her every second of every day," her dad whispered and Emerson held on tighter. "I thought it would get easier. I thought that maybe someday she would be simply a happy memory."

Emerson looked up to find that Roger was crying too. She'd never seen her dad cry. Not even at the funeral. "And?"

"And then something amazing happens with one of you girls, or a hummingbird lands on the feeder, and I remember that she's gone." He cupped her face. "But then I remember that you're here and she is such a huge part of you. I know I'm not your mom, and I know that you outgrew needing me a long time ago, or maybe I made it so that you couldn't count on me, but I'm here now."

"I've been dating this mule-headed, stubborn, God-he's-such-an-idiot man," she admitted.

Roger smiled. "Sounds like true love."

"It is, Dad," she said miserably, burying her face in his chest. "And I am pretty sure he loves me too, but he's a chicken and took a job as a beefcake and doesn't want a long drawn-out ending so he left."

"Sounds like a certifiable asshat to me," Roger said and Emerson laughed. She laughed so hard water started dripping from her eyes.

His hand stroked her hair, just like her mom used to. "Oh, sweetie, don't cry."

"I'm not a crier," she sobbed into his Hawaiian shirt.

"I know." He delivered comforting little pats to her back. "You're a tough girl, just like your mom."

She looked up through blurry eyes. "Mom cried all the time."

"Yet she was adamant that she wasn't a crier."

chapter
seventeen

A few days later, Emerson woke up to find she was not alone, but being watched.

She rubbed her eyes and remembered she was on the couch—at her dad's place. Her head throbbed, her lids were scratchy when she blinked, and that cold, empty feeling had settled in her bones. "What time is it?"

"Almost eight," Roger said.

Emerson shot up, shaking her head to clear the sleep-induced fog. "Eight?" She never slept in that late. Actually she hadn't slept at all since she'd heard that Dax had indeed left. He'd texted her to explain that he'd still come up for Street Eats and she'd texted him back one word.

Crumbs.

He'd texted back that he was sorry. And that had been that. And Emerson was working hard to move forward like he was obviously doing. But it didn't mean that she didn't feel the loss with every breath.

She threw the blanket back and sat up. "I have to get Violet ready for school."

"Violet's ready," her sister said, plopping down on the cushion next to her. She was in a light green dress, pigtails with coordinating bows, and cute white flats—which couldn't have taken a fairy tour of the yard this morning. She looked showered, school ready, and adorable.

"Did you get dressed by yourself?"

"Dad helped me pick out the dress and stuff," she said, swinging her legs. "But I showered myself. And washed my hair."

"I can tell." Her hair was crunchy from the residual shampoo.

"Violet and I had a long talk the other day and decided that girls who were old enough to go win ribbons and go to Disneyland were old enough to dress appropriately for school and use their real name." He handed Emerson a steaming mug of coffee. "Breakfast is on the table, toast and eggs, nothing fancy but it's edible. Violet, go grab your lunch so we can head out."

Violet kissed Emerson on the cheek, then hopped down, her flats slapping the wood floors as she ran.

Emerson looked at Roger, who was looking smart and business ready in his loafers, slacks, button-up shirt, and . . . Emerson rubbed her eyes. "What happened to your hair?"

"Mary at the Prune and Clip cleaned it up a bit and a lady at the winery said I look like George Clooney." He beamed and Emerson felt her chest squeeze.

"You look good, Dad," she said quietly.

"Ah, like George Clooney," he corrected, grabbing his laptop bag off the chair and car keys off the wall hook. "I get off early today so I can pick up Violet." Who was magically waiting by the front door—lunch and school bag in hand. "We'll be home early to help with the prep work. Oh, and the guy at the auto body shop called while you were asleep. The truck will be done this afternoon. I told him we'd pick it up by four, then I figured maybe the three of us could get some root beer floats on the way home."

Emerson's throat tightened at the memory of the last time they'd had floats. "That sounds fun, but you don't have to do all this."

Roger leaned down and kissed her on the forehead. "Yeah, kiddo, I do. And I want to. You've been taking care of us for so long, let us take care of you this time."

"But I'm . . ." She trailed off before she could say *fine*. It had been four days since Dax left and she was so far from fine she didn't even know what direction to move in. Other than one that led her to the backup tray of baklava her dad had helped her make last night.

"Fine. I know you are," he said, setting his bag on the floor. "But your mom always said that it was our job to make it magical." He sat next to her, his expression sad yet hopeful. "Let me make it magical for you, Fairy Bug."

"Okay," she said, resting her head on his shoulder, desperately wanting to be that same little girl who believed in magic and fairies and happily ever after. Her dad pulled her in tight and gave her the kind of hug that made her feel safe, loved, and gave her hope that maybe there was still some magic left out there for her.

"Love you, kiddo," he said, kissing the top of her head. "To the moon and back."

"And every star in between."

"You've got one shot. You can either sit there all day, staring a hole through that scope, knowing the target isn't going to get any clearer, and waiting for the sun to set. Which really makes things difficult." Dax looked at Gomer through the binoculars. The kid was twenty feet up, wedged into the side of a cliff, and contemplating if he had the shot. Same position he'd been in over an hour ago. "Or you can take the shot."

"Yes, sir," Gomer's voice came through the headset.

"Was that a 'yes, I'll take the shot, sir'? Or you're still thinking about it?"

"If he doesn't take the shot, I'll shoot him," Jonah said. He sat next to Dax in the bunker at the county shooting range, sipping on his coffee. The rest of the team had been tested and cleared, passing the long-range field exercise with ease.

All except Gomer, who was still on the ledge, waiting for the wind to blow his direction. Hitting an orange-sized target at five hundred yards was impressive, but Dax knew that Gomer had the chops. FNG issues aside, the kid had something—and Dax needed him to figure that out.

"And I only get one shot, sir?" Gomer asked.

Dax closed his eyes. "How many bullets were you given?"

"Two."

"Good, so if you were given two and missed the first shot, how many remain?"

"One shot," Gomer said.

"And now that we all know how to subtract, take the shot, and soon, or I am going to grab a beer and you'll have to walk home. Understood, Deputy?"

"Yes, sir."

Dax set the headset down and looked at Jonah, who was looking back all kinds of amused. "The kid just psyched himself out. He didn't think the first shot through, rushed it, then scrambled around to find a better angle and now he's hesitating."

Jonah leaned back in his chair. "Is that what you're doing? You rushed the first shot and now you're hesitating?"

"I already cleared the entire field." And he'd done it in record time. Six bullets, six targets, in under six seconds. Jonah's little army of deputies had practically pissed themselves.

"I was talking about why you're sitting here when Emerson is across town setting up for her cook-off."

"Street Eats," Dax corrected and, yeah, he knew what Jonah meant. He'd spent the entire week trying to forget about it, with no such luck. He was the one who'd blasted his way in, gotten her to open up, then he'd hurt her. Badly.

Emerson had finally allowed herself to lean on someone else, and he'd taken the support right out of her foundation. Because he'd hesitated. He'd seen the look in her eyes, heard the confidence in her voice when she'd said she loved him, and it was like he couldn't breathe through the admission.

It was so unexpected—*she* was so unexpected—and her words so completely terrifying that he froze.

"You going to call her? Tell her you want another shot?" Jonah asked.

"What's the point?" Dax asked, knowing he'd blow that one too. "You and I both know that my kind of job doesn't afford the lifestyle that she's looking for."

Jonah laughed at that, hard and long until Dax shot him a look that would have a smart man running. Jonah proved that wisdom didn't always come with age, because he choked on another few laughs, even patting his chest. "Sorry, you said *lifestyle* about a woman who wears Converse, offensive tank tops, and drives a food truck."

"I meant that she's got plans, knows what she wants, and trust me, it's not me." Dax shook his head. "Plus, she's already got a hundred people weighing her down."

Jonah studied him, seeing way too much. After a minute, he shook his head slowly, releasing a low whistle while he did it. "Oh man, this is even worse than I thought," Jonah said, sitting back. "You told your woman, the one who loves you, what she needs and what she wants? Rookie move, bro."

"She's not my woman," he mumbled. "And how do you know she loves me?"

Because she might have told him that in a heated and emotional moment, but Dax hadn't told anyone else. No matter how emotional he'd been after. He hadn't had the time—or the heart.

Emerson loved him, and Dax didn't have a clue what to do with that information—how to process it in a way that would fit into his plan. He'd done the plan A thing, was on to plan B, and even if he managed to come up with a plan C, D, or Z, he didn't know how to reconcile that reality with the role he'd been playing the past few weeks.

So he froze. Watched her walk out of his house and did absolutely nothing to stop her, then jumped on his bike and headed off toward his new life. Only he got there and it didn't feel much like a life at all. His apartment was bare, his new team, although nice enough guys, felt like cardboard fill-ins, and his bed felt empty. And his chest—

He didn't even want to go there.

"According to Shay, who got the entire story," Jonah said, enjoying himself, "Emerson wanted to be your woman, only when she told you, you ran away like a little girl."

Dax's head throbbed at the idea of Emerson talking to her friends. So did his heart. Not that he was concerned if they thought he was an ass, since it would be an accurate assessment, but that the most private woman he knew was hurt badly enough to have to go to them.

And he'd done that to her.

"I didn't run," he said. He'd driven his motorcycle like a grown-ass man. "I went to start my new job."

Jonah snorted. "You don't want that job. Protecting a bunch of entitled suits? You'll be bored in three months."

"You think that sitting here watching Gomer stare at a freaking orange target all day will excite me?" Dax asked.

"No, but based on that sorry look you've been sporting all day, I think Emerson excites you. And you know that. Just like you know that she might be the one who saves you."

"All that in one look, huh?" he said drily. "Man, Sheriff, you've got talent."

"Oh, it's not just any look. It's the look guys like us get when an incredible woman says she loves you. The look that says your biggest fear is you're not loveable. Or worse, maybe you are but you know deep down that you don't deserve it. How could you, after everything that happened?" Dax could see the familiar pain in his brother's eyes. "I get it. Trust me."

Dax did. Jonah too knew what it felt like to carry the weight of someone else's choices. A few years back he'd made a gut decision that ended up in the deaths of a couple of teenagers and a fellow officer. Jonah had come home, but the guilt was always right there with him.

Dax had doubted if his brother would ever get past it. But somehow he had. He'd found whatever answer the universe had to explain away something as messed up as two dead kids, and he'd found peace. Even more, his brother had found happiness. And love.

"You want to know the only difference between you and me, Dax?" Jonah asked. "I blew the first shot with Shay, and the second, but I decided that I would go back as many times as it took to get it right, because Shay was worth it. But you? Rather than take another shot, you ran, because running hurts less than her figuring out that you were right."

Dax sat back and rubbed his hand over his chest, trying to ease the itch that had been gnawing at him all week. It didn't help. Nothing he seemed to do helped. Not even running. That made it worse.

"But here's the thing with love," Jonah said. "That scenario could never happen."

"Why not?"

"Because in love, the man is never right," Jonah said. "Never. Let me repeat, in case you still don't get it. The man is never right, and even if he is right, he knows it's better to go to sleep with a sexy woman next to him than cuddle up with his ego on a cold couch. Egos don't wear lace. Remember that and everything else is easy."

Easy, Dax thought. Everything with Emerson was always easy and natural. Chaotic and crazy and unexpected—but easy. With her he felt like everything was all right, that he was all right.

He loved that she never judged or demanded. She'd accepted him, broken parts and all. And wasn't that the definition of love?

"Yeah, I know that look too," Jonah laughed. "Equally as scary but lacking in that heart-ripped-out-of-your-chest feeling that always made me want to puke."

"I still might puke." Dax stood and looked at his watch. Because she'd asked him if he trusted her and he'd said yes. And trust was a two-way deal, he knew that. Yet when she went for honesty he let doubt creep in.

He'd hesitated.

Because of the connection. He'd hesitated because he'd recognized that look—it was the same one he'd seen Jonah give Shay, his grandpa give his new wife, ChiChi, and he knew if he went for it and misjudged, it might kill him.

So he'd reassessed, tried to find a different avenue, an angle that wasn't there, and spent so much time weighing risk to motives that he missed what was standing right in front of him.

His golden opportunity.

Emerson had put herself out there, offered him a chance to be a part of her team, no guarantees but an honest-to-God chance at finding happiness, with her. And instead of fully engaging, he'd changed position before really giving it a shot.

He wanted that second shot. Needed it.

"Emerson is stubborn," he said to Jonah, who was just smiling.

"Almost as bad as I am. Hell, I'd only give me one shot. What if she does the same?"

"Did you cuff her in front of the mayor and throw her in jail?"

"What the—?" Dax narrowed his eyes. "No."

Jonah waved a carefree hand. "Eh, then you should be good. Buy her a kitten, though, just in case."

"A kitten?" Dax asked. "Are you screwing with me? I'm not buying her a kitten so you can get rid of one of the nine thousand in your house."

Jonah shrugged. "Your call, but I'd go with Patches. He's a Siamese-Bengal mix. Won't shut up but took on a coyote a few months back and won. He's missing a leg. A real badass. Sounds like Emerson's type."

A bullet blasting through metal cut through the air and Dax turned his head. Gomer had taken the shot, and it was all Dax could do not to run down there and look to see if he'd made it. "Tell me he hit orange."

Jonah picked up the binoculars and laughed. "Nope, went wide and hit my cruiser." Jonah looked at Dax over the lenses. "Poor FNG hesitated so long he talked himself right out of his second chance."

"You going to give him another shot?" Dax asked, not amused by the irony.

"Nope. You are."

Dax looked up and Jonah patted him on the back. "You can tell him Monday morning when you report to work—as his mentor. That way the kid sweats it out a little."

Dax hugged his brother. "I don't know what to say."

"Try 'Affirmative, awesome brother of mine. I will report to work first thing Monday morning, here is my hand, let's shake on it,'" Jonah said in his best Dax impersonation. Dax laughed and took his brother's hand.

An overwhelming sense of right went through that shake, because everything Dax had lost when he'd walked away from the army was standing right in front of him. He was already a part of the best brotherhood on the planet.

Dax pulled Jonah in for a one-armed bro-hug, followed by the more masculine proud-of-you smack to the back. "Missed you."

Jonah paused, and so did Dax. It was the first time he'd said those words to anyone in his family since enlisting.

"Missed you too. And I'm glad you're finally home," Jonah said thickly and Dax realized that he wasn't home. Not quite yet. But he was finally ready to start the journey. And he knew just who he wanted to take it with.

"Now go, before you have to bring Emerson a kitten *and* a Shetland pony."

chapter
eighteen

By the time Emerson set the last of the cupcakes on the tray, she had chocolate batter dried on the tip of her ponytail, orange-zest-stained nails, and enough ouzo frosting on her apron to pass for a drunken cupcake. She also had a heartache that burned as hot as the Sahara that made fully enjoying this moment hard.

"The toppings are prepped, the orange slices are candied and ready to go on the cupcakes, and the troops are waiting for orders." Roger pointed to the cluster of tyke-sized #GOGREEK hats sitting on the steps of the food truck with promotional shirts on. "Look, even their uniforms are ironed."

That wasn't all. Each girl had hand drawn a sign for the competition, proclaiming Pita Peddler the best streatery in wine country. They'd also handed out over two hundred fliers to tourists who had come out to taste some of the best eats in the country. Including several corporate scouts interested in finding new potential franchising opportunities.

And the crowd reflected their hard work. Peering out the window, Emerson could see the bright colored trucks lined up side by side, stretching all the way through the parking lot of the Napa

County Fairgrounds. Bold flags flapped in the wind as the crowd of foodies took in the quirky menus and vinyl-wrapped trucks boasting their mascots. Thousands of street food enthusiasts had turned out—and a good handful were swarming her truck, waiting for the window to open so that they could sample the menu she and Harper had labored over.

"Thanks, Dad," Emerson said, wondering how so much had changed in just a few short weeks. Her sister was happy, her dad was on to an exciting new chapter, and Emerson had opened the first truck in her soon-to-be Greek streatery fleet.

She'd also fallen in love, had her heart broken, and yet somehow she was surviving. It still hurt every time she breathed, and even thinking about Dax made her stomach knot, which happened every time she slowed down, but she was pushing forward, and her family was there to help her.

"What do you think Mom would say?" she asked, wondering if Dax was allowing his family to help him or if he'd decided to go it alone.

"I think she would say the nachos are ingenious, the baklava tastes just like your great-great-grandmother's, and that the lamb needs more salt." Roger wiped his hands off on his apron and pulled Emerson in for a hug. "She'd also say that you are an amazing chef and an amazing daughter. Then she'd wipe her eyes on her sleeve and blame it on the onions."

Emerson laughed and did a little wiping of her own. "Yeah, she would. And she'd be wrong on the lamb. It's seasoned perfectly."

Roger smiled but added a sprinkle of salt. "It looks like people are already starting to line up, and the girls did a great job handing out the fliers." Harper had the brilliant idea to make up coupons—a buy-an-entrée-and-get-a-cupcake-free campaign to bring in a crowd. And from the looks of things, it was working. "I'd say we've got less than ten minutes until opening."

"Okay, give me a minute." Emerson took a breath and forced her heart rate to slow. She wanted to be in the moment, experience how it felt when everything finally came into focus and things that had seemed so impossible just a few weeks ago were suddenly real.

This was her time and she didn't want to miss a second of it.

"I'm ready," she said.

Emerson opened her eyes and turned around, and everything slowed to a stop.

Dax stood in her truck, dressed in full camo fatigues, wraparound glasses, and his army cap. He looked big, bad, and combat ready. There was also a duffel bag at his feet that had her going lightheaded.

"The truck looks great," he said. "And the food smells amazing, even the green stuff."

"You came here to try my food?" she asked and a painful laugh escaped her lips. "Or is this some twisted *I am a man of my word* moment? Because I meant what I said, I've got this."

She didn't want his crumbs. She wanted it all: love, magic, all of him.

"I came here to give you this." His face was carefully blank, not giving a thing away as he handed her a one-page, handwritten letter.

She swallowed hard and took the paper. Her heart was hammering too fast for her to make sense of anything, so after a few lines she gave up. "What is it?"

"An application."

Her throat went tight. "But you already have a job."

"I quit that one," he said, removing his glasses, and when his piercing blues met hers, she stopped breathing altogether. "This is for a new job. One here."

"With Jonah?"

He shook his head. "With you."

Not sure how to take that, she lifted the paper again, but she was shaking so bad it was impossible to make out anything beyond a few words, like chopping and sous. She looked up. "You want to be my sous chef?"

"Today I do. And tomorrow, if you'll let me, I want to be your pillow. And the next day your first and last customer." He took her hand in his and trapped it against his heart. The beat was steady and sure. "The day after that I want to cook you dinner. It won't be perfect, but I'm willing to try. And that brings us to Thursday, which means I'd be your co-leader."

"And Friday," she asked, hating how her voice shook, her heart so heavy with hurt she was too afraid to hope. "What happens then? Because we did all of that, and it wasn't enough for you."

"Friday," he said, his voice so raw she had to look away. Gather her thoughts. But he wasn't having it, waiting until she was ready to look at him again. And when she couldn't, he lifted her chin until she was gazing into his eyes. "Friday, I want to be your fun. I want to take you for a ride down the coast, maybe pitch camp on some isolated beach, and spend the entire night telling you just how amazing you are. And just how sorry I am."

"Sorry doesn't take away the hurt," she said. "You hurt me, Dax."

"I know. I had everything I wanted right in front of me, but grabbing it meant staying *here*. In my hometown."

"We could have worked it out," she said, taking a step back, but he didn't let go of her hand. "I was scared too but I was willing to risk the ache for a shot at something amazing."

"Did you know I was the only person who came home on my plane who didn't have a family member waiting for them at the airport?" he asked quietly. "Not because they didn't want to, but because I didn't tell them I was coming."

His words were like an arrow to her already broken heart. Dax was surrounded by more love than one could imagine, yet he chose to stand alone. It was so incredibly sad—and terrifying.

"The truth is, I wasn't ready to come home," he said and she could hear the shame in his voice. "I didn't know how. Everything was exactly the same, except for me. No matter how hard I tried, I didn't seem to fit here anymore. But then I met you, and damn, Emi, you were so warm and real and the perfect distraction. In fact, your big heart and smart mouth had me so distracted I didn't even realize that you'd become my safe haven. You accepted me for who I was, at every moment, giving me the time I needed to figure things out. I just figured it out too late. And I hurt you, and for that I will forever be sorry."

As much as she wanted to say it was okay, that she was okay and wanted nothing more than to spend every day with him, she couldn't. She deserved someone who was willing to stay and fight. For love and for her.

"What did you figure out?" she asked.

"That I had already come home. I came home that first night in San Francisco." He cupped her face. "I was looking for a place to fit in, but I found you. With you I fit. With you I am whole. You're my home, Emi."

"My home is crazy and you need easy," she reminded him.

"I need you," he said and she almost believed him. "Emerson Blake, you are my kind of crazy. Please tell me I'm yours, because I love you."

"You let me walk away," she cried, everything inside of her breaking all over again. "My whole life I have clung to everyone I've loved, fought to spend every second with them. That's love, Dax. And I told you I loved you and you threw it away, then watched me leave."

"I did," he said. "And I can promise you that will never happen again. And you know how I am with promises." A little bead of hope bloomed at his sweet words, because even though he'd crushed her world, he'd always come through on his promises. Always. "Just give me one more chance to be the kind of partner you need."

NEED YOU FOR ALWAYS

Emerson felt the first tears well up at the intensity in his words and expression. "What would you do if I gave you another chance?"

"I don't have a ring," he said and, *sweet baby Jesus*, right there in the middle of the Pita Peddler Streatery, dressed like a hero for hire, Dax dropped to one knee. Emerson's heart dropped to the floor.

"Dax," she whispered, her hand covering her mouth. "What are you doing?"

"This is me going all-in," he said, looking up at her as if she was the only thing in his sights. "I don't know what the future holds, but I know that I love you. I love that you love the people in your world with complete abandon, and that you never back down. And I love that you hide green stuff in my eggs because it's good for me. And I love your tough side and your soft side, and I especially love your backside." She choked out a laugh. "I love you, Emi, and I'd love it if you'll let me be your foundation, your fun, and your family."

Dax looked deep into her eyes and all of the hurt and anger faded because she saw the truth in his eyes. The way he loved her was the same way she loved him.

Unconditionally.

"Knock knock, Emi," he said.

"Who's there?" She laughed but it came out more of a sob, as hope and something warm and safe filled her chest.

"Al."

"Al who?"

"I'll promise you always if you just give me the chance to win your heart."

"You already have my heart," Emerson said, tugging him to a stand. "You had it before I even knew it was gone."

"Thank Christ," he said, pulling her into his arms and wrapping her up in his love. "Because you already have my heart, and if I didn't have yours, things might get weird."

"You know how I hate weird," she whispered as he covered her mouth with his, his hands threading in her hair and holding her to him. And Emerson let herself be held, gave herself over, because when she closed her eyes she could feel the truth: all the avenues led straight to Dax. And if that wasn't proof that magic existed, then she didn't know what was.

acknowledgments

A deep and appreciative thank-you to all of the men and women who risk their lives and sacrifice time with their families to protect our freedoms.

As always, a special thanks to my editors, Maria Gomez and Lindsay Guzzardo, and the rest of the author team at Montlake for all of the amazing work and support throughout this series.

Finally, thank you to my fabulous agent, Jill Marsal, for always being in my corner. And to my daughter and my amazing husband, you guys are my world.

Read on for a sneak peek of Marina Adair's next
romance set in St. Helena

Need You for Mine

Available Spring 2016 on Amazon

Need You
for Mine

HEROES OF ST. HELENA SERIES

MARINA ADAIR

chapter
one

There wasn't a person on the planet who Harper Owens couldn't friend. The problem was, there wasn't a single man in wine country who hadn't already sentenced her to a lifetime in the friend zone.

Until now, she thought giddily, staring up at her Mr. Tall, Dark, and—*ohmigod*—Mine.

It had taken her eighteen long months of casual conversations, lots of lash batting, three new shades of lipstick, and finally a well-orchestrated flash of cleavage, but Harper was about to get her kiss.

From Clay Walker. Respected pediatrician, a Doctors Without Borders frequent flyer, and on top of being revered by every kid and parent in town, the guy Harper had been hot for since he moved to St. Helena with his son nearly two years ago.

"Thank you for walking me home," Harper said as they stopped in front of the yellow-and-white Victorian storefront on Main Street. She pointed to the upstairs window of her apartment. "Do you want to come up? I have some wine in the fridge."

Clay checked his watch. "I wish I could, but I promised the babysitter I'd get her home by ten," he said, and didn't that warm her heart.

He was such a good dad. Devoted, involved, loving, and—*holy cow*—was he looking at her boobs?

Was Dr. Dreamy checking out Harper Owens's cleavage?

She watched his eyes to see if they'd dart again, and they ended up doing a minidip—not enough to be called an ogle, but enough that she decided it was the bra, which took her from a moderate *B* to a sexy *C* in one shimmy.

St. Helena rolled up its welcome mats at dusk so there weren't many people out. Just Harper and Dr. Dreamy, alone on the lamp-lined sidewalk, the gentle spring breeze wrapping around them as they stood under the twinkling lights of her grandmother's shop—and the million or so stars overhead. So she shimmied again and—*bingo*.

He was sizing up the goods. Which meant this was a premeditated escort.

With the latest crime spree including senior citizens, barrel tipping, and indecent exposure in the community fountain—all related events—Clay hadn't offered to walk her home for her safety. He'd offered to walk her home so he could make his move.

And since her body hadn't been moved on in far too long, she was ready.

"There is something I've been meaning to ask you, but there was never a time when Tommy wasn't around, and I didn't feel comfortable calling you at work," Clay said, that deep voice rolling over her and lighting the anticipation that had been simmering since he'd pulled up the bar stool next to hers, offered to buy her a drink, then started asking all the *right* questions. "So when I saw you at Spigots tonight, I figured it was perfect timing."

"Perfect," she repeated, stepping closer and looking up into his deep brown eyes. It was perfect. The perfect place for their perfect first kiss. The perfect moment to take their relationship from *I teach your kid how to paint* to *I know how to make you pant* in a single brush of the lips.

NEED YOU FOR MINE

"I'm going to San Diego for a conference the second week of May and I'm scheduled to be the keynote speaker. It's a weekend conference, right on the beach."

"San Diego is beautiful in the spring," Harper said as if all of her knowledge about the coastal city hadn't come from the passenger seat of her mom's car when she was nine and headed toward Mexico for a month-long artist retreat on native beading.

"It is," he said. "And the conference is only one night, but I was wondering if you were free."

"The second weekend in May?" That was the worst possible time for Harper to get away. It was spring inventory prep at the Fashion Flower, the couture kids' boutique and art store she managed, and she was the only person who could handle the delivery. But a weekend away? With Clay? Naked? "I'm all yours."

"Really?" He put his hand on her shoulder and smiled.

At her.

It wasn't the same smile he gave her when picking Tommy up from class, or even the one he'd flashed when seeing her around town. This smile was different. He was looking at *her* different. As if she were special. As if she were—

"A lifesaver, Harper. That's what you are." Clay released a long, relieved breath. Funny, since she had stopped breathing altogether. "Tommy's mom can't take him that weekend, and his sitter is only fifteen, hence the reason I need to get her home by ten. I didn't know who else to ask and you are so good with him."

"You need me to babysit? Tommy?" She had to ask because she'd had a drink or two, and her brain wasn't functioning on all cylinders, but she was pretty sure he'd just demoted her from quirky-but-cute art teacher to backup babysitter. And her competition didn't have a driver's license.

"That would be great. He really adores you. You know?"

Oh, she knew. She knew this moment so well she wanted to cry.

It was just like senior prom when Daniel McCree passed her a note saying he wanted to ask a special girl. Only after Harper had mentally picked out her dress, shoes, and the perfect place to lose her virginity had he explained that the "special girl" was Janie Copeland—the captain of the dance team and Harper's neighbor.

Harper had delivered Daniel's invite on her way home, then received a record eleven more invites to the prom that year. None of them were addressed to her.

"Tommy would probably be more comfortable at my place. You can sleep in my bed, if that works for you," Clay offered, and Harper had to bite her lip to not laugh at the irony. He looked at his watch again. "I'm late. Can we work out all the details later? Kendal's mom flips if I get her home after ten."

"That's the great thing about thirty-year-old women," she pointed out brightly, holding on to that smile even if her cheeks hurt from the weight. "No curfew."

"Something to keep in mind," he said with a wink. "Oh, and you have some kind of punch on your dress."

Harper looked down at her favorite daffodil-colored dress and saw the bright red splotch, right below her minuscule cleavage he'd been eyeing all night. And if *that* wasn't humiliating enough, he pulled her in for a hug. Not a dual-armed embrace, bodies touching kind of event. But a side-hug/pat-to-the-back combo that bros gave each other. "Thanks, Harper. I owe you," he said and headed back toward the bar.

Unless he was offering up a tangled sheets kind of favor, Harper wasn't interested. In fact, Harper wasn't interested at all. She didn't want a favor. She wanted passion, connection, adventure, to *be* wanted.

And speaking of wanted, she wanted cookies.

Not the kind with sprinkles that her grandmother made, but the kind that only a strong, sexy man could provide. And she wanted a baker's dozen, she thought as she fished out her keys to open her grandma's shop. The scent of rosewater and lavender greeted her as she stepped inside and felt as though she were transported back in time. The Boulder Holder was a lingerie shop specializing in vintage seduction for the curvy woman—it also had a great stain remover in the storage closet.

Still at a complete loss, or maybe not so complete, since looking back, the intimate questions Clay had asked earlier were all standard résumé info for applying nannies, Harper closed the door behind her and reached to disarm the alarm—which was already disarmed.

"Dang it, Baby," Harper mumbled, making a note to reprimand the closing manager for neglecting the alarm again. And, apparently, her job, since there was a vast collection of high-end merchandise hanging outside one of the changing room doors.

The whole point behind hiring a closing manager was so that her grandma could work fewer hours, let someone younger lift heavy boxes and stock the store. Clovis needed to stay off her knee so it could heal from its most recent replacement surgery, but if Baby wasn't keeping the store working at night, then her grandma would have to put it in order before opening. Which defeated the purpose.

Frustrated, Harper grabbed the stain cleaner and a rag from the closet and walked over to the large gilded mirror on the wall at the far end of the dressing rooms.

Normally being in her grandma's shop, surrounded by all of the bright fabrics and bold designs, could erase even the worst of days. The shop was every girl next door's haven—sexy with a touch of sophistication, and a brilliant kaleidoscope of intimates from time periods usually forgotten. A new adventure to be found on each hanger.

Not tonight, she thought, taking in the image staring back at her in the mirror.

Tonight, Harper felt like a big, stupid banana in a specialty candy store.

"Think of the bright side," she told herself, pulling her arm out of her dress and slipping it off so she could get at the stain easier. "At least he friended you before you showed him your panties."

The ability to see the bright side of even the worst situations was Harper's gift. It was how she'd made it through her eclectic childhood—and how she kept her smile genuine. And being thought of as a babysitter didn't even touch Harper's worst list.

"If you'd gone at him in those panties, I bet he'd have forgotten all about curfew," a distinctively male voice said from behind her.

Harper spun around, the scream getting stuck in her throat along with her heart, which had lodged itself there first. Acting on reflex, she threw the only thing she could reach at the tall, dark—emphasis on the dark—and dangerous-looking shadow. Only the shadow's reflexes were skillfully honed, because he caught the flying object with one hand. Leaving her nearly naked and him holding her favorite daffodil-colored dress.

"Whoa," the unfamiliar and unwelcome voice said from the dressing room doorway. The male face, though, all it took was two seconds for *that* to register.

Harper's fear turned to immediate embarrassment, because standing in her grandma's darkened shop, holding her dress and a slinky red robe, four hours after closing, was the only man in town who hadn't put Harper in the friend zone. Because he was the only man in town who Harper hadn't bothered to friend.

St. Helena firefighter, bro of the year, and legendary ladies' man—Adam Baudouin.

"What are you doing here?" Harper demanded, looking up at him, and he could see the fire lighting her eyes.

A good question. One Adam had crafted a great answer to when she'd first turned around in that pink, teal, and gold-embroidered number with the tiny matching thong, which looked as if she'd recently escaped the Copacabana. Then she'd tossed her dress at him and things had gotten interesting. Little Miss Sunshine wiggled a lecturing finger his way, which caused everything in silk and lace to do a little cha-cha in its own way, and Adam's mind went to a bad place.

An incredibly good bad place.

Oh, Harper was all sunshine and freckled up top. But she was a secret freaking bombshell below. High breasts, tiny waist, curvy hips, long, lush legs that went on for miles. All that silky skin and willowy allure was as surprising as it was intoxicating. Who knew she kept all that hidden under her Rainbow Brite attire?

Not the dildo with the kid who'd ask her to babysit, that's for sure. Because if he'd seen the view Adam was privy to, the guy would have taken her inside the shop—and right up against the wall.

"Apparently, I'm just in time for the show," he said, looking down into her face. With her pert nose, twinkling blue eyes, and wild mass of waves piled on top of her head, she was cute, he decided. The crazy kind of cute.

"There's no show," she said. "And what are you staring at?" When he looked his fill in response, she rolled her eyes and crossed her arms. "They're called boobs, Adam."

"Oh, trust me, I know, Sunshine," he said, stepping closer and, being the expert on that subject, sized her up in a single glance. Firm, perky—the perfect little handful who wished she was a *C*. That explained the creative clothing choices. "Just wasn't sure if you knew, with your outfit and all."

"What's wrong with my outfit?"

"You look like a yellow crayon who stepped in grape juice."

She looked at him in disbelief, then outrage. "I do not! That dress revealed more secrets than Victoria's new catalog."

He held up the dress and she grimaced. "Secrets or not, the only thing you're going to attract with this dress is honeybees, not a hookup."

"Yeah, well, I'm not looking for a hookup," she mumbled, snatching her dress back. And because he already knew that, just like he knew one more frustrated huff would have her popping right out of that bra, he let her take it. Even turned his back when she slipped it back on. Because getting a boner for Pollyanna wasn't a smart move.

"But if I were . . ." she said so quietly he turned back around. She was once again in the yellow jumper, zipped up to her sternum, and fiddling with the little silver heart charm dangling from her necklace. "Are you saying I have to change how I look to get a guy?"

"No." He actually liked the crazy cutie exactly like she was. Her blinding fashion sense was loud, quirky, and kind of adorable. Except, he remembered, those of the adorable-crazy-cuties variety tended to want more than he was willing to give. So he checked himself, then gave a silent lecture that she wasn't asking about *his* preferences, but Dr. Dildo's. "However, if you want *that* guy with the kid, then yeah, you got to up your game."

She looked so incredibly confused he reached for the front zipper of her dress to show her.

She smacked his hand away. "Hey."

"You asked for my help, so let me help," he said, grabbing a red belt off the silk robe and tying it around her waist, cinching it in and showcasing her flat stomach. When she no longer looked like a chewing gum wrapper, he tugged the zipper south, far enough that the collar of the dress opened and slid down one arm.

Her shoulder was now exposed as well as a nice hint of her Copacabanas. "You need new lipstick."

"My lipstick is not the problem. This is the third color I tried this month and the saleslady at the drugstore said it is the perfect shade."

"First problem with what you said was drugstore, since we both know that the saleslady in question is Mrs. Peters, who hasn't changed lip color since Carter left office." He undid her hair, which was held up by a chopstick. Not a decorative one, but a wooden one from the takeout place down the street.

"My curls are out of control, I wouldn't do that," she said, her hands coming up to her head. He intercepted them mid–helmet pose and set them back at her sides, squeezing her wrists so she knew to leave them there. And miracle of miracles, she actually listened.

"You have slept-in bed waves, not curls," he corrected and, *yup*, one pull and all of those melted-chocolate waves came tumbling down to her midback. *Like walking sex*, he thought. "Back to the lipstick. Are you really wearing pink with glossy shine and glitter?"

She shifted on her feet. "So?"

"So it's a problem." He handed her a tissue and waited while she wiped it off. Then he put his fingers in her hair and gave it a little shake and stepped back to study his work. "Better. But still missing something."

"Wow, you sure know how to sweet-talk a woman," she mumbled, and that's when he realized what it was. Sunshine was looking self-conscious, which he'd never seen before. She usually marched to her own beat and flashed those pearly whites at anyone who looked at her strangely—her version of flashing the bird. Only good-girl style. But right then, standing there looking bed rumpled and sexy as hell, she was uncomfortable.

So Adam did the only thing he knew would work. Okay, the second thing, since what he wanted to do wouldn't be appropriate— she wasn't looking for a hookup. So he slid his fingers deeper into her hair and kissed her.

And *holy shit*, Harper Owens with her warm smile and rainbow dreams might look like the kind of girl one would bring home to Sunday dinner at the parents', but she kissed like she'd rock your world on the car ride over.

And back.

She made a soft little mewling sound that drove him crazy, because it was half-surprised and wholly aroused. Without warning, she pulled his lower lip with her teeth, sucked on it for a good minute, and he manned up in the most embarrassing way. But then her hands were on him, threading through his hair, playing with the ends at the back of his neck, and he forgot what the problem was.

Forgot why crazy cuties were a bad idea.

"Adam?" she purred, and he started walking backward into the dressing room when he realized she wasn't moving with him. She also wasn't kissing him anymore. In fact, she looked all prickly.

"Adam?" a sultry voice teased from the other room. "Where are you?"

Harper cleared her throat and took a step back. A big step back. "He's out here, Baby."

Four things hit Adam simultaneously. First, he'd come here tonight with the stacked blonde he'd met at the bar for a private lingerie show and a fun game of Spin the Spinner. Second, he'd almost had sex with a girl named Baby. And third, he'd just made out with the weird art teacher—and he'd liked it.

Hell, based on the tent in his pants and the way he was gasping for breath, he'd more than liked it. His lips still tasted like some kind of fruity umbrella drink, and he wanted another sip.

Which brought him to the last revelation of the night. Harper Owens was a closeted hottie. And if she'd disliked him before, which he could only assume since she'd never looked twice at him until tonight, then she'd hate him now.

Her hair was magically back up in its messy twist, her dress was zipped to the neck, and she was shooting glares frosty enough to cryogenically freeze his nuts for decades to come.

"Oh, hey, Harper," Baby said, stopping at the entry to the dressing room. She was in stripper heels, fishnets, and three leather straps that strategically crisscrossed her body. Her hair was ratted, her lips ruby red, and she should have had him revving to go. Only Adam was too busy watching Harper. "What are you doing here?"

"I was about to ask you the same thing."

about the author

Marina Adair is a #1 national bestselling author of romance novels. Along with the St. Helena Vineyard series, she is also the author of *Sugar's Twice as Sweet*, part of the Sugar, Georgia series. She lives with her husband, daughter, and two neurotic cats in Northern California. She loves to hear from readers and likes to keep in touch, so be sure to sign up for her newsletter at www.marinaadair.com/newsletter.